The Marquess had made his stance clear.

He was content—insistent, even—on carrying on in the same manner. Yet what else could she expect? He did not see her—but how could he? He saw only what she had shown him. What she had become—for him.

Suddenly the truth was blindingly clear. She could not stay. Could not pretend that nothing had changed inside her. The pain she felt now was nothing to what such a course would lead to. Before long she would be writhing beneath an unbearable weight of unrequited caring and burgeoning resentment.

Hardwick had no future. Not with the Marquess. Not even without him.

Yet she was more than Hardwick, was she not?

She would never find out if she stayed.

AUTHOR NOTE

Are you a collector? Although I admit to a taste for research books, I don't have anything to rival Lord Marland's superior weapons collection. Then again, neither have I made his mistake of pouring all my passions into a room full of ancient swords and gleaming battleaxes—or hefty tomes and old maps, as the case may be!

I'm not *über*-organised either—unlike Miss Chloe Hardwick. But that's the beauty of writing romance—the chance to explore all sorts of fantasies! Uptight Chloe may seem like an odd choice to turn the Marquess away from his obsession with instruments of death and towards life, but their quest to find a mysterious spear turns into a journey of discovery for both Chloe and Lord Marland. I hope you'll enjoy the trip along with them, as they learn to let fear and hurt drift away and hold onto love—and each other—instead.

UNBUTTONING
MISS HARDWICK

Deb Marlowe

First published in Great Britain 2012
by Mills & Boon, an imprint of Harlequin (UK) Limited.
Harlequin (UK) Limited, Eton House, 18-24 Paradise Road,
Richmond, Surrey TW9 1SR

© Deb Marlowe 2012

ISBN: 978 0 263 89248 2

Harlequin (UK) policy is to use papers that are natural, renewable and recyclable products and made from wood grown in sustainable forests. The logging and manufacturing process conform to the legal environmental regulations of the country of origin.

Printed and bound in Spain
by Blackprint CPI, Barcelona

Deb Marlowe grew up in Pennsylvania with her nose in a book. Luckily, she'd read enough romances to recognise the true modern hero she met at a college Halloween party—even though he wore a tuxedo T-shirt instead of breeches and tall boots. They married, settled in North Carolina, and produced two handsome, intelligent and genuinely amusing boys.

Though she now spends much of her time with her nose in her laptop, for the sake of her family she does occasionally abandon her inner world for the domestic adventure of laundry, dinner and carpool. Despite her sacrifice, not one of the men in her family is yet willing to don breeches or tall boots. She's working on it.

Deb would love to hear from readers! You can contact her at debmarlowe@debmarlowe.com

Previous novels by the same author:

SCANDALOUS LORD, REBELLIOUS MISS
AN IMPROPER ARISTOCRAT
HER CINDERELLA SEASON
ANNALISE AND THE SCANDALOUS RAKE
  (part of *Regency Summer Scandals*)
TALL, DARK AND DISREPUTABLE
HOW TO MARRY A RAKE

To Valiant Husband:

For braving trolls and spiders beneath decks,
for technical support, for 'just stopping by',
for liking my friends, for all the late pick-ups
at the gym, for not damaging my calm,
for having the best laugh and sharing it so often,
and for a thousand and one other reasons.

I know how lucky I am.

Prologue

'**M**iss! He's coming!'

Over the relentless pounding of her own heart, Chloe Hardwick caught the excitement in the maid's tone. She inched a little closer to her desk, straightened her spine and settled her new spectacles more firmly on her nose.

Clearly this was a woefully insignificant re-action.

'Miss!' How was it possible for the girl to shriek and whisper at the same time? Her shivery delight grated on Chloe's already strained nerves.

'Oh, heavens!' From the passageway, the maid hissed again. 'He's nearly here!'

Chloe swallowed an empathetic surge of panic. Her day of reckoning had come. It was time to own up to her lies, to confess her deceit to The Marauding Marquess.

It's only a nickname.

None of his infamous conquests, reportedly gathered on the battlefields and in the bedrooms of Europe, would come into play here at Denning Castle. She repeated the reassurance in her head even as she pinned the girl with a stern stare. 'Thank you, Daisy. That will be all.'

The disappointed maid flounced away from the door. Making a small concession to her nerves, Chloe ran a finger along the row of buttons marching down the front of her jacket. The garment might be supremely unstylish, but as always she drew strength and a sense of security from her unusual attire, as if the string of tightly spaced fasteners were a line of soldiers standing firm between her and the world. Breathing deeply, she ignored the sounds of arrival, pulled a file from the neat stack at the corner of her desk and bent over it.

'Hardwick!' The shout echoed from below, followed by a set of footsteps advancing up the stairs. They paused as Chloe's unwitting employer called to an unseen servant. 'There is a loaded wagon coming along behind. No one is to touch it until I am available to supervise. Is that understood?'

He didn't wait for an answer. The footsteps were nearly upon her now. 'Hardwick!' he called again. 'Did you get it, man?'

Chloe sensed, rather than saw, the large form that erupted into her small study.

'Hardwick?'

This was it. The moment she'd been preparing for—and dreading—for nearly sixteen months. Nervous energy coursed through her. She closed her eyes and tried desperately to quell it. When she opened her eyes, however, she saw that the quill she held trembled in her hand. Deliberate and slow, she set it down and rose to her feet.

'Lord Marland, welcome home,' she said to the quill. 'How pleased we all are to have you back.'

She forced her gaze up, across her desk and the short expanse of carpet…and stalled at a pair of slightly dusty cavalry boots.

Oh, my.

Chloe did have a weakness for a man in boots—and this set had her swallowing back a sigh of admiration. Plain, black leather, climbing high at the knee and cut away in the rear, worn from use and moulded to a set of muscular calves…

'Yes, yes. Thank you.' The Marquess of Marland cleared his throat. 'I'm looking for Hardwick.'

She raised her eyes, then—up and up, over the tall and powerful figure that dominated the small room—and stalled again.

He looked nothing like she expected—so

much *more* than the portrait in the gallery downstairs. He was magnificent…and wrong. Broad of shoulder, wide of chest and sleekly muscled, Lord Marland looked as if he'd stepped from the pages of history. A Viking warrior, perhaps, or a knight of old, nothing like the few gentlemen of noble birth she'd had a glimpse of before. Even his hair bespoke of ages past: thick, chestnut locks left to grow just past his shoulders and caught up in a queue at his nape. Chloe couldn't help herself. She ran her gaze over him, mentally stripping away the buff breeches and brown superfine. He belonged in leather, or armour. Perhaps a kilted plaid from across the nearby Scottish border. But, no, then he wouldn't be wearing those wonderful boots…

He cleared his throat once more and Chloe started, yanking herself back to reality.

'Hardwick?' he repeated. 'Where might I find him?'

Summoning every bit of willpower, each ounce of determination she possessed, she met his bold, black gaze and answered him. 'I'm Hardwick, my lord.'

The marquess blinked. For a single, thrilling instant, he allowed his interested gaze to wander over her, as she'd just done to him. Then he blew out a breath, his impatience clear. 'As fond as I am of games, Miss…whoever you are, I've no time for them today. I need to talk to

Hardwick immediately. Mr George Hardwick. *My* Hardwick.'

Chloe wanted to look away from his dark eyes—even if only for another glimpse at his broad and powerful frame—but she didn't dare. Everything she had worked for came down to this moment. 'Mr George Hardwick—my adoptive father—grew ill right after you went abroad, my lord. He's been confined to his bed and fighting a wasting illness ever since.' She breathed deeply. 'For all intents and purposes *I* am your Hardwick, sir.'

He drew himself up, impossibly straight. The scorching look he sent her way should have seared her skin. She met his burning gaze and braced herself for the explosion.

It didn't come. Instead the marquess froze. His obsidian eyes flared wide for a second, then he whirled. In an instant he was gone. She could hear him sprinting down the stairs.

Chloe knew where he had gone, but for the life of her she couldn't follow. *Please*, she sent the silent plea out. There was nowhere for her to go. She needed the safety of this position more than she would ever be able to admit out loud.

Her knees buckled. She dropped into her seat and let her head fall into her hands.

Braedon Denning, the seventh Marquess of Marland, pushed impatiently through the layers of tarpaulin separating the new wing from the rest of Castle Denning. *His* wing. The legacy that he meant to leave to the future—and his brother and father both be damned.

The breath he hadn't known he'd been holding burst out of him. He sucked in a lungful of air tainted with sawdust, tinged with the acrid tang of paint, but tasted nothing more than sweet relief.

All looked as it should. His fury abating, he walked across the vast, grey-stone floor. The intricate, inlaid pattern of Italian marble was just as he remembered from the designs. Halfway across, he looked up, noting the curved niches spaced around him and the scaffolding running up one wall, reaching up to the first signs of the second-floor gallery.

'Hell and damnation,' Braedon whispered the words, just to hear the echo come back to him from the domed ceiling. He'd expected the worst, but it rather looked as if the wing was ahead of schedule. Even the separate entrance was in place, as he had specified. Eagerly, he strode through the pedimented door to examine the place from the outside.

It was perfect, each stone block a masterpiece of precision. Braedon walked every foot of the perimeter without finding a single flaw. His anxiety and irritation began to dissipate, leaving room for jaded curiosity to grow. When he circled back around to the entrance and found the unknown chit waiting on the top step, he was able to examine her with his usual, careful detachment.

Even that didn't help. Here was a woman that did not fit into any of the usual classifications. She was tall, that much was clear. But every other womanly detail was hidden away. Trim figure or curves? Impossible to tell under the box-like garment she wore, cut in severe lines. Rather like a gentleman's morning coat, without the cutaway front. The skirt was made of the same material, and hid just as much, although Braedon surmised the legs beneath must be mouthwateringly long.

Could she know that such a get-up merely made a man itch to know what was underneath? Was that her game after all? Braedon eyed her warily. He'd grown up in a ruthless and manipulative environment, and learned early that dark and dangerous gifts often came wrapped in shiny packages. Staring hard at this odd specimen, he couldn't help but wonder if the opposite would hold true.

'The Aislaby sandstone was a wonderful choice,' she said as he drew near. 'Nearly a perfect match for the rest of the exterior walls.' She cut a glance in his direction and reached out to touch the golden stone. 'Though we only narrowly avoided a disaster, when the quarry sent word that we would have to wait a year for enough stone to finish.'

Braedon watched her hand. She caressed the stone as if it were a living thing and could feel her approbation.

'And yet all appears to be proceeding according to schedule,' he said, gesturing about them. 'Why is that?'

'The quarrymen had heard of your departure for the Continent,' she responded with a shrug. 'Thus they judged your project to be a lower priority than some of their other customers.' She turned and met his gaze squarely. 'I convinced them otherwise.'

Braedon crossed his arms and regarded her with amusement. 'So I'm to believe that *you* have been directing all of this…' he paused and lowered his voice to a timbre that had set seasoned soldiers to shaking in their boots '…all of *this*, practically since the day I left?'

She dropped her arm and drew herself up straight. 'Believe what you like, but it is simply the truth.'

'I want to see Hardwick.' It came out an order.

'He's awaiting you, somewhat anxiously,' she answered calmly. Her eyes grew sad. 'But I ask you to go softly with him. You'll find him much…diminished.'

'Why wasn't I told?'

'At first, I merely wished for a chance to

prove myself. And we hoped that Father's health would improve. A few months at the most...' Her voice trailed off and she regarded him with irony. 'Your trip was initially to be much shorter, if you'll recall.' She sighed. 'And the longer your absence stretched, the more difficult it became to tell you the truth. I decided merely to do my best and confess my sins when I must.'

'And now you have.' Braedon strode past her through the large door.

She followed, right on his heels.

'The columns of veined alabaster are due to arrive next week. Once they are in place, work on the gallery will begin to move quickly.'

He was moving quickly, but she kept pace with him and her clipped conversation outpaced them both. 'Your arrival now is propitious. The plasterers have questions about the trim on the niches. I have a few sketches from Mr Keller. I would appreciate it if you would choose between them.'

That brought Braedon up short. He turned to glare at her. 'Brian Keller is an architect of keen eye and remarkable skill. He's also a womanising rogue of the first order. Am I now to accept that for—' he paused to count '—fifteen months—'

'Nearly sixteen,' she interrupted.

'For sixteen months, Keller has been taking orders from *you*?'

'No.'

Braedon's mouth curved in triumph.

'He's been collaborating with me, which is something else altogether.' She chuckled. 'I admit, he was reluctant at first, but I won him over.'

'How?' He couldn't hide the suspicion he felt.

She merely smiled. '*He* wasn't able to get the Aislaby delivered in time.'

Braedon huffed. 'Look, Miss…Hardwick?'

She nodded.

'Perhaps you do indeed have a gift for organisation—or perhaps merely for manipulating men.' He continued on past her wordless protest. 'But George Hardwick was more than merely a manager for the building of this wing. He was in charge of my *entire collection.* Do you have any idea what that means? How far behind it must be?' He moaned and increased his pace again.

Miss Hardwick, on the other hand, drew to a sudden halt. 'Come with me, my lord.' Turning abruptly, she headed for a corner of the room. Behind a hidden door she revealed a narrow passage and a door with double locks. From her pocket she produced a ring of keys.

'Stay here,' she said as the door opened onto a dark room. She entered and within moments light flared and grew.

It was a workroom, he saw, as she lit one

lamp after another. Neatly hung brushes and small tools ringed the walls. Crates of many sizes were stacked against the wall. Near the back sat a desk covered with papers, parchment and books. And in the middle of the room, on a long table, revealed as she peeled back layers of cushioning muslin…

Braedon rushed forwards. It was a bronze short sword, tinged with the greenish patina of extreme age. Reverent, he lifted it. Months ago he'd found this treasure in a Hungarian curiosity shop, filth-encrusted and looking as if the proprietor had used it to pry open tins of food. What he held now was a masterpiece.

He ran a finger along the half-circle of high-relief carvings just past the hilt and leaned closer to the light to examine the sharpened edge of the blade. 'Who?' he asked. 'Who restored it?'

The pride with which she beheld the weapon answered the question for him.

'How?'

'My father has been working with me. His speech is slow and his body seems to be gradually betraying him, but his mind is as keen as ever.' She crossed to the desk and lifted a file. 'I've done a bit of research. There are notes here on its possible age, construction and use, that sort of thing. I also jotted down a few ideas on how you might wish to display it.'

He looked up, his eyes narrowed. 'What of

the others I sent? The Egyptian dagger? The carved-ivory scabbard?'

'All here, my lord.' One by one she revealed the pieces he'd gathered over the last months, scavenged from collectors, pawnshops and junk heaps across Europe. Each one shone with new life and had been treated with the veneration it deserved.

He was impressed, despite himself. When he spoke again, he allowed respect to replace the animosity in his tone. 'There is no doubt you've done a fine job here, Miss Hardwick. I have a full appreciation for the work you've done and I thank you for it.'

The relief he caught shining through those spectacles forced him to go on quickly. 'A problem remains, however. I was woefully indulgent in staying away so long. A huge amount of work and a long list of duties await my attention now. I was counting on Hardwick to carry on with the collection, to take my place with some of the legwork and travelling. There is much involved in acquiring pieces like this: correspondence, business savvy, negotiation skills, the ability to travel with ease.' Braedon sighed. 'I had written your father about a piece I had particularly longed for—a rare Japanese pole arm recently brought back from the Orient. I hate to think that my chance at it is gone.'

Without a word, the girl produced another key

and crossed to a tall armoire in the corner. She opened it to reveal a gleam of metal emanating from a long-hafted weapon.

Speechless, he stared. He rushed over to pull the piece into the light. Time passed as he traced reverent fingers and a sharp gaze over the masterfully crafted samurai blade, the long tang and longer staff. He looked at her in awe. 'How did you do it?'

'I followed the instructions you sent my father. I took William, your sturdiest footman, along and one of your tenants, a young woman recently widowed, as a companion. We made an effective team.'

Braedon knew there was more to the story. There were a hundred questions he should ask, but he couldn't tear his gaze away from the incredible piece in his hand. 'We'll enlarge one of the niches,' he said suddenly. 'Design it around this piece—it will be one of the highlights of the collection.'

'Actually—' the girl crossed to the desk again '—I saw a magnificent display case in a private collection of manuscripts once. I made a few changes and came up with this. We could place the whole thing right in the centre of the room.'

He stared at the gorgeously rendered, ornate sketch. 'You designed this?'

She nodded.

Braedon eyed her closely again. He fought

back a short-lived twinge of disappointment at the idea of never probing beneath all of that packaging she wrapped herself in. He couldn't help glancing over his shoulder, back in the direction of the main house. He was back at Castle Denning, wasn't he? The place where he'd grown used to being denied what he wanted most. He shrugged off the thought. In any case, it wasn't his habit to pry into others' secrets, any more than it was to share his own.

The magnificent design caught his eye again and he made his decision.

'Well, then, Miss Hardwick—how would you like to stay on as *my* Hardwick?'

Chapter One

One year later

'Miss?' The head carpenter poked his head into her workroom. 'Would you have a moment? You might wish to see this.' He jerked his head in the direction of the weapons wing.

Clutching her correspondence, Chloe instantly left her desk. 'What is it, Mr Forrest?' She groaned. 'Not the gallery floor again, I hope?'

'Now, miss,' the carpenter said with a chuckle, 'it does no good to always expect the worst.'

Plaster dust swirled about her skirts as she followed the man, ducking under scaffolding and stepping around stacks of wood. But there were far fewer obstacles than in months past, and in only a minute he paused to wave triumphantly at one of the niches set into the first-floor walls.

'Ooohh.' She sighed in delight.

Forrest nodded. 'That Italian you brought over talks as fast as a river floods, and I vow he's as tetchy as a cat with a sore tail…but he does beautiful work.'

That he did. The scalloped levels of the domed top beautifully echoed the colours of the ceiling, pillars and floor, while the framing and the interior panels had been covered in gorgeously ornate plasterwork. A large blank space awaited the installation of a specially designed display case.

'That does end the day on a good note, doesn't it?' Mr Forrest grinned. 'I'm the last straggler here, miss, save yourself. Do you want to lock up after me?'

'Oh, yes. Of course.' With a last lingering look, she tore herself away. She bid the tradesman a good evening, then, closing the heavily panelled doors after him, she leaned against them and took in the results of two years of hard labour.

Nearly complete. It seemed an impossibility. Yet Lord Marland's wing stretched out before her, a dusty, slightly cluttered promise of magnificence. Only details remained to be completed: the niches, a bit of work on the second-floor gallery, the intricate trim and moulding about the walls. Then, of course, the displays would need to be arranged and set up—oh, who was she fooling? There were still a hundred small tasks that needed doing, but the end was drawing undeniably near.

The thought had her pulling out her crumpled letter. Her old friend knew that the wing was nearly finished—and he hinted that it was time for her to leave Northumberland.

She looked up again, taking in marble and stone, pillars and dome, and clutched a fistful of buttons on her formidable jacket. She'd been so fortunate in this project—and in this position. Here, she had the best of all worlds. Tucked up safe behind her spectacles and boxy skirts, she'd also been utterly challenged and completely absorbed. The work had brought her closer to her stepfather in his last days and provided an outlet for grief and an escape from loss when he'd passed on, mere weeks after Lord Marland's return.

Never could she have imagined such a perfect hiding spot. She'd thrown herself into both the collection and the construction, reinforced her persona and buried her true self deep, far beyond the chance of discovery. She'd proved herself to the marquess, too, and they had gradually developed a quiet bond of respect. She'd found herself as close to that elusive state— happiness—as she'd been in a long, long time.

'Hardwick!' Lord Marland's voice echoed like thunder from the passage beyond the wing.

'Hardwick?' The door swung open and the marquess leaned in, his dark gaze meeting hers across the vast chamber. 'There you are.' He strode in, and the wrench inside her was both familiar and surprisingly strong. He was garbed casually, as if he'd come from his work, in waist-coat and shirtsleeves rolled high. He'd left his coat behind again. It was a familiar sight, yet it hit her hard, a bubbling rush of pleasure and pain that bloomed in her chest and raced with frothy abandon through her veins.

What was wrong with her? She shook her head and, tucking her letter away, moved to meet him midway. 'Good evening, my lord.'

'And to you. I wished to tell you…' His words trailed off as he caught sight of the completed niche. Silent, he went to stand in front of it. When he turned away, long moments later, he was grinning. His eye roamed about the room and then back again. 'It truly is going to be magnificent, isn't it?' he asked softly.

'It truly is,' Chloe agreed. She stared at him, caught by the light in his eyes and the way that the sun's last rays burrowed in his long hair, carving lighter channels along certain strands. He was her employer. He was pleased. She was also, of course. Hadn't she just stood in that same spot and sighed over the intricate beauty of the *stuccatore*'s work? Yet the the marquess's euphoria irritated her. She shook her head again. She was being irrational.

He met her gaze at last. 'About that Druidic dagger…' he began.

'I don't recommend that we pursue it,' she said abruptly.

He paused. 'I was going to say the same thing. I have it on good authority that it's a fake.'

She nodded. 'I had heard the same.'

His gaze wandered again, travelling about the room, fixing on the marble veining of a pillar here, a delicately turned newel post there. This was nothing unusual. They often discussed business here at the end of the day and the marquess was often distracted, cataloguing the progress made. Chloe was used to it; preoccupied as he might seem to be, he never missed or forgot a single detail of their conversations.

And yet—there was that phrase again. Something had changed, but she could not quite get her finger on the pulse of it. She only knew that her heart rate was ratcheting, her skin felt tight and she realised suddenly that tonight she could not stand here, calmly talking about the collection while his attention fixed on everything but her.

'Would you mind walking as we talk, my lord? If you have more to discuss, that is.' She made her request with a lift of her chin. 'I promised Mr Keller I would find a sketch of a certain Roman medallion in the library.'

'Of course.' The marquess looked surprised, but trailed obligingly along. He had a few more questions about displays and possible acquisitions and Chloe felt a certain guilty satisfaction when his focus remained on her.

In the library, their discussion wound down. She'd just found her illustration when the marquess stood to take his leave. 'That should be enough to occupy you for a day or two,' he said with a wry twist of his mouth. 'I'll be busy for a few days with the bailiff's latest idea to keep the sheep from wandering into the mud flats. I'll check back with you then, if there isn't anything else.'

He stood, the scrape of his chair sounding loud in the quiet room. He clearly expected that there would *not* be anything else. And why wouldn't he?

He turned to go without another glance and Chloe marvelled at the differences that existed between them. For her, isolation was a necessity—the price she was willing to pay for the security of a respectable position and the blessed feeling of safety. Lord Marland, on the other hand, seemed to revel in his solitude— and to actively encourage and increase it. Chloe didn't know if this behaviour originated with some pain in his past or from simply never having experienced otherwise. Either way, her heart ached for him.

But she would never break his trust by allowing him to know of it. The marquess was an intensely private man, she'd discovered, and nothing displeased him more than someone—anyone—trying to edge past the barriers he kept firmly in place. So instead, she did what she did best. She watched him closely, learned all that she could and became exactly what he needed most. She took on his burdens and eased his mind about the project closest to him. In short, she became the absolute best Hardwick she could be.

Sneaking another glance at him, she suppressed a sigh. Sometimes being Hardwick was very hard indeed.

'Lord Marland—wait!'

He pivoted on a heel, brow arched in surprise. She knew how he felt. She'd shocked herself.

'Ah, could you wait a moment? There is something, actually.' She twisted her fingers around each other to keep them away from her buttons.

He waited.

'It's just…the new wing is so nearly complete…and the collection is in splendid shape… and I know you are not interested in opening the collection to outsiders…'

'No. I am not,' he said flatly.

'I didn't mean to argue the point.' Chloe ducked her head. Reaching into her pocket, she touched the letter from her oldest friend. 'It's only—it's been suggested that I might seek another position. That you might not require my services any longer, after the project is finished.'

'What?' He reared back. 'Who's been spouting such nonsense?' His shock and outrage were sincere, to her utter gratification. 'Not Mrs Goodmond, I hope?'

Surprised, Chloe shook her head and placed her book on the table between them. 'No, it was—'

She stopped, her mouth open, unable to continue, when the marquess took a seat directly across from her. He stared up at her with a kind expression of sympathy and understanding. 'Your position must be an awkward one, Hardwick. You've talents that put you beyond a woman's normal sphere. No doubt you will run into more than one narrow-minded fool who will push you towards a more accepted mould.'

He reached out suddenly and grasped her wrist. Chloe's mouth dropped again in wordless shock, even though her coat covered the spot. Her bones felt small and fragile beneath his large hand. His grip was both firm and tender. Warmth radiated from his hand and she could not suppress the shiver that ran through her.

'Don't listen to them, Hardwick,' he said, insistent. 'Any woman can run a household or pop out a parcel of babes, but your skills are unique. You have a fine, clear mind, a gift for retaining and arranging information, and the damnedest ability to inspire people to meet your high standards.' He shook his head. 'This wing, this collection, they are incredibly important to me, and neither would be in so grand a shape were it not for you.'

He gave her arm a squeeze and, sitting back, let her go. Chloe flushed with surprise and pleasure. He'd given her compliments before, on a job well done, but this level of warmth and approval was new—and intoxicating.

'Not everyone is meant for the intimacy of marriage or the rigours of child-rearing,' the marquess reflected. He smiled at her. 'Embrace your differences, Hardwick. Don't allow anyone to make you feel inferior.'

Elation abruptly drained away. Stricken, Chloe blinked at the marquess. Inferior? She might have spent the last months moulding herself to best fit his needs, but she'd never considered that the process would render her unfit for anything else.

She cleared her throat. 'I'm afraid you've misunderstood, my lord. It is not Mrs Goodmond, but a friend of mine who worries… He fears that there soon may not be enough work for me here.'

He leaned back. 'What sort of friend?' He frowned. 'And what could he know of the state of my collection?'

Incredulous—and a little exhausted from the constant swing of her emotions—Chloe narrowed her gaze. 'An old family friend. And he possesses the same scant information that the rest of the antiquities community does.' Seeing his frown deepen, she leaned forwards, her hands on the table. 'And no, I have not been talking out of turn.' She raised a brow. 'Surely you've realised the curiosity our work here has stirred? With tradesmen and specialists coming and going—not to mention the aggressive number of acquisitions we've made—it's caused a stir.'

'I don't like to think of people speculating about me.' He shot her a conciliatory glance. 'Or you.'

'Well, I'm afraid a certain amount of speculation is unavoidable, my lord.'

He sighed and climbed to his feet. 'In any case, tell your friend that his concern is premature. Such a notion is absurd. Put it from your head, Hardwick. No one could display this collection like you will—you've designed half of it yourself, for God's sake. And the collection is far from complete.' He gave a curt nod. 'There's plenty more work to do here.'

Uneasy, she watched as he nodded a dismissal and left the room.

She bit down on her lip hard to quash her wildly fluctuating feelings. Forcibly, she unclenched her fists and turned back to her illustration. She should be thrilled. She *was* thrilled, she told herself firmly. Against all odds, this position had given her exactly what she wanted: a perfect blend of safety and responsibility, anonymity and respect. Truly, she was grateful that there was no need to contemplate leaving it.

She sneaked a peek over her shoulder, after the marquess.

Yes. She had exactly what she wanted.

And if she were wise, she would keep reminding herself of the fact.

'Skanda's Spear? Do I have that right?' Chloe asked, nearly a week later. She tossed a book onto a pile of others, already discarded. 'I can't find a mention of it in any of my journals or references.'

Something was off again today. She dug her fingers into her temple, trying to sort the odd sensation. Something in the air, perhaps.

No. Chloe might deceive the world—after all, what were her spectacles, her dress and all that which made up her odd persona, if not for deception and evasion? But she did make it a policy to be honest with herself. And that was the rub. Reluctantly, she had come to the conclusion that whatever strangeness had been haunting the place lately…was coming from her.

Tranquillity had deserted her. The unflagging energy she normally focused on her work had begun to unravel. Since she'd spoken with the marquess in the library, she'd been beset with unfamiliar doubt, yearning and the rolling echo of his words in her head. *Marriage. Babes.* It wasn't that she'd never contemplated such things for herself. It was just that she'd been so intent on finding a place and position of safety and security, that they had always felt very far away. Now Lord Marland's words had jerked them right to the front and centre of her mind.

Did she want such normal, feminine things? The part of her that melted at the thought knew she did, but the pragmatic side of her couldn't find a scenario in which it could happen, while the dark, doubting bit of her soul threw out the marquess's other words—words like *unusual* and *inferior.*

She rubbed a hand against her brow. She was awash in conflicting new feelings and desires— and suddenly unceasingly aware of an older one.

Bracing herself, she glanced over at her employer.

She couldn't ignore the truth any longer, any more than she could ignore the jolt of longing

and resignation she felt every time she looked
at the marquess. When had it begun? Irrelevant,
she supposed. Some time in the months since
her stepfather's death she'd allowed grief to
inevitably loosen its hold on her heart. She'd
grown comfortable with Lord Marland, had
begun to esteem his dedication and reserved
humour just as she'd always admired his broad
shoulders and incredible strength. Yearning
had escaped the realm of fantasy and daydream
while want had awoken and swirled up and out
of her, tiny tendrils, reaching for the marquess,
seeking to bind him to her.

She ducked her head, worried that he might
catch a hint of her shifting feelings, but another
quick glance showed him still occupied and
oblivious. Straightening, she stared at him out-
right for several long moments.

Still nothing. Lord Marland's barriers worked
both ways, she realised. They, together with
her mannish attire and severe coiffure, had
succeeded in making her invisible. To Lord
Marland she was Hardwick, more function than
flesh and blood. He no more noticed her breath
catching or her heart pounding than he would
suffer such afflictions himself—which was to
say, not at all.

Today they sat together in the workroom,
she at her desk, while he—an artist's vision

of a warrior tamed—bent over a rusty cavalry sword, painstakingly cleaning the pierced guard.

'You won't find Skanda's Spear in any reference books,' Lord Marland chided her.

'Then how do you know of it?' she asked carefully. His attention still hadn't wavered from his task, so she eased her spectacles off and allowed her gaze to roam over him.

Though he sat still and focused, the marquess loomed large in the enclosed space. From corner to corner, the air pulsed with the energy of leashed strength, of capable male. He had, as usual, lost his coat some time earlier in the day. Beneath the linen of his shirt, muscles bunched and flexed as he worked. The old, scuffed cavalry boots, his favourite and hers, were planted wide on either side of his chair as he worked. His hair—good heavens, the fantasies that she'd built around that hair—had begun to pull loose from his queue. One long strand hung before his eyes as he leaned in close to his work.

He sat back suddenly and grinned at her. She whipped her gaze back to her desk and pushed her spectacles back onto her nose.

'Whispers,' he answered. 'The Spear of Skanda has been but a myth, a legend spoke of in whispers trickled down through the ages.' His eyes flashed in the candlelit room, nearly as dark as the elaborate black embroidery on his waistcoat. 'Lately the trickle has become a river. People are talking about it once more. I've heard more than one report saying that the Spear has been brought to England by an unknowing nabob.'

She looked up again, and cocked her head at him. 'What doesn't he know?'

'The extreme value of what he holds, it is to be hoped,' he answered sardonically. 'And if he's unaware of just what he has, then it's unlikely he's aware of the curse.'

Chloe groaned. 'It's cursed, too?' Heart thumping, she returned his grin. 'Bad enough you charge me with finding a will-o'-the-wisp weapon that may or may not exist, but must it be cursed as well?'

The marquess's expression grew suddenly stern and unexpectedly intent. 'I want that spear, Hardwick.' He slapped down the oiled cloth he'd been using with a muffled thump. 'If it has indeed surfaced, then I must have it. No other weapon could be a more perfect centrepiece for my collection.'

Mesmerised, Chloe stared. Since the day he'd agreed to let her stay on, Lord Marland's manner had been cool, unflappable and frustratingly distant. As passionate as she knew him to be about his weapons collection and the elaborate wing they were constructing to showcase it, she'd seen evidence of it only in his unending dedication to the project. He'd never given her so much as a glimpse of what lay behind his obsession or how he truly felt about it and she had learned not to ask. This sudden flash of emotion set her to blinking. She felt as if she'd caught wind of something far more rare than Skanda's alleged spear.

'You've amassed a network of sources that puts even your father's to shame. Use it. Track it down,' he ordered, retreating into bland politeness once more. He gestured towards the papers on her desk. 'I know you'll find it. You've never failed me yet.'

He turned back to his weapon, running slow fingers over the length of the curved blade. A shiver of longing skittered up Chloe's spine, tightening her nipples and setting her insides to sizzling. She suffered a vision of those big hands touching her with such precision.

Abruptly the marquess flourished the sword he'd been working on, slashing bites out of the air with practised ease. 'This is interesting,' he said, caressing the pommel. 'A hodge-podge of a piece, with the lion's head and the fancy basket guard. A cavalry sword, I'd guess, but the blade…' He ran careful fingers along the curved edge. 'It is unmistakably from an earlier weapon. Repaired after battle, perhaps?' He stared at the thing, musing. 'Scots made, in all likelihood. Not fit for display, but excellent for practice.' A slow smile spread across his face.

'It puts me in mind of the first old blade that I ever found.'

Chloe's heart leapt, though she was careful to keep her expression neutral and her gaze fixed on her next book selection. She had no idea what might have brought on this unusually candid mood, but she had no wish to inadvertently put an end to it. 'Is that how you began your collection?' she asked casually.

'Have I never told you the tale?' A wry grin put a lie to the innocent question.

'Not that I recall,' she replied, turning a page and keeping her tone absent. All of her insides were aflutter at the idea of Lord Marland sharing such an important piece of his past.

'Ah.' For several long moments he said no more. The workroom filled with a companionable silence, broken only by the distant clatter of workmen and the rasp of the polishing stone over his tarnished blade.

'I was young—perhaps twelve years at most,' he said eventually. 'I was exploring the eastern boundaries of my father's land. Near the shore there are long stretches of rocky ledges that eventually expand into cliffs.'

Chloe glanced up. 'Yes, I'm familiar with the area.'

The marquess looked surprised. 'Are you?'

She shrugged. 'I enjoy the seaside.'

He stared at her a moment.

Inexplicably, his startled expression began to irritate her. 'It may come as a shock, my lord, but I do continue to exist once I step out of this workroom and beyond the new wing.'

'Yes, of course.'

She raised her chin. 'I find the sea to be soothing. Ever changing and yet constant at the same time—it comforts me. I go whenever I can, especially in the months since my father passed.'

Lord Marland blinked.

What was she doing? She was breaking their code, the unwritten rules that had allowed them to exist in harmony these many months. But there truly was something different about her today. Her inner landscape was shifting and the words would not stop bubbling out. 'Some day I hope to have a home of my own, near the sea.'

A flash of bleakness darkened his expression, just for an instant. Chloe winced. She'd gone too far.

Charged silence stretched between them. Breathless, she waited.

He'd turned back to his work. 'I found a cache, built of stone,' he continued as if she hadn't spoken, but he'd lost the open, contemplative tone that he'd started with. 'It contained a musty old sporran, a disintegrating bit of plaid and a heavy, gorgeous broadsword, corroded by the sea air.' A sigh escaped him. 'I could barely lift the thing, but I thought it the most marvellous thing I had ever beheld.'

Out of the corner of her eye, Chloe caught a small flutter of movement. Silently cursing the ill-timed interruption, she turned her head towards the door. She expected to find yet another workman with a question or problem—but to her surprise, she discovered a strange woman standing there.

Chloe stiffened. In an automatically defensive gesture, she reached to tug her coat straight.

The woman caught her eye and smiled. 'You would have thought it was a sultan's treasure that he had found—' she spoke as if she had been included in the conversation all along '—instead of a pile of mouldy discards.'

The sword clattered to the table and Lord Marland was up and bounding to the door before Chloe could blink an eye.

'Mairead, you minx!' He lifted the woman off her feet in an exuberant embrace. 'I was expecting you this morning.'

'The roads were muddy from yesterday's rain. It slowed us a bit.' She returned his hug with enthusiasm.

Chloe stood, feeling extraneous. Lord Marland's sister, of course. She had the look of her brother and the same appealing vitality. The square family jaw was softened in her case, while the strikingly high cheekbones were not. Lighter hair and a mouth more lush than wide combined to make her a strikingly beautiful woman.

The excited babble of happy greetings continued. Chloe spared a moment to wonder if the housekeeper had been apprised of this visit. She certainly had heard nothing of it.

'You came through the wing,' Lord Marland said eagerly. 'What do you think?'

'It is magnificent,' his sister declared. 'As striking and elegant as you could possibly have managed.'

'And it doesn't match a stick of the rest of the house.' The grin he flashed at her held a definite boyish quality. 'Father would have despised it, would he not have?'

'Heartily.' She laughed. 'That's what makes it all the more grand.'

'Come.' He tugged her towards the door. 'Let me show you all that we've done.'

'Of course, Braedon, I'm eager to see it—but won't you introduce me first?' Lady Mairead made an elegant gesture towards Chloe.

'What?' The marquess turned back with a frown. 'Oh, yes—of course!' Without the slightest discomfort he beckoned the forgotten Chloe forwards. 'Mairi, I'm delighted to make you acquainted with my invaluable assistant, Hardwick. Hardwick, my sister, the Countess of Ashton.'

The curiosity on the countess's face gave

way to shock. 'Hardwick?' She rounded on her brother. 'Do you mean to tell me that, all of these months you've been writing and expounding on the many talents of your Hardwick, you forgot to mention that she is a *woman*?'

Lord Marland shrugged. 'Does it matter?'

Chloe's face flamed. Caught between pleasure at the compliment—second-hand though it might be—and the ignobleness of having her femininity so casually dismissed, she found it impossible to do more than bob a curtsy in the countess's direction.

Lady Ashton gave her a sympathetic glance. 'Please…Miss Hardwick?' At Chloe's nod, she continued. 'Pay no mind to my brother. He has always been the perfect embodiment of every exasperating male quality.'

Chloe could not help but silently agree.

'I won't bother to defend myself,' the marquess said with a sigh, 'since I can't be sure just what I've already done to push the two of you into an unholy feminine alliance. Come, Mairi.' He pulled his sister's arm through his. 'There's so much I want to show you.'

'Gladly, Braedon. I've much to share with you as well.' She smiled at Chloe. 'It was lovely to meet you at last, Miss Hardwick. I can scarcely wait to get to know you better.'

'Thank you, my lady. I look forward to that as well.'

Refusing to glance at the marquess, Chloe turned back to her desk. But as the pair made to leave she was struck by a sudden thought.

'Wait!' She felt the flush climb over her face. 'My lord, that first blade, the one that you found in the rocks—it would make a poignant addition to our displays. But I don't believe that I've seen it. Do you know where it is?'

Lord Marland's expression closed and his shoulders tightened. 'Lost, I'm afraid,' he replied.

'Sold, you mean.' Chloe was startled to hear the bitterness in Lady Ashton's voice. 'Thanks due to Connor.'

The marquess merely shook his head.

'Sold to cover the licentious—and expensive—habits of our departed brother, Miss Hardwick.' It was pain that put the twist in the lady's lovely mouth, Chloe thought, along with an unexpected dose of resentment. 'He, you understand, was the perfect embodiment of every loathsome male quality.'

'Hardwick,' Lord Marland broke in, his tone distant and dismissive once more, 'put your ear to the ground and see what you find out about that spear.' Turning away, he tugged his sister along with him. 'Come, Mairi. Let's get you settled in. On the way, you can tell me what you think of my marble inlay. And later, I plan to bore you with a description of each and every display that will occupy all of my wonderful nooks and crannies.'

'I don't know why you've gone to such incredible—and incredibly expensive—detail, Braedon, when you don't intend on allowing anyone to actually see all of your hard work.' Lady Ashton glanced back one last time as they moved towards the door. 'Or has *your Hardwick* convinced you to open your weapons wing for public display?'

'Never,' he responded firmly.

'Why so much bother, then, if no one will see it?'

'I will see it, dear Mairi. I will frequently walk in here and gaze with utter satisfaction on my private contribution to the Marland legacy.'

'Ah, you intend to gloat then, do you?'

'Each and every day.'

Their voices faded. Chloe stared after them for a long minute while her pulse settled and the sharp stab of yearning in her breast shrunk to a dull ache. Clearly her own altered feelings didn't matter. The elaborate mask she'd been so comfortable hiding behind worked too well. Lord Marland looked at her and could see nothing but quiet, stark and efficient Hardwick.

Surely that was as it should be? The marquess had looked at her—*touched* her—with warmth and admiration for that narrow side of her. She wrapped her arms tight about her middle, as if to hold in all the formally dormant aspects of her nature that were clamouring to be let out—and clamouring to show Lord Marland an altogether different side of Chloe Hardwick.

With a sigh, she turned back to her work. But nothing was accomplished for a good while. She was caught up, instead, contemplating a project of another nature.

Chapter Two

⤜⥈⤛

True to his word, Braedon dragged his sister all over the new wing, filling her ears with his ideas, describing all that they'd already accomplished and much that he still had planned. Poor Mairi bore it well, but as the afternoon wore on, her eyes began to glaze.

He took pity on her—and on himself, too, for his mind wandered repeatedly back to Hardwick. There had been something different about her these last weeks, had there not? Or perhaps he was transferring his own uneasiness on to her, for he had to admit, the idea of her searching for a new position had shaken him.

It was one reason he'd been so excited to hear the news about Skanda's Spear. Not the main reason, but he had to admit that he'd considered that the challenge of finding that elusive artefact would leave Hardwick with no time to think of leaving.

With a smile for his sister, he held out his arm. Escorting her back to the library, he poured her a good, stiff drink and set about discovering what crisis lay behind her unexpected trip home.

'You've utterly transformed this room,' she marvelled, looking about her while she trailed a hand over the back of the new sofa.

'This is where I work.' He nodded to the behemoth desk he'd brought in and grinned at her. 'I had to do something. This is the only room I can spend any amount of time in.'

'You'll have no argument from me.' Mairi gave a theatrical shudder. 'They always make me nervous, all of those dead animals glaring at me with their glassy, accusing eyes.' She crossed over to the high bank of windows he'd had installed. 'All of this lovely light.' She sighed. 'If it were me, I'd go right through the place. Rip out all of that dark panelling and lay all of those poor creatures to rest in some high, sunny meadow.' She shuddered again. 'Far away.'

'I don't know.' Braedon shrugged. 'I feel a certain, perverse satisfaction, walking through those rooms every day.'

'Because *you* are here to enjoy them and *they* are not?' Mairi asked with her usual terrible clarity. 'Or because they provide such a marked contrast with your tasteful, new and modern wing?'

'A bit of both, I'd say.' And because all of those gloomy rooms served as an inescapable warning. Those dark walls might echo with memories of his desperate unhappiness, but they were also a reminder of the invaluable lessons he'd learned. 'In any case, I don't plan on redoing the rest of the old pile.'

'You surprise me,' she said with brows raised. 'I would have thought that you would grab at the chance—if only to thumb your metaphorical nose at Father.'

'Ah, but I think leaving it the way that it is accomplishes the same purpose. You know how the old man loved Denning. The only thing that ruined his pleasure was the disparity of the place—his beloved Jacobin manor shoved up against the old North Tower like a malformed appendage.' He allowed his mouth to twist into a grin. 'Well, now I've thrown the new wing into the mix, and we've *three* different styles shoved cheek by jowl together.'

His sister didn't even try to hide her snort of delight. 'You are right,' she said fervently. 'He's likely spinning in his grave.' She trailed a hand along the thick curtains and her expression grew devilish, her smile crafty as she glanced his way. 'It's likely a good idea to wait before you redecorate, in any case. What better gift could you give to your bride, after all, than an entire castle to do with as she pleases?'

Braedon's amusement burst like a bubble. 'Leave off, Mairi. All the fun and privilege—and expense—of modernising the place will go to your cousin Franklin, as eventual heir.' He waved a hand. 'And much joy may he have of it.'

Her face fell. 'Don't tell me that you are holding on to that old saw?'

'Old saw?' he repeated sardonically. 'Which one? I dare say I have a death grip on several.'

'It's no joking matter, Braedon.' Mairi's voice tightened, taking on the shrill edge it had nearly always held in the past, when she was forced to live each day with unending tension and constant vigilance. 'They are gone now,' she said with intensity. 'You cannot let them shape your life. You cannot hide away up here.'

'I'm not hiding,' he retorted, stung. 'I've come home and I am fulfilling my duties. I am working!'

'As what? A reclusive hermit? You are all alone.'

'And happy to remain that way.'

Mairi was becoming distraught. 'Don't say that,' she whispered. 'Of course you must marry! I don't want to think of you alone. I cannot bear the thought that you will never find someone to be happy with.'

He didn't want to upset her. He summoned a smile and nodded at her. 'Well, then, of course I shall,' he said lightly. 'Eventually.'

But he knew he would not. Mairi had got it backwards. But how to tell her that the brother she knew was largely a fabrication? She had her ways of dealing with the difficulties of their childhood and he'd developed his own. He'd discovered early that exposing too much of himself left him open to ridicule from his father—and worse from his brother. Distance had become his saving grace, both emotionally and physically. It had kept him going until adulthood, when he'd bought himself an army commission just as soon as he was able.

The military had been demanding, but hard-edged reserve had stood him in good stead in the field, almost as much as his skill in tracking down, harassing and capturing French pay wagons and supply caches. He'd been moved eventually into more strategic and diplomatic posts, where he'd learned to add practised charm to his bag of tricks. He'd done well, but it had been a tense and exhausting way of life.

And now—at last—he had the freedom to shape his life exactly as he wanted it. Shockingly, he'd found he enjoyed the role of marquess far more than he had expected he would. As loath as he had been to return to Denning, he had found life here to be almost enjoyable now that he held the title and lived here on his own.

In fact, everything important was easier here. He was the master, and nearly everyone expected him to hold himself detached. The pretence so essential in the army and in the diplomatic arena was simply not necessary. He didn't have to work so hard to hide. Tenants tugged their forelock and deferred to his opinion. They didn't require unending caution or the light, easy banter that served so well to keep society at a distance. He had his duty, a few acquaintances, his collection and Hardwick to share his enthusiasm.

So, no—there could be no marriage. How to maintain defences in such an intimate relationship? Even to imagine the sort of work required made him shudder. His father and brother might be gone, but the lessons they had taught had served him well: don't ask for anything. For God's sake, never give anything away. Keep the exterior calm and the interior guarded and you could not be hurt.

But he had given the correct answer and Mairi's face had lightened—in direct contrast to the dark turn of his thoughts.

'Eventually is not soon enough, dear brother.' Her gaze grew mischievous. 'I confess, I'd thought to nag you until you joined me in Town.' She tilted her head. 'But now I am entertaining new suspicions.' She glanced towards the door, then back at him with widening eyes. 'You must tell me all, Braedon… Are you hiding your bridal candidate up here with you?'

Now he laughed. 'You're the mad one in the family, not I. Sorry to disappoint, but I've no secret bride stashed away.' He gestured grandly. 'However, you're more than welcome to make a search of the cellars and attics.' He grinned at her before he took a long swig of his drink.

'Cawker.' She rolled her eyes. 'I'm talking about *Miss* Hardwick.'

The brandy came back up with far more velocity than it had gone down. Eyes watering, he sputtered and glared at his plague of a sister. 'Hardwick?' he choked. 'You truly are mad.' He ignored the rush of…what?—Interest? Excitement?—that surged at the unexpected notion.

'I'm not mad. She's a woman—and one who apparently shares your odd interests.'

'She is in my *employ*,' he stated firmly. It was not arousal stirring to life at Mairead's ridiculous idea. It was merely the old, latent curiosity—the wonder at what Hardwick was trying so hard to hide. 'And a very valuable employee she is, too, so please keep your wild notions to yourself. I won't have her scared off because you cannot keep your imagination in check.'

He drew breath, ready to scold her further,

but his sister turned and crossed her arms in defiance. The lace at the end of her sleeve fell back just as the sunlight streaming though the windows slanted across her. It illuminated clearly the large bruise above her elbow, a stain pulsing darkly against her fair skin in the exact shape of a man's hand.

Fury roared to life inside him. He rushed her like a maddened bull, though he forced himself to be gentle as he grasped her arm.

'What's this?' he demanded, his voice gone rough. Her skin felt so soft, her bones so fragile cradled in his broad fist. 'What have you done, Mairi? Have you finally pushed Ashton too far?' He needed a target for the rage clawing its way through him.

She yanked her arm from his grasp and stepped away. 'Don't be ridiculous. Ashton would never hurt me.'

Braedon's fists tightened at his sides.

'No!' she cried. 'I can see what you are thinking and I would never serve my husband so ill. It was just a…misunderstanding. A small flirtation that got out of hand.'

There was no keeping all that he felt from his face. Dismay. Disillusionment. Disappointment.

'Don't look at me like that, Braedon.' She gave a soft sob and he was seized with the urge to pull her close, tuck her away in his embrace and shield her as he'd always done.

He didn't. Couldn't. 'Does Ashton know?' But he already knew the answer—knew that that had been Mairi's idea all along.

'He challenged the man—no, not to a duel. Fisticuffs, at a training salon. Ashton beat the dastard to a bloody pulp and then he packed his things and fled to his hunting lodge in the Highlands.'

Braedon sighed. 'I take it back, Mairi. You're not mad, you're merely trying to make your husband so.'

His sister lifted her chin. 'These bruises are badges of honour, brother dear.' She let loose a defiant bark that was supposed to be laughter. 'At least I know he feels something for me. My marriage may not be sunshine and roses, but it is passionate and deep.'

Braedon closed his eyes.

'Think what you like, but at least I never have to wonder if Ashton even sees me.' She jabbed a finger high. 'At least I'm not like Mother, sitting alone up there in the solar day after day, while my husband forgets my very existence!'

'I understand.' Weariness swept over him. 'Of course I do.'

Mairead had turned back to the view outside the window again. She stood straight as a rod, but she suddenly appeared to shrink in on herself. 'I'm afraid,' she whispered. 'I'm afraid I've pushed him too far this time.'

'You should be. A man can only take so much, my dear.' Feeling a hundred years old, Braedon poured another drink and tossed it back. 'Listen. I'm only going to say this to you once. Once,' he emphasised, and refrained from gazing longingly at the door. 'Ashton will be back, I'm sure. Wait for him here, if you wish, but you had better use this time to think long and hard on what sort of marriage you want, what sort of wife you wish to be.' He set his glass down. 'The man cares for you, my dear. I can see it. Everybody can. But now is the time for you to finally believe it—or to let him go. God knows, the *ton* is full of married couples who exist in a state of polite estrangement.'

She made a wordless sound of protest.

'You cannot keep testing him this way, Mairi. Decide now,' he continued ruthlessly, 'before it is too late.' He sighed. 'And what of children? Will you treat them the same way? Will you leave them anxious and wary, never knowing what to expect from you? How to approach you?'

'Braedon!' It was a whispered cry of despair.

'Think about it. You have some serious decisions to make. Make them here, if you wish. Stay as long as you like.' He deliberately firmed his tone. 'But I won't have you making mischief.'

'I wouldn't.' She sounded small now, as well.

'Your mind will be busy enough. Look around, talk to the housekeeper, the vicar's wife, perhaps. Find some project to keep your fingers occupied as well.'

She did not turn to meet his eye. 'Thank you, Braedon.'

He fled. With a measured tread that belied his inner turmoil he strode quickly through the gloom. He felt for Mairi. It was never easy, coming home to Denning. Yet it was a damned sight easier than growing up here. He sighed. He was doing what he could to change things, but he and Mairi would always carry the burdens of their childhood. It was just a damned shame that her marriage must also be marked.

He found himself in the soothing quiet of his weapons wing. Some instinct had him pausing beneath the vast glory of the dome. Braedon closed his eyes and let the empty silence of the place ease him, push him further away from the turbulence brought on by his sister's distress. Yet her words echoed in his mind. She accused him of hiding? He snorted, thinking of Mairi's histrionics and Hardwick's manufactured, forbidding aspect. There were ways and ways of hiding.

And suddenly it was Hardwick's image filling his head and making inroads on his carefully maintained borders. Her earlier words sprang to mind. She'd been irritated—because he had not known of her preference for the sea? He tried to recall if he'd ever before seen Hardwick irritated. She was always calm, competent, serene. He'd grown used to—hell, he'd come to count on—her silent efficiency.

Damn Mairi anyway, for her outlandish suggestion. Of course he'd wondered about his assistant. Occasionally he had surprised a delighted laugh out of her, or caught a glimpse of her hard at work, her lips pursed in concentration and her hair falling in tendrils about her face—and he'd known that there was *something* there. But he hadn't looked too deeply. All these months he'd tucked away his curiosity, banished the occasional urge to know what Hardwick was hiding beneath all that severe tailoring and daunting effectiveness. The more he'd come to value her skills, the less inclined he'd been to meddle. Now his interest had been piqued again and it had brought along the image, lush and vivid, of him starting with those damned buttons and peeling her layers away, one by one.

Flushed and hot, he banished the vision and headed for the workroom and the blade he'd abandoned there. He grasped the hilt and lunged, stabbing a thrust through an imaginary opponent. What he needed was a bit of practice to conquer such wayward thoughts.

And that was why Mairead was wrong. He'd no need to hide. He'd faced war, both at home and abroad, he'd swum through the murky waters of diplomatic intrigue and he'd survived social manoeuvring that made politics look like child's play. And he'd yet to meet the obstacle he couldn't conquer with determination and a damned good weapon.

He glanced over at Hardwick's empty desk. Surely this one would be no different.

It had taken a couple of days, but Chloe had at last tracked down the hint she needed regarding Skanda's Spear. She clutched the table in relief. She needed to maintain her usual impeccable work performance, for her attempts to attract the marquess's attention in other ways were resulting in mixed success, at best.

She'd thought that seeing him outside her usual sphere might be a good beginning, so she'd 'arranged' to run into him in different spots about the house and the grounds. Lord Marland had looked intrigued, the first time, and then increasingly resigned, but in each instance, he'd merely nodded, exchanged a brief nod and moved on.

So she'd tried bringing up other topics of conversation. He'd followed easily when she'd asked about the estate, talking with enthusiasm about the improvements he was undertaking at his bailiff's advice. But then he'd caught himself and cast her a measuring glance. Later he'd resisted speaking of his sister and flatly refused to discuss the weather, each time turning the conversation back to the collection or, repeatedly, the Spear of Skanda.

Yesterday, though, she'd experienced a greater measure of success. She'd eschewed her usual, severe chignon and worn her hair loose down the back of her neck. She'd gone about other business as usual, but several times she'd looked up to find him staring intently from a distance. Near the end of the day they'd been debating the merits of open and closed cases for a set of ancient flint knives when his argument had stuttered to a stop. She'd glanced up in surprise to see his gaze fixed on the curl that had fallen forwards over her shoulder. Without another word he had stood and stalked from the workroom.

She had grinned for the remainder of the evening and taken it as a sign, however small, that he did feel a degree of attraction for her. It gave her real hope. They were so compatible in other ways. And she certainly felt more than enough heat for him.

But today she needed to focus on her work. She had a feeling that the marquess knew more about this mysterious spear than he was saying, but it wasn't her place to ask. Now at last, in his vast library she'd finally discovered that Skanda was one of several names for the Hindu war god.

She'd even found an illustration, complete with a depiction of his favoured weapon—a spear with a wide, spade-shaped blade. Her heart lifted. She knew of several experts who might be of immediate help for this sort of artefact. She'd just bent closer to study the image when she was distracted by several flashes of light dancing across the bookcase in front of her.

She knew what that meant. Skanda was forgotten as she tore off her spectacles and made her quick and stealthy way to the large windows. She eased herself into position. See without being seen, that was the trick. There. One small step more… Her breath hitched. Her heart began to pound as if she was the one about to engage in combat.

For combat it was to be. Lord Marland moved below, pacing the levelled bowling green that he had long ago appropriated for his more… unusual pastime. He gripped the newly restored cavalry sword in one hand, sunlight flashing with each restless slash of the blade. A predatory gleam lit his eye as he watched his sparring partner ready himself for their match.

The twitching started up again, deep in the secret recesses of Chloe's belly, a tympani that pulsed loudest between her legs and sent echoing tremors along all of her limbs. The thrumming began each and every time she saw the marquess like this—a hunter, a warrior clad incongruously in thigh-hugging breeches and high, worn boots. He'd cast his coat and waist-coat aside, leaving only thin linen and a few tantalising glimpses of browned skin and broad torso. Chloe's mouth went dry.

Lord Marland was warming to his task, each practised lunge and thrust showing her more. All those sculpted muscles and masculine planes and angles. She closed her eyes, wondering how they would feel beneath her fingers.

The clash of steel signalled the opening of battle. Chloe took a risk and edged a little closer to the window. The combatants were engaged, their focus locked intently on each other. She allowed hers to fix on her employer. He was magnificent, a figure straight out of legend. He was an expert in his warrior's dance of strength and strategy, and she was enraptured. She was...

Caught.

The weight of someone's gaze rested on the back of her neck, growing more palpable by the second. The tiny hairs there rose high. Someone was staring at her as intently as she was watching the scene below.

Grasping for a veneer of nonchalance, she turned. For the second time in as many days, she confronted Lord Marland's sister poised on the threshold of a doorway.

'I had wondered how you managed it.' The countess's expression was mobile, fading from surprise and interest into something that resembled mischief.

'My lady?' Chloe did not move from the window.

'Living up here, tolerating the isolation. Getting along with my singularly uncommunicative brother. But now I see.' Lady Ashton's mouth quirked. 'You fit right in because you are just like the rest of this family—gifted at hiding what you don't wish to face.'

Chloe stiffened. 'I'm sorry, but I don't know what you mean.'

'No matter.' Still smiling, the countess stepped fully into the library. 'I'm in no place to criticize, in any case. I heard the clamour and merely wished to see the show.' She crossed the room to stand at the window by Chloe's side. With considerable enjoyment she watched the fight below, but after a moment she leaned abruptly over the sill. 'Braedon's partner—is that Sir Thomas Cobbe?'

Chloe realised she'd been edging away. 'It is.' She gave up and moved back to stand next to the countess. 'He comes to train with Lord Marland as frequently as his schedule will allow.'

'I heard he was the best. Knighted after he became sword master to the Prince Regent and his set, was he not?' She winked in Chloe's direction. 'Of course that was years ago. He may be a bit older than Braedon, but I met him once in London. Poor as a church mouse, but I should say he'd be more than able to hold his own in battle. And he's just as sword-mad as my brother.'

Her eyes twinkled in good humour. 'I'm beginning to wonder if we might find some common ground as well.' She looked over her shoulder at the books Chloe had spread over a table and her spectacles lying conspicuously on top. 'What was it you were working on, before you were so understandably distracted?'

Chloe took another step back towards her work. 'Lord Marland wishes to acquire an elusive weapon, a spear. I should perhaps—'

She was interrupted by a clash of steel and a low grunt that echoed up from below. Lord Marland's opponent had sunk to one knee. But the fight was far from finished. Though his sword was locked with the marquess's, Sir Thomas suddenly held a wicked-looking dirk in his other hand. He aimed a vicious swing at Lord Marland's knee.

'Oh, that's hardly cricket, is it?' the countess cried.

Her heart flopping like a fish, Chloe gasped as her employer jumped back, the blade missing him by a hair. Sir Thomas lunged to his feet and the battle raged on, as fiercely as ever.

'They are marvellous, aren't they?' Lady Ashton murmured. 'Just look at Braedon. Fully engaged, utterly alive. Battle brings it out of him.' She sighed. 'It was ever thus. It is only in these moments that he allows himself to step out of the shadows and into the light.'

Chloe said nothing, though part of her burned to encourage the countess, to push and pry and question. The strange feeling was back again, alive in her gut, urging her to give in to the temptation. But she shouldn't. She knew Lord Marland would find it intrusive. And therein lay her particular genius.

Chloe knew how to blend, to fade. Transforming herself into what was needed most was a strategy that had allowed her to survive all the difficult periods of her life. It was just such a tactic that had convinced the marquess to grant her the secure haven of this position. And after so long, she knew what Lord Marland wished for and needed her to be. So she did what she'd become so adept at doing: she swallowed her curiosity, tucked away all of her wonder and excitement and unslaked desire. She was Hardwick. Calm, detached and efficient.

Safe.

She breathed deeply. The warriors outside had reached a *détente.* They'd discarded their weapons and were pouring tall drinks as they relived their skirmish.

'Enough of them!'

Chloe started when the countess reached out to tug her away from the window.

'Come, Miss Hardwick. Let us spend some time getting to know each other.'

'I'm sorry, my lady, but your brother was most insistent about the spear...' Chloe began to make her way back to her work-strewn table.

'He always is,' Lady Ashton said with a roll of her eyes. 'But answer a question for me— when was the last time you took an afternoon for yourself?'

She hesitated, pursing her lips. She had taken a day, spent the morning walking along the sea-shore and the afternoon shopping for essentials in the village. But when had that been? 'Months ago,' she admitted.

'Well, you are overdue then, are you not?' The countess's smile was pure wickedness. 'I can be quite insistent, too, you know.'

Chloe glanced again at the books and corre-spondence awaiting her. Her duty was clear. Yet those other voices were calling, too, and for the first time she wondered if duty—and safety— was enough. 'Perhaps for a short while.'

'Come!' Lady Ashton was triumphant. 'I want to hear it all—how you came to be my brother's right hand. And perhaps I shall share with you how I escaped Denning when I ca-joled Lord Ashton into asking for my hand.' She waggled her fingers and extended her arm.

Pushing aside her last reservation, Chloe took it and allowed herself to be led away.

'And that,' the countess said later, her voice full of laughter, 'is how I convinced Lord Ashton that he could not bear the thought of life without me.'

Chloe only kept her jaw from dropping by taking a sip of her tea. Among the servants at Denning, Lady Ashton had the reputation of a certain...instability. But she quite liked the countess. She and Lord Marland's sister were comfortably ensconced in the lady's apartments with a tray from the kitchens. 'I don't know how you dared,' she said after she'd got over her shock.

'In truth, I had him in a frenzy by that time. He was nearly half-mad with desire and took only the slightest of pushes.' Lady Ashton's smile faded and Chloe caught the hint of sadness that coloured her expression. 'But enough about me. I want to learn about you.' She looked her over closely. 'Months since you've taken a day off?' Impishness chased any lingering melancholy away as she leaned forwards. 'You must enjoy your position enormously. Your father held it before you, did he not?'

Chloe nodded. 'He met Lord Marland abroad, years ago, and was hired as your brother's factor. He travelled, doing research and acquiring pieces. When the marquess decided to begin building the new wing to house his collection, he asked Father to come and take charge.'

'But where were you while your father was working overseas for so long?'

'He was my stepfather, actually,' Chloe confessed. She ran her finger around the edge of her cup. Surely it couldn't hurt to share this small bit of her history. The countess could discover any of the same information if she asked her brother. 'But he treated me as his own and we were very close. After my mother died, he was distraught. He wanted to leave England for a while, to help him forget. I went to school. He wrote me the loveliest letters, filled with the sights he'd seen and the treasures he'd found. When I was finished with school myself, I took a teaching position at the establishment.'

'How happy you must have been when he returned.'

She couldn't suppress the smile that bloomed at the thought. 'Ecstatic, I should say. We had not seen each other in years. I was thrilled to leave my position and to come here to act as his assistant.' She looked up. 'It was as if we'd never parted. I'll always be grateful to your brother for those lovely months I shared with my father before his death.'

'How lucky you were,' Lady Ashton said wistfully. 'I rather thought that Ashton was my chance at such a relationship. We had such a wonderfully satisfactory courtship and after our marriage we grew even closer.' With a heavy sigh she set down her tea. 'Thick as thieves, we were, so impatient to get back to each other at the end of the day. I finished his sentences and I vow that he knew what I was going to say before I could finish thinking it…' Her words trailed off and her gaze came unfocused. Chloe knew she'd left these rooms altogether. She sipped her tea and left the countess to her memories.

But in a dazzling change of mood, Lady Ashton whirled and fixed a determinedly hopeful smile upon her. 'But the bloom does fade. A common enough situation, I would guess.' She leaned forwards. 'What would you recommend, Miss Hardwick, for a couple grown distant from each other?'

Chloe's cup rattled in the saucer. 'Why ask me?'

'My brother's letters are full of praise for you, dear. He raves about your uncanny skill at reading people, at your ability to handle any situation or solve any problem. I thought you might have a suggestion that could help me.'

She flushed. She shouldn't answer, shouldn't meddle. Almost without thought, she ran her fingers down the row of buttons on her jacket. She'd forgotten herself, crawled too far out of her shell. She needed to get back.

Yet the countess's pain was apparent and remarkably like her brother's. She pursed her lips together.

'You miss him, it is obvious,' she abruptly blurted. 'I'd wager that he feels the same. Perhaps he only needs a reminder of the closeness that you once shared.'

'A reminder?' Lady Ashton arched a brow. 'I remind him quite regularly, Miss Hardwick.'

Chloe tried not to flush. 'Something only you would know, I meant.'

The countess sat back with a frown. 'A secret?'

'A secret wish, perhaps. A regret? Something that you would understand the significance of, more than anyone else.'

The frown deepened and her eyes narrowed. 'That is a very interesting notion, Miss Hardwick. I shall set my mind to it.'

Several long moments of silence passed. Chloe quietly set her cup down. She started to rise, but jumped when Lady Ashton gasped out loud.

'I know just the thing!' The countess had gone pink with excitement. 'It couldn't be simpler—or more perfect! Miss Hardwick, you are brilliant!'

'I am truly glad I could help, my lady.' Chloe got to her feet. 'I should get back now, though. Thank you for a lovely visit.'

'Oh, you must forgive me once more.' Lady

Ashton rose as well. 'First I steal you away and then I neglect you. But you must not worry that Braedon will berate you, Miss Hardwick. I doubt we'll see either hide or hair of him until dinner and then we shall present a united front. He'll be helpless against the two of us.'

Chloe paused and placed her hands on the back of her chair. 'Dinner?'

'Indeed. The vicar and his wife are to join us. And Sir Thomas, of course.'

Chloe bit her lip. 'I'm afraid that I do not normally join the company at dinner.'

The countess frowned. 'How do you normally take your meals?'

'On a tray in my room. Or sometimes with the housekeeper in her apartment.' She shifted. 'I've found that the servants are not really comfortable having me in their hall.'

The countess's eyes flashed. 'I see that I've come not a moment too soon. Well. This will not do.' Her smile welcomed Chloe in as a conspirator. 'Pull your best dress out of your closet, Miss Hardwick. Dust it off. You shall be at the formal table tonight. I need you to even out the numbers.'

A mad surge of disappointment froze Chloe to the spot. 'I cannot, my lady.'

'Why ever not?'

'I have no dress to wear. All of my garments

are...' She made a small gesture down the length of her protective coat and heavy skirt.

'What, *all?*' Shock had apparently robbed the countess of further words.

Chloe nodded.

'How can this be? No—never mind.' Lady Ashton was already across the room and pulling the chord to summon a maid. She appeared to become more agitated by the minute.

Chloe instinctively moved to soothe her. 'Don't fret, please. No one here will fuss over uneven numbers. Or perhaps I can send a footman with an invitation to one of the other neighbourhood ladies...'

'Stop right there, Miss Hardwick!' The countess's tone was firm. 'How efficient you are. No wonder my brother values you so highly. You step right in and do what needs to be done, don't you?'

'That is a basic, if sweeping, description of my duty, my lady.' Chloe's mouth twisted wryly.

'Not today it isn't.'

A soft knock sounded on the door. Daisy entered, but the countess waved her out. 'No, I need Brigita, please. Have her come at once.' She crossed the room to close the door behind the maid, but her dresser was already hovering outside in the passage. 'Brigita! Come in, I am in dire need of your wisdom.' Her foreign serving woman entered and the countess firmly shut the door on the befuddled maid even as she swept her hand in Chloe's direction.

The pair of them took up a side-by-side stance, identical expressions of displeasure on their faces.

Chloe took a step back. 'What is it?'

'What do you think?' the countess mused. 'Jewel tones, I should think.'

The formidable Brigita nodded.

'The dark purple, then.'

'No, my lady—not with that pearlescent skin and dark hair. She needs the ocean-blue.' This was said with heavy Germanic finality.

Chloe began to understand what was going on. She took another step back. 'No, my lady...' But she paused. Changing her hair had had a measurable effect on the marquess. What might happen if she changed...everything? She looked down at her costume. Could she do it? Step outside of the disguise? Leave herself vulnerable?

Her eyes closed. Images sprang to life in her mind. Lord Marland at practice, all muscle and might. Leaning over her desk, eyes glowing over a renovation. Sitting across the workroom in companionable silence. Gripping her arm and smiling up with warmth and support.

She nearly trembled with sudden yearning. She could do it. Because she wanted all of that again—plus the promise of more. Not so long ago she'd thought that she was grateful to have

landed close to happiness. Truly, she was changing inside—because now close wasn't enough.
She wanted to be happy—she wanted to wallow
in it. And she quite desperately wanted to make
Lord Marland happy, too.

She thought they had a chance at it. A spark
did exist between them. She knew it. Just as
she knew he had been ignoring it nearly as
diligently as she had been urging it to life. A
complete change of appearance might be what
she needed to blow his resistance to shreds, to
obliterate the barriers he'd placed between them
from the beginning.

Only one thought gave her pause. To what
end? He was a marquess. Would he even consider a relationship with his assistant? She bit
her lip. He'd never exhibited any need to live
by any strictures except his own. His words to
her the other day had certainly encouraged her
to look beyond society's expectations.

'Oh, yes, Miss Hardwick.' The countess was
waiting, all kindness. 'This is a momentous day.
Not only has my taciturn brother offered me
advice, but for perhaps the first time, I am taking it. Today you have been of invaluable help to
me.' Her voice softened. 'Today you have given
me hope.'

All of her new feelings whirled inside of her,
urging her on. 'But what of—?'

'No.' Lady Ashton raised a hand. 'Now I am

going to go start my own preparations. *You* are going to put yourself in Brigita's hands.'

Chloe wanted to do it. But all of her old instincts still had a voice, too. She might be risking the safety that she'd worked so hard for. 'What if Lord Marland doesn't approve?' It came out in a whisper.

The countess grinned. 'Approve?' She ran a practised eye up and down Chloe's long form. 'I think that my brother is going to thank us. In fact, I believe he'll be on his knees before us both.'

Whoosh went her insides, roiling again. That mental image crowned all the others and drowned her worries in a flood of excitement.

'Come, Miss Hardwick.' The countess beckoned. 'It is time for you to step out of the shadows.'

Her words resonated through Chloe, as sharp and loud and long as the strike of a bell. She met Lord Marland's sister's eyes and nodded.

Chapter Three

The vicar's lady was excessively fond of her cats. At least, her incessant ramblings about them made it sound that way to Braedon. Her obsession could not be healthy—he'd learned the hard way, as a child, the dangers of emotional dependence on something so fragile.

On Mrs Goodmond's other side, Thom tossed back another drink. Unobtrusively, Braedon changed position, trying to wiggle his toes. He couldn't begrudge Mairi her dinner—not as he'd been the one to suggest both a project and an acquaintance with the vicar's wife—but he couldn't help pining for his favourite boots and a pint down at the Hog's Tail.

He'd just shifted again, seeking relief for his cramped toes, when he saw Thom's eyes alight. Ah. Mairi must have arrived. He turned towards the door. Now they could be seated and he could rest his aching…

Tight shoes were forgotten as he realised Mairi wasn't alone. She stood poised just inside the parlour door, another female—a tall, slender beauty—at her side.

Mrs Goodmond fell silent. Thom stepped up close beside him.

'I thought I was going to have to change your nickname to the Mouldering Marquess, stuck as you've been up here, with no opponents or conquests to speak of, but I see that you've been holding out on me.' His sparring partner nudged him with an elbow. 'Who is she?'

Braedon opened his mouth to inform Thom that he had no idea who the strange woman might be, when his sister drew her forwards to greet the vicar. Just the smallest thing, a change of expression, the fading of nerves into a gentle smile of greeting—but it tilted Braedon's world right off its axis.

'Hardwick,' he breathed. The earth rolled beneath his feet. No. It jerked to a halt, leaving him stumbling on alone.

'Hardwick?' scoffed Thom. 'Nice try, Braedon, but I'm not that gullible.'

Hardwick. It was she. He didn't know how he could be so certain. He'd never seen *his* Hardwick smile so widely. He'd never seen her hair shining so richly, left to lie in gleaming sable curls long past the sweet curve of her nape. He only knew that it was Hardwick standing there, as foreign and exotic as an ocean naiad in a gown containing every changing colour of the sea.

Thom let loose a long, low breath. 'By all that's holy, that *is* Hardwick!' He shot Braedon an accusatory glance and moved to intercept the two women.

Cursing wildly in his head, Braedon made his excuses to the vicar's wife and followed. Some of the anxiety returned to Hardwick's expression as he joined the small group.

Good. Some primitive part of him did not want her to be comfortable. Mairi crowed with delight in her handiwork and Thom was at that very moment expressing his own approval of the surprise, but Braedon was feeling unaccountably...furious.

Why? He breathed deeply, pushed back, tried to impose the emotional distance that was such a vital component of his equilibrium, but it fell apart each time he looked at her and the anger in his gut raged a little higher.

Again, he forced himself to consider why. Because the two women had cooked this up between themselves, without his knowledge? Because Thom was acting like a randy stallion who'd just scented a new mare? Or because *this* was what Hardwick had been hiding all of these months—and he'd never had the faintest idea?

He still hadn't spoken a word. She sent another nervous glance his way and he stepped closer. 'Hardwick,' he began. His voice had gone rough as gravel. He had half a mind to order her back to her room and into her regular, daunting uniform.

'Lord Marland.' She inclined her head.

'I gather that I am now meant to compliment you on your changed appearance?'

Her hand rose and hovered uncertainly for a moment over her bodice. He recognised the movement and suffered a small-minded sense of victory.

But Hardwick raised her chin and lowered her hand. It was just as well, for there were no buttons, only miles of skin and a sophisticated gown of the most gorgeous changeable silk. Beautiful blue shot with green, the dress flowed over her like the ocean it was meant to represent.

And then she smiled at him. 'Of course you are not obligated, my lord, but should you choose to offer a compliment, I will be glad to accept it.'

He snorted. 'You don't need me to tell you that you look beautiful this evening, as I'm sure both your looking glass and my sister have already done so.'

She tilted her head. 'I am sure that it should not be so, but the fact remains that a compliment from a gentleman always means more. So I will thank you—even for that half-hearted attempt.'

Glowering, he took a drink. 'I am reminded of the adage about a leopard never really changing her spots.' He lifted his glass. 'And find myself hoping it is true.'

She frowned. 'I'm not changing my spots, my lord. Following your analogy, I would say that I am merely shifting my pelt about to showcase a new side.'

'Turning yourself inside out is more like it,' he grumbled.

Hardwick laughed. 'Nothing so dramatic, I promise.'

His sister had noticed his ire and moved to intercept. 'Do forgive us for the delay,' she announced to the group at large. 'Shall we all go in to dinner?' She took Braedon's arm and left Hardwick to be escorted by the vicar.

But before Mr Goodmond led her away, Hardwick stepped close and sparkled up at him. 'You may yet get a glimpse of my insides, Lord Marland, but not before you display a bit of your own.'

Frowning, Braedon led the company in. His agitation didn't fade as they took their seats. He'd known something was in the wind, but he'd done his best to ignore it. He shook his head.

Hardwick already had so many fine and useful qualities—now she displayed beauty and wit as well? Any other woman and he'd be intrigued. But this was Hardwick! Didn't she see? Changing herself forced other things to change, too. He suppressed a snort. Show his insides? She should know him well enough to realise he'd avoid such a thing at all costs.

He sighed. Surely this was a temporary aberration, provoked by Mairi, no doubt. He would wait and things were sure to go back to normal.

But finding his balance proved impossible. The distance lens through which he normally viewed life had flipped completely—and focused itself firmly on his assistant. He barely ate, could scarcely concentrate on Thom's sporadic attempts at conversation. He could only stare at the magnified brilliance of Hardwick.

She looked so soft. The close-viewing lens roamed over her, highlighting glowing skin, every bit as lustrous as the pearls enhancing her gown, cataloging the plush and creamy bosom so gratifyingly displayed. Her eyes sparkled brilliantly blue. Where were her damned spectacles?

Her laughter drifted down the table and Braedon stifled a flare of outrage. How could this be? Surely it was not *jealousy* burning in his gut—over Hardwick?

She glanced his way again, just the lightest,

fleeting brush of their gazes. She coloured and looked away.

No. He wasn't jealous. The notion was too ridiculous to be entertained. And yet he couldn't help but wonder—from where had come that glow, lighting her face from within? Why had he never seen her smile so, before now? He couldn't look away.

He wasn't alone. Thom stared unabashedly. The vicar kept shooting her small glances of bemusement. Even Mrs Goodmond frowned repeatedly in Hardwick's direction. As the next course came out, the vicar's wife laid down her utensils and cleared her throat.

'Miss Hardwick, I wondered if you intend to engage a chaperon to stay here at Denning along with you.' She gave a nod towards Mairi. 'Lady Ashton lends you countenance, of course, but I'm sure her stay is only temporary.'

Hardwick frowned. 'I hadn't thought to, Mrs Goodmond.' She set down her own silverware and met the woman's eye directly. 'In truth, I hadn't even considered such a thing. When I first came to Denning, my father was here as well. After his death, I was so distraught, and then so busy, that it never entered my mind that I should need a chaperon.'

'Well, it entered mine,' the lady returned somewhat waspishly. 'But Lord Marland has been so busily engaged in restoring his estate and you seemed so occupied with the new wing, and so I thought… There was talk, of course, but, well, I let the matter drop.' She leaned back in her chair and bestowed a sternly disapproving look, first upon her husband, then upon her victim. 'And now I am picking it back up.'

Hardwick stiffened. 'I've only changed my dress, Mrs Goodmond. Not my character.'

The lady sniffed. 'Appearances matter, Miss Hardwick. And now that your appearance has changed…a chaperon is in order. I only hope it is not too late.'

Braedon had heard enough. 'I respect your position, of course,' he said with a nod to the vicar. 'But Hardwick is a member of my staff and I don't appreciate interference in how I run my household.'

'Now, everyone take a breath,' Mairi interrupted as Mrs Goodmond puffed up, ready for a fight. 'I am sure that my brother will do all that is right and proper, ma'am. He usually does.' She smiled. 'Now, he tells me that you manage several charitable projects in the area. Will you tell me about your work?'

Braedon ducked his head. It had been a long time since he'd had to reach for the numbness that had protected him so long ago, but he could use a good dose of it now. How heartily he wished this night over. Tomorrow he would have a talk with Hardwick, clear the air and insist that they return to the normal, comfortable state of things.

Chloe bit her lip and stared at her plate. This scenario had not played out as she'd hoped. Lord Marland appeared only annoyed at her transformation, not intrigued. Why was he so resistant?

She caught him tossing her a quick, scowling glance and thought perhaps she could guess why. She'd been so caught up in the swirl of her new feelings that she'd forgot that only her inner landscape was in upheaval—and had been even before the countess had arrived. Everything inside Chloe was shifting as fear receded and curiosity and confidence began to grow. She was changing, nearly by the minute. Lord Marland was not—and neither was his view of her.

She sucked in a breath and hoped that she had not made a colossal mistake.

Her head came up as she heard her name.

'—and I understand now the high praise you included in your letters, Braedon,' the countess said. 'And I find myself in complete agreement. Why, I've only been here a few days and Miss Hardwick has helped me with a particularly sticky problem.'

The marquess mumbled something incoherent.

'You'll recall the matter we discussed,' his sister said brightly. She turned to Mrs Goodmond. 'I'm happy to say that the solution will lead to a large project of my own. You see, my husband's birthday approaches.' The countess caught Chloe's eye. 'Growing up, he's mentioned that such occasions were never marked. But this year I intend that it should be.'

Understanding dawned. The secret, the regret that she had mentioned as a way back to intimacy with the earl. She nodded.

'I'd like to make it a grand event. An occasion suited to his particular tastes. A celebration of every masculine delight.'

From Sir Thomas came a great guffaw. The countess turned a saucy eye on him. '*Nearly* every masculine delight, then.' Her smile faded. 'It shall be a great deal of work. I suspect I must find an assistant of my own, when I return to Town. I can only hope to find someone half so competent as Miss Hardwick.'

Chloe straightened, lightning-struck by the obvious notion. She caught Lord Marland's eye, but he quickly glanced away. No, she thought, staring hard at him. She had not made a mistake. She hadn't been wrong to pursue this position when she'd had such a great need of it, and she wasn't wrong to heed her changing needs now. But perhaps she had tried the wrong tack. Perhaps, now that she had delivered the marquess such a shock, she should let him taste her absence.

'Oh, but you've given me a lovely idea, Lady Ashton!' she said. 'I'm due some time away from my position, as you pointed out earlier. So why do I not come to London to help you?'

The countess grasped her hand and gasped in delight. The Goodmonds exchanged a glance. The marquess, however, gave a snort of derision that echoed around the room.

'Oh, would you?' Lady Ashton cried. 'It would be just the thing! You are a model of organisation and efficiency—with your help I'm sure I could not fail to please my husband.'

Lord Marland eyed his sister with obvious irritation. 'Don't be ridiculous, Mairead.' He turned to Chloe with the same hostility. She fought back a shiver as he raked a critical eye over her. 'I know I asked you to find some way to keep busy, but I never meant for you to turn Hardwick into a pet project.'

Chloe stiffened. Now she was becoming agitated.

'You are the one being ridiculous, Braedon,' Lady Ashton responded. 'Miss Hardwick is a person, not a project. A young woman with hopes, dreams and feelings.'

'And responsibilities. I need her here. The collection—'

'Will be fine in your capable hands,' Chloe

said smoothly. 'The wing is in the last stages of construction. Most of the collection is ready, or waiting on the completion of our custom-built display cases. Surely I could be spared for a few weeks?'

'Famous!' the countess exclaimed, with a clap of her hands. 'I'm so relieved!' She squeezed Chloe's hand again. 'I promise that it won't be all work and no play. We shall have plenty of time to shop and meet new people, to go to the theatre and the parks. It will be a grand time all around. What do you think?'

Chloe's heart leapt. Underneath the table, her free hand gripped her napkin until her knuckles were surely whitened. It sounded terrifying—and divine.

'Now that is the outside of enough,' Lord Marland scoffed. 'You mean to take Hardwick to Town and thrust her amongst the *ton*?'

His mockery made Chloe blanch.

'It would be nothing but an unmitigated disaster.'

Lady Ashton clenched her jaw. 'I think that you underestimate Miss Hardwick.'

'No, I believe that you overestimate the fashionable set. Hardwick is no empty-headed society chit. What does she care for fashion and furbelows?' He gestured in her direction. 'Hardwick can estimate mortar to the last brick.

She deals in stone blocks and steel blades, not crowds and gowns and gossip.'

Chloe stilled. The marquess surely didn't intend to be cruel.

'I know your tricks, in any case, Mairead.' Lord Marland's voice had gone heavy with warning. 'You won't leave it at a party and be done with it. You'll turn this jaunt into a husband-hunting expedition—and what will that gain Hardwick? She's not that sort of woman. She'll be left with naught but dashed hopes and broken dreams.'

Jagged and intense, the pain ripped through her. His disregard was so casual and immediate. So easily he summed her up and dismissed her.

She could scarcely believe how much it hurt. But worse was her suddenly bleak vision of their future. The marquess had made his stance clear. He was content, insistent even, on carrying on in the same manner. Yet what else could she expect? He did not see her—but how could he? He saw only what she had shown him. What she had become—for him.

Suddenly the truth was blindingly clear. She could not stay. Could not pretend that nothing had changed inside her. The pain she felt now was nothing to what such a course would lead to. Before long she would be writhing beneath an unbearable weight of unrequited caring and burgeoning resentment.

Hardwick had no future. Not with the marquess. Not even without him.

Yet, she was more than Hardwick, was she not?

She would never find out, if she stayed.

And just like that, Chloe decided. It was going to hurt. It was most decidedly not going to be safe. But she was going to go.

She stood. 'Upon further reflection, I've changed my mind. Lord Marland, I hereby tender my resignation.'

Over his sputtered protests, she turned to his sister. 'Lady Ashton, I would be pleased to accompany you, to assist you with your project.'

And to take the chance to discover just who Miss Chloe Hardwick truly was.

Chapter Four

❦

'A post from London, my lord.' Billings hovered in the doorway to the workroom. 'The messenger said it was urgent.'

Braedon winced as he looked up from the rack and ruin of Hardwick's desk. The constant pressure of his grinding jaw had given him a headache. 'Does he wait for an answer?'

'No, sir.'

Impatient, he beckoned the man forwards. Billings, unable to hide his distaste, picked his way past stacked crates and piles of books and papers strewn on the floor. Braedon sighed. Hardwick had not been gone a month, but her well-ordered system and intricately organised process was disintegrating about his ears.

'The completion of the wing is not progressing quite as smoothly since Hardwick left us, is it?' Billings handed over the thick vellum and stared at the shambles of the desk. 'Shall I send down a maid to assist you, my lord?'

'No, no,' Braedon refused irritably. 'I shall set it all to rights, eventually.' He was tired of hearing Hardwick's name, weary of having to excise her from his thoughts. It was ridiculous to fixate on her now that she had gone. She'd been right under his nose for months and he'd barely allowed her to register on his mind. And why?

Perhaps because he had known better.

Yes, occasionally he had looked at her—like a man looks at a woman. But he had never really seen—never *allowed* himself to see. Because he had never wanted to view her as a person, and he could ill afford to frighten her away. He had needed her, damn it. Needed her to smooth the construction on his blasted wing. To put the last, elegant touches on his collection. To be his sounding board and the one person who shared his enthusiasms. He had needed her—and he had not allowed himself to think too deeply about the *why* of the thing.

He paused, fingers poised to tear open the letter, and frowned up at Billings. 'Do we not have another candidate for Hardwick's replacement coming to interview today?'

'We do, sir. Shall I place him in the library when he arrives?'

'It would be best. I don't wish to scare another

off before we can even begin.' The irritation simmering beneath his skin threatened to boil up again. 'Does this one have any sort of credentials?'

'A background in mining, I believe.'

This time Braedon cursed out loud. Mining, land management, insurers. None of the men applying for Hardwick's position knew the first damned thing about how to manage a collection like his. They had no knowledge, no reverence, no art in their souls—and he'd yet to find one of them who possessed Hardwick's skills at managing men. He banged a fist on the desk, sending papers sliding in every direction. Damn it all to hell and back! He'd had the perfect assistant and now she was off in Town, organising parties.

'Never mind all that!' Brian Keller, his architect and builder, burst into the room. He pointed an accusing finger at the correspondence in Braedon's hand. 'There's no time for it. I have urgent need of you.'

Braedon frowned and brandished the letter. 'You don't even know what it is.' Neither did he.

'I don't care. The *stuccatore* has quarrelled with one of the carpenters. I've tried to calm him, but he refuses to finish the decorative reliefs over the niches. You must come and be properly intimidating or this wing will never be done!'

Happy for an excuse to push away from the desk, Braedon started around it. But something pulled him to an abrupt halt. He frowned at Keller. 'Is that how Hardwick would have handled it?'

'Lord, no.' Keller frowned back.

He waited.

Keller cast helpless hands into the air. 'I don't know how she did it. She would have listened to them complain, just as I have, but somehow, in five minutes she'd have taken them from the brink of mayhem to laughing and clapping each other on the back, vowing to buy each other a pint at the end of the day.'

Braedon blinked. 'How the hell am I supposed to do that?'

'I don't know!' Keller looked him over. 'You're the Marauding Marquess, for God's sake! You've sniffed out enemy supply dumps and strategic secrets all over the Continent. Sniff out a solution for us now. Or at least use that air of arrogant command.'

The door was thrown open. It hit the wall with a crash and rebounded as two men pushed their way through, their voices raised in argument. The *stuccatore*, his hands waving, cursed wildly in Italian. The carpenter shouted his protest that he could not even understand what it was he was accused of. Keller waded in and even Billings raised his voice as he tried to re-store order.

Braedon stared at the ascending chaos and silently cursed Hardwick. *Arrogant command?* He'd rather snatch up one of the multitude of weapons lying about and scare the devil out of the lot of them. Struggling for control, he sank back down to perch on the desk. He had not stooped to using a weapon to intimidate since his brother was alive and living at Denning, nor felt such impending rage.

Connor. Hardwick. Shocking to think that they might have so much in common. And yet his brother had been an expert at hiding nasty surprises inside shiny packages. Hardwick had gone about it differently, concealing all the bright, appealing bits of herself behind grim efficiency, yards of forbidding material and a row of formidable buttons.

A rustle distracted him from his resentment and the rumpus before him. He still held the letter in his hands. He tore it open and began to read.

His fists clenched tighter, the further he read. This was the final straw. Weeks of restraint and control gave way before a great, rushing wave of anger. Skanda's Spear—confirmed on England's shores? Pursued by a host of collectors? Damn Hardwick! Bad enough that the finishing of his wing was descending into disarray. He needed her to help him obtain that weapon. He needed her expertise, her resources, the network of contacts that she'd inherited from her father and expanded on her own.

He *must* have that spear, had to have it as the centrepiece of his collection. No one could understand what it meant to him, how everything he'd heard of it resonated within his soul. It was as if someone centuries ago had looked into the future and seen how this particular weapon would stand as a symbol of all of his victories, his triumphs over the layered and varied darkness of his life.

He felt swamped by a familiar, hated feeling of frustration. Truly Hardwick was Connor's *doppelgänger*, promising him that which he most wanted, then snatching it away.

He tossed the letter aside and stood, deliberately hardening his heart. By all that was holy, he'd never, in all of those years, allowed Connor to beat him. He'd be thrice-damned before he let Hardwick do so. She'd made him promises. Damned if he wasn't going to make sure she kept them.

Without hesitation he ploughed through the cluster of quarrelling men. Surprised, they fell back and fell silent.

The *stuccatore* aimed a querulous remark at him in Italian.

'Yes. Where are you going, my lord?' Keller asked.

'I'm leaving you in charge, Keller. This collection is missing two important pieces—I'm going to fetch them both.'

Chloe left the printer's shop, a beautifully realised sample invitation in her pocket and a smile on her face. She stepped out, heading for the Strand and the confectioner's, her last stop for the day. As she went she withdrew a list from her pocket and consulted it. Satisfaction, thick, warm and comforting, wafted over her. Plans for Lady Ashton's birthday ball were proceeding well. This might be the most unusual, the most talked-about event in years, but it was going to happen without a hitch. She was well ahead of her schedule. Already she'd hired the musicians, interviewed extra help for the countess's kitchen staff and…

And she was doing it again.

She came to an abrupt halt, right in the middle of the pavement, her back arching as if the thought had been a blow between her shoulder blades. Pedestrians grumbled as they stepped around her, but Chloe remained frozen, caught by harsh truth.

She was doing it again. Nearly a month she'd been in London, working with Lady Ashton on her plans to surprise her husband. She'd debated ideas, made notes and begun to organise the thing with her usual ruthless efficiency and attention to detail. She'd also paid calls with the countess, gone driving in the park and attended two lovely dinner parties. She'd begun to learn Lady Ashton's ways and to anticipate her needs. She was well on her way to becoming the countess's perfect companion.

What she had *not* done was that which she had left Denning to do. She had not taken a single step towards discovering more about herself.

Cold humiliation chased her former satisfaction away as Chloe started trudging forwards again. She must stop this. She'd left Denning for this chance. Almost irritably, she quelled the sudden leap of her heart—an instinctive reaction to the mere name of the place—and brushed away the memories of passionate black eyes, large hands and worn boots. She'd left all that behind, and for good reason. She'd exchanged the impossible dream of Lord Marland for the prospect of a real life, abandoned the safety of her role as Hardwick for the opportunity to find Chloe. It was time she stopped hiding behind the care of others and discovered her own needs and desires.

Another fresh swell of shame rose inside her as she stepped into the confectioner's shop.

The place was charming, done up in rich creams and soothing blues. Warm draughts and rich smells surrounded her, but it was the sight of the woman she spotted in the kitchens, pacing behind a swinging half-door, that sent a stab of envy through her gut.

Older than Chloe, but not by many years, the woman was wrapped in a voluminous apron. She strode the substantial length of a pine table, examining row upon row of delicate pastries even as she issued orders to a beleaguered staff. Her words were sharp, her tone urgent, but the look on her face as she turned to begin tucking her creations into pretty boxes…it was beautiful. She nearly glowed with pride and contentment.

There, thought Chloe. There is a woman who understands herself.

Perhaps Chloe's gaze carried the weight of her envy, for the woman glanced up suddenly. She called out further orders in rapid French as she wiped her hands and came through to the shop to greet Chloe with a smile.

'Good day to you,' she said. 'You are Miss Hardwick, yes?' At Chloe's nod she continued, 'I am Madame Hobert.' She swept a hand towards a small table set up at the end of the display case. 'You are to discuss an order for Lady Ashton's ball, I understand?'

'I am. It is a pleasure to meet you, *madame*.'

She moved to take a seat at the table. 'Your shop is charming.'

'*Merci.*' The confectioner gazed about with satisfaction as she sat. 'It is just what I have wanted, since I was a girl.' From a pocket she produced a pencil and paper. 'Now, can you tell me what the lady has in mind?'

'Of course.' Ignoring the surge of envy the woman's words sent thrumming through her, Chloe took out her own notes and leaned forwards. 'The ball is to be in honour of the Earl's birthday and we are planning something special. Lady Ashton admires your artistry, but she asks for your discretion, as well.'

'Ah.' Madame smiled. 'There is to be a surprise?'

'Many surprises,' Chloe said with a grin. 'Most important, the countess wishes you to create a grand dessert table, in the old style. She wishes an entire tableau done in sugar-paste sculpture, with the theme of an English Hunt.'

The confectioner's eyes widened in delight. 'But how wonderful! Oh, but the creations my father made in Paris, long ago! He was truly an artist. And I have all his moulds—I shall be thrilled to use them once more.' Her brows lowered as she thought. 'A hunt! Yes. Yes. I know just the thing!' She fell silent, clearly caught up in the idea.

'Of course, Lady Ashford wishes to order

other desserts as well.' Chloe outlined the ideas they had settled on.

Madame was all nods and smiles. By the end she was nearly clapping her hands in delight. 'How marvellously well you have planned.' Her face fell a little as she sat back from her notes. 'Ah, you have inspired me, Mademoiselle! Already I have ideas for entirely new creations that will serve your theme.' Her hands began to twist together. 'Alas, I have a large order to fill today and two of my bakers are ill at home. But please, send the good lady my deepest apologies and assure her that I shall have a selection for her to approve by tomorrow.' She stood, clearly anxious. 'Will it do, do you think?'

Chloe stood as well. 'Certainly, *madame*. You must meet your obligations, of course.' She stared a little wistfully over the confectioner's shoulder. She'd never spent more than a minute or two in a kitchen. *Madame* must have grown up in one. Yet how had the woman known that she loved it enough to make it her life's work? And now that she had, how difficult did she find it to handle the business side of her enterprise? What if one or both of those things might be something that *Chloe* had a passion for? How could she know?

She couldn't—unless she finally did what she'd come here to do. It was time she began to embrace possibilities and explore…everything.

The confectioner took a step towards the door, clearly intending to escort her out, but Chloe stopped her with a shy smile. '*Madame*, I admit I've no kitchen experience, but I've a willing spirit and two good hands. Would you mind if I volunteered to help you? Would you permit me to help you fill your order?'

Madame Hobert chuckled as she continued towards the door. When Chloe didn't follow, she turned. Obviously perplexed, she began, 'Your offer is much appreciated, Miss Hardwick.' She stopped and ran an assessing eye over her. 'But…why?'

'I'm new to Town…' Chloe faltered and bit her lip. Lifting pleading eyes, she started over. 'The truth is that I'm a stranger to myself, *madame*. I came to London…well, to start over, you might say. I'm searching,' she said with a shrug. 'Searching for myself and for a way forwards. And I've made a vow that I would explore new ideas and possibilities.'

Madame's brow furrowed. 'You wish to become a confectioner?'

'No,' Chloe said slowly. 'At least, I don't think so. But a businesswoman—yes, I think that I might enjoy that, very much. I would like to learn, and perhaps to ask you a few questions.'

The confectioner's face softened. 'In that case, miss, let us get you out of that long-sleeved spencer and into an apron.'

* * *

Three hours, two cramped hands and a sore back later, *Madame*'s order was complete and at least a few of Chloe's questions were answered.

'Well?' The older lady's eyes danced as she tied up the last box and raised a brow at Chloe. 'You wished for an experience. I think we have given you one, *non*?' She smiled. 'How do you feel?'

Chloe set down her pastry bag. She licked creamy filling off the back of her hand and considered. 'I feel pleasantly tired,' she answered. 'And incredibly sticky,' she continued, looking down at herself with a rueful eye. 'And reasonably sure I could handle the running of a business—provided I found one that evoked the sort of interest and passion that baking clearly does for you.'

One of *Madame*'s assistants, silent until now, made a coarse, heavily accented remark about *Mademoiselles* who made it a practice to combine experience and passion.

Madame Hobert gaped. The other assistant gasped. Chloe giggled—and before long the lot of them had dissolved into fits of helpless laughter. Thoroughly tickled and grateful for the release, Chloe laughed until tears came to her eyes. It wasn't until the repeated clearing of a masculine throat finally broke through the noise that any of them regained a measure of control.

'*Bon soir, monsieur,*' *Madame* called. She moved toward the dark form filling the doorway to the kitchens. 'I am so sorry, but we have closed for the day.' She continued to chatter as she went. Still giggling, Chloe wiped flour from her chin and turned to watch.

Laughter died away. About her, the kitchen grew hot, then abruptly and inexplicably cold. Time slowed and her heartbeat with it. Yet something else within her quickened. Hidden deep, tucked somewhere behind her heart, a small and withered hope plumped suddenly with life.

Chloe straightened—and met the stormy gaze of the Marauding Marquess.

Chapter Five

For well over a year, Braedon recalled irritably, he'd never had to think twice about finding Hardwick. Half the time, it had seemed, he'd merely had to think of her and she'd appear, springing out of the Northumberland mists as if summoned by his want of her. The other half she'd been either in the new wing or in the workroom, right where he expected—and needed—her to be.

They were a far cry from there now, weren't they?

Bad enough he'd had to follow her to London, but she hadn't been safely ensconced in Cavendish Square with his sister. No—he'd had to trek through Town to find her covered in flour and playing at *patisserie*.

A Frenchwoman—the owner of the shop,

he assumed—hovered before him. Her nattering might as well have been the buzzing of a gnat. For Braedon was caught, held fast by Hardwick's great blue eyes, locked in place as her gaze met his and he wondered how the hell he had ever missed the shards of gold that turned her eyes molten and reached out to stab him straight in the heart.

Every other damned person in the world wore spectacles to see. Oh, but not Hardwick. She'd worn them to keep others from seeing her.

The Frenchwoman still talked unceasingly, trying to shoo him away. He should listen to her. Hadn't he learned long ago to rely on himself? He'd discovered with brutal clarity that it was best not to ask or expect anything of others.

But there was the stalled construction of his wing. And the strange silence or half answers from his usual correspondents and contacts whenever he tried to raise the topic of Skanda's Spear.

He wanted that artefact, with an urgency that had begun to burn deep in his gut.

So he waved the buzzing Frenchwoman off. 'Not to worry, *madame*,' he said. 'I have not come for something sweet. I am here for Hardwick.'

That broke the spell. Hardwick blinked, frowned and looked away. Manfully, Braedon stiffened his spine and told himself that there was no need to slump in relief.

It was short-lived relief, in any case. For Hardwick was crossing the room. Her cheeks were flushed and her chin smudged. Her hair, arranged in another, softer style, had begun to tumble loosely down to frame her face.

'Lord Marland.' Her tone was as cool as the slow, curious look she slid over him.

He heated up anyway, from the abruptly tingling top of his head to the soles of his shining Hessians.

'What are you doing here?' she asked.

'I've come for you,' he repeated irritably.

One of the women behind her let loose an incredulous, undeniably Gallic snort. The Frenchwoman shushed her.

'Mairi sent me,' he said, swallowing a curse. 'My sister, Lady Ashton,' he said in an aside to the shop owner. 'She received the message that Miss Hardwick would be delayed and did not wish for her to walk home alone at this hour.'

'How very thoughtful.' Hardwick's voice was muffled. She was occupied in unwinding the apron that enveloped her. 'But would not a footman have sufficed?' With a sigh of relief she pulled the thing over her head and dropped it on a nearby table.

Braedon experienced a sudden and fervent longing for her old attire and its marching line of buttons. Surely they had been charmed, those glossy, gold buttons. They had to have possessed some sort of supernatural power, to have for so long and so effectively hid the graceful swell of that bosom. They'd done the job a damned sight better than the gown she wore now, in any case. Though most conservatively cut, with long sleeves and a high neckline, the rich druggett clung to her ample curves from shoulder to hip and displayed the smooth, feminine curvature of her arms.

'I volunteered,' he said past the unexpected dryness at the back of his throat.

'How kind you are.' Without meeting his gaze, she turned to take her leave.

He waited at the outer door, fiercely recalling his purpose and watching as she spoke to the women. He was drumming impatient fingers when she finally quit the kitchens, pausing in the shopfront to don a spencer against the evening chill. That garment possessed a line of buttons in the front, but they were no damned use. The cat was out of the bag, so to speak, and there was no going back.

Damn it all to hell, but he wished to go back. He'd like nothing more than to lock Hardwick back behind her stark, bulky clothes, heavy spectacles and severe hairstyle and back into her position as his assistant. Everything would be so much simpler. He'd just snap his fingers and order her to quell the chaos at home and to find that spear here in Town. Instead he must stand here and pretend not to notice her unveiled charms. He was going to have to go against his every inclination and strike up a conversation with her. And somehow he was going to have to find a way to *ask* her to do what she'd already promised to deliver.

'Shall we?' Her goodbyes accomplished, she approached him with a tight smile.

He made his bows and they set off. The sun hung low in the west, setting the sky ablaze. Evening made its advance and all along the Strand shopkeepers either barred their doors or lit their lamps in welcome, depending on the nature of their business and the needs of their clientele. From the direction of the river crept tendrils of fog, curling languidly around their feet as if to hold them back.

Ignoring it, they pushed on in silence and Braedon grumped inwardly at yet another discomforting change. He could not count the times he'd sat silent and relaxed with Hardwick in the past, but the ease was gone and the quiet between them felt…heavy, perhaps. Fraught with the expectation of…something.

Clearly she felt it, as well. For the first time in their acquaintance, Hardwick was the one to break the silence. 'What brings you to London, my lord?'

'The collection does.' He breathed a sigh of relief. There. The subject was broached. Now things could begin to progress normally.

'I see,' she answered.

He waited. In vain. She made no further comment or question.

Braedon was flabbergasted. At a loss. He'd felt sure that mention of the collection would set things back on to an even keel between them. The collection was what they had talked about—*all* that they had talked about.

'I hope that everyone at Denning is well,' she ventured at last.

'Yes,' he said shortly, still trying to work out what had gone wrong. 'Keller and the workmen all send you their best.'

'How kind of them!' Her face lit up. 'I hope you will do me the favour of sending my fondest regards when you return.'

He grunted. He was damned well going to return *her* to Denning and she could tell them herself.

Silence descended again and Braedon grappled with the awkward feel of it. Good God, but he'd felt more at home in the midst of fields of Frenchmen intent on skewering him. He'd moved more comfortably through the conniving machinations of Europe's heads of state. But he'd be damned before he allowed one changeable chit to unsettle him or to distract him from his objective.

An intuitive chit, too, he suspected. He had to wonder if she suspected his motives, for as they reached the quieter streets of Mayfair she began to pick up her pace. By the time they turned off Oxford Street onto Princes Street she was nearly trotting.

She wouldn't get away that easily. He cleared his throat.

But she'd caught sight of Ashton House ahead and put on a spurt of speed. She raced for the steps of the house like a thoroughbred heading for the finish.

'Thank you so much for the escort, my lord.' Breathless, she refused to meet his eye. 'How late it has grown. I must hurry up to change. Will you be joining us for dinner, then?' she asked, taking the first step.

'No.'

She murmured a platitude and turned to go. Cursing under his breath, Braedon reached out and grasped her arm.

And nearly had his fingers singed off for his temerity—by a jolt that hit him right through his glove and her sleeve. A jolt that travelled in jagged sparks from his fingertips and along his arm. It took a detour through his chest for the purpose of stealing his breath before striking straight down to set his nether regions to twitching. He snatched his hand back.

Hell and damnation, had he never touched Hardwick before? In all the time they had spent together? He couldn't recall, but worse was the uncertainty that it might not have mattered—before.

'Listen, Hardwick. I think perhaps you have an inkling of why I have come.' He ignored the aftershocks coursing through him and the strain on her face and ploughed ahead. 'I want you to come back to Denning.' He tucked both hands behind his back and rocked back on his boot heels. 'Come back and take up your position again. You were comfortable there, were you not? And damned good at it, too. Come back— and help me finish what we started.'

Chloe heaved a sigh and ducked her head, unable to meet Lord Marland's expectant gaze. She shouldn't have tried to outrun his request. She'd known it was coming, almost as soon as she'd turned to find him glowering at her over Madame Hobert's kitchen door, but she'd been too distracted to come up with a polite response.

They'd all been distracted, she rather thought, by the startling contrast he made, looming darkly against the delicate pastel background of the shop. Good heavens, but she'd only been gone a few weeks and already she'd forgotten his utter masculinity, the sheer height and breathtaking width of him. Even dressed more formally than she was used to—in Town, she supposed, he could not get away with leaving a trail of neckcloths and waistcoats behind him—he took her breath away. A hundred other gentlemen might be wandering the streets of London this moment in buff breeches, black superfine and shining Hessians, but none of them made fashion so superfluous, or made a woman look past it to the powerfully elegant form beneath.

None of them moved in quite the same way he did, either. Not a wolf set among the sheep of the city's populace, but something more primitive and sleek. A jungle cat, perhaps, prowling toward the West End. Walking at his side, she'd felt at once supremely protected and in undeniable peril.

He shifted and she realised that he waited, still, for her answer. And grew more impatient by the second. She recalled her wandering thoughts and looked him in the eye. 'I thank you for the compliments, my lord, and for the offer, but I am afraid that I cannot agree to it.' Turning, she made to enter the house.

'Wait.'

She glanced back to find his expression fixed. 'If the issue is how you have…changed…' he waved a hand '…then of course you may continue to please yourself.'

The set of his jaw told her that pleasing herself in this case would be akin to punishing him. The realisation helped to harden her resolve.

'I'm afraid you have it backwards, Lord Marland,' she said quietly. 'It is because of all the ways that I have not changed that I must decline.'

She glanced away. At all costs, she had to keep him from realising the terrible truth of that statement. For parts of her were rising in rebellion, urging her to give in, to make him happy and go back to the security of Denning and her role as Hardwick.

She shook her head. Watching him closely, she took a step up. Away. She could not go back. Would not.

He let out a huff of irritation. 'Fine. But plague take you, Hardwick. I wish you would stop looking at me like that.'

She frowned. 'Like what?'

'Like I'm about to devour you. Like you are afraid of me,' he said roughly. 'All I am asking for is a conversation.' He placed his fingers to his temple and pressed. 'I don't suppose it will kill either one of us.'

She swallowed. *Now* he wished to talk to her? The irony was painful, but she supposed it was the least she could do. 'I suppose not.'

'Not in there.' He scowled at the house. 'I don't want Mairi sticking her nose in again.'

Chloe bit back a laugh. 'Where, then? And when?'

'Now.' He cast a despairing look up and down the wide street, but brightened as a lady opened the gate from within the circular garden in the middle of the square.

'Just a moment,' he called to her as she struggled with her easel and canvas. 'Allow me to assist you.' He left Chloe and rushed to hold the gate wide and help the lady balance her load. Brushing off her thanks, he cast a cheeky grin in Chloe's direction and swept a bow to indicate she join him.

She went and, nodding her head, took the arm he offered.

'Come along, deeper in,' he urged. 'I don't want my sister catching sight of us and interfering.' He cast a disparaging eye upon her new bonnet. 'And she'll know those feathers and furbelows at once.'

Chloe tugged her arm away and glanced around. The evening light was fading and shadows deepened the gloom here beneath the trees. 'I hope you are not bringing me in here merely to malign my millinery choices, my lord.'

'What? Lord, no.' He gave her hat another dubious glance. 'As far as I'm concerned you are free to don breeches and boots and masquerade as a Bond Street Beau, should you wish.'

'Thank you, no. I don't wish.' She'd had enough of masquerades, though she didn't know how to make him understand it.

'Ah, this should do.' They'd reached the centre and the equestrian statue of the Duke of Cumberland. Several stone steps surrounded the plinth. Lord Marland stood on the first one and tucked his chin into his chest. Chloe watched, fascinated, as he began to squirm. A minute of struggle and a few gratifying flexes of his broad chest and he had wiggled out of his coat, unaided. 'For you,' he said, flourishing the garment and spreading it over the middle step. 'Please, have a seat.'

His scent drifted over her as he repeated his earlier sweeping gesture of invitation. They struck her hard, those hints of bay and citrus and something vaguely alcoholic. She shivered even as his grin lit up the dusky clearing.

'Good God, but it feels good to be rid of that thing.'

She laughed at his fervent tone and sat. Her heart pounded, sounding loud in her ears as she watched him settle next to her. Was this not exactly what she'd wished for a thousand times, during those months at Denning? The chance to talk—to *really* talk to Lord Marland?

She raised her gaze to his. His colour was high, his expression…wary?

A nearby rustle of skirts snapped their spines straight, their eyes apart. A young lady strode by, her maid trotting behind. The girl cast a mildly curious glance over them, but didn't alter her pace or pause.

The pair passed on towards the north gate, their voices fading. The marquess relaxed, leaning his elbows onto the step behind him. The vivid colours of the garden were fading with the light, leaving a singular sense of intimacy. Glad for the respite, Chloe drank in the isolation, allowed the birds' sleepy chirps to ease her nerves. Gradually the familiar, companionable silence that she was used to sharing with the marquess drifted over them.

'Ah, there it is,' Lord Marland said on a long exhale.

She tilted her head, questioning.

He shook his head, closed his eyes. He began to breathe deeply, as if he could take in the peace of the scene with his every breath.

Chloe, on the other hand, only wished to observe him. Absorb him, like water through thirsty pores. She was terribly aware of the size of him, sitting so close. His scent made a haven as it stole over and around her.

She'd seen him like this before, she realised. Still and at peace with his surroundings. Always in the evening. Outside or at a window. And always alone.

'You enjoy the sunset,' she observed abruptly. 'Does it hold a special meaning for you?'

She'd shattered the spell—and his peace. He opened one eye and frowned at her—a serious look of displeasure. If she had still been his Hardwick, she had no doubt that he would have reprimanded her.

She thought he meant to ignore her instead. Avoid the question. But he sighed with resignation and closed his eyes again. 'I like to take a moment in the evening,' he said. 'To pause and reflect. To revel in the victory of making it through another day.'

His answer only raised more questions. He did not mean to give her the chance to ask them, though. He opened his eyes and sat up, dispersing any remaining tranquillity of the moment with a sharp frown.

'The new wing has slipped woefully behind schedule,' he pronounced.

'What, already?' Surprise made her ignore his accusatory tone.

He nodded. 'The porcelain work on the cabinet for the Japanese pole arm is still not complete. The workroom is a chaotic mess and progress on the gallery has ground to a halt.'

Chloe blinked. 'What's happened in the gallery?' she asked, unable to deal with more than one of these complaints at a time.

'The craftsmen bicker like children!' he huffed. 'I don't know how you got a day's work out of them. Your Italian *stuccatore* has quarrelled with one of the carpenters and neither will finish the job!'

'Which carpenter?'

He merely blinked.

She sighed. 'It will be Mr Forrest, most likely. Listen,' she urged, 'it is simple enough. You must take Signor D'Alesio aside and assure him that, despite his personal shortcomings, Mr Forrest is the only artisan capable of work that will compliment his own genius. Then you must take the carpenter aside and give him the same assurances. You must encourage them to co-operate for the sake of their work.'

'*That's* how you convinced them to get along?'

Chloe rolled her eyes. 'These men are artists, my lord, and can have the temperaments that go along with it. They require these little comforts.' She bit back a smile. 'What did you do? Take up a broadsword and threaten to skewer them?'

'I considered it,' he answered. In all seriousness, it appeared. He fixed her with a steady look. 'I won't lie, Hardwick. It's all falling apart without you. Are you sure you won't consider returning?'

Why did this question not get easier each

time it came? She wished he hadn't asked it. The marquess exerted a nearly irresistible pull. His even gaze spoke to her of contentment and security. She wanted to enjoy the gentle, tidal tug of excitement that he stirred within her— without the struggle of internal debate. But he was asking—and he was asking *Hardwick*. And, perhaps because she was being forced to make her decision yet again, she was realising that Hardwick was truly behind her.

She sat a little straighter. It was true. Hardwick was gone and in her place was...who? She didn't quite know. A fledgling, perhaps. A young woman who had discovered in the last weeks that she loved a ride in a fast phaeton and that she hated stewed herring. Who had found only today that she enjoyed baking—when it was confined to an afternoon's activity.

Lord Marland didn't know this girl—and Chloe wasn't at all sure that she wished for him to do so. Having just discovered her, she was feeling rather protective.

She looked up at the marquess and suddenly it was easier to give him her answer. 'I'm sorry, my lord, but I will not.'

'It is a matter of money, then?' he growled. 'A problem easily solved, then. Consider your salary doubled.'

She felt her face colour furiously. 'It is not a financial matter.'

'Then what?' he demanded.

She cut her glance away for an instant. 'I fear that is my business, sir.'

Frowning, he slumped backwards. Several conflicting emotions showed on his face before he settled on one of contrition. 'I suppose I should beg your forgiveness.' She jumped as he suddenly pounded his fist on the stone. 'Damnation, you must know I hated to ask!'

She considered. 'Yes, I suppose I do.' She'd never known him to ask for help—or anything else—from anyone. Denning must indeed be in disorder for him to take such a step. The image in her head gave her pause for a moment, before she pushed it away.

'Yet I had to try. The situation demanded it.'

Her own patience began to wear thin. 'Lord Marland, are you attempting to convince *me* to apologise? Because I assure you, I shall not. I have every right to leave a situation I am no longer comfortable in—even yours. And I beg you not to ask again, for I have no intention of going backwards.'

She skidded back in alarm as he suddenly launched himself from the pedestal. In a blur of strong, smooth motion he went from reclining beside her to towering above. Chloe stared in astonishment as he began to pace in everlengthening strides before her.

She couldn't help but flinch when he halted

abruptly and pierced her with his fierce gaze.
'Very well, then. Enough about Denning. But
you must brace yourself, or prepare to forgive
me. For I'm determined to importune you about
another matter.'

He stepped forwards and crouched down. He
was so close—enough so that she could feel the
heat emanating from him and see the need conflicting with pride in his expression. He reached
for her hands and clutched them tightly together
in his.

She made a sound, of shock perhaps, and he
dropped them immediately. They fell to her lap
and he leaned in further, bracing himself on the
stone on either side of her.

'It's the Spear, Hardwick. Skanda's Spear. It's
here. In London.'

That caught her attention. 'You've had it confirmed?'

His eyes shifted. 'Nearly.'

'More whispers,' she said, suddenly impatient.

'The whispers have turned to shouts. I had
several letters of elation and jubilation. Everyone interested in antiquities was abuzz with the
news. And then—silence. My further inquiries
have gone unanswered or ignored.'

Chloe understood. 'It will be a race, then.
They will all be after it.'

'Yet I mean to have it.' His voice had grown

rough. 'There are no words to explain how much I need to have that spear for my collection.'

She stared in wonder. She'd never seen him like this, so open and raw. She felt trapped by his arms and the urgency of his emotions, yet she felt no urge to escape.

'It won't be easy,' she whispered.

'That's why I need your help. You have amassed a web of connections that would put a spider to shame. I know I've no right to do this. And you have no inclination to listen, perhaps. But I'm asking for your assistance anyway.'

And she discovered with some surprise that she wished to give it.

He'd always been so far away when she had been Hardwick. The distance between them had come by unspoken, but mutual agreement. She'd broken that silent pact when she had destroyed the barrier that was her stark persona. She'd done it even knowing that the consequence would be the loss of Denning, of their working relationship.

Now she saw that he had lowered his own blockade, if only a little. This was a rare glimpse of the man behind the remote and forbidding Marauding Marquess.

She found that she wanted to see more.

And yet…she forced herself pause. What of her own mission?

It took but a moment for her to know one

thing with certainty. Chloe did have something in common with Hardwick: she wanted to know Lord Marland nearly as intensely as she wanted to know herself.

She straightened—and blushed when she came within inches of his encompassing, waiting form.

'I will make a vow, should you require it, right here and now.' He pitched his tone low and earnest. 'I will not allow the search to hinder the help that you are giving to Mairi.' The look he ran down the front of her made her feel restless and hotly aware. 'And though I cannot begin to understand it, I promise that I will not interfere with your…transformation.'

Grateful, she nodded.

He drew breath. 'I—'

She placed her fingers against his mouth. His lips were soft. Like silk. Warm, living silk. His breath stopped—and she found herself pleased. 'Yes.' The rest of her words had disappeared.

'Truly?'

The one-word question emerged on a searing breath. The sensitive pads of her fingers picked up the heat and sent it winging along the roadmap of her nerves, awakening every cell within her. She'd never been so aware of every part of herself—or of the nearly painful sting of connection between them. 'I'll help you find the Spear.'

How often she'd imagined him as a warrior of old. He looked every inch of one now, staring so intently down at her in the disappearing light. He reached out for her again—and she gasped at the heat ignited inside her when he grasped her by the waist and lifted her to her feet as easily as if she were a child.

Somehow her hands had come up. They rested lightly against the thin linen of his shirt. Beneath her fingers she could feel his heartbeat. Her own filled her ears, drowning the comforting lullaby of sleepy bird sound.

'Thank you.' His simple words vibrated against her fingers, as well as in her ears. They started a chain reaction. She was trembling in the deeper shadow cast by his large form—and then she was caught unaware by something entirely new.

He smiled.

A hundred times she'd dreamed of this moment—the instant that he looked at her with more than an ancient weapon on his mind and polite expectation on his face. Now it was here, and it was—shockingly, impossibly—far more thrilling than she had dreamt.

Never would she have considered that the rarity of his smile might be a good thing, but the thought crossed her mind now. It transformed him completely and captivated her utterly. She was caught. Not frozen. Warmed, rather, by the

sunlight that was his pleasure, approval and regard. It stunned her, that smile, and brought
to life every fantasy she had ever indulged in.
Knights and Vikings paraded behind her eyes,
followed quickly by stolen kisses and impas-
sioned embraces. Heat rose to the surface of
her skin and she lost herself in the promise and
potential and possibility that lived in the creased
corner of his eye and the turned-up edge of his
mouth.

Possibility. The word struck a chord inside
her that released her from his spell. Her mind
began to spin and tumble. She stepped back,
smoothed her skirts to hide her confusion,
ducked her head to keep from revealing the
revolutionary notions erupting inside her.

'Come.' He gathered up his coat and slung it
over his arm. 'Let's get you back before Mairi
begins to worry.'

Chloe nodded. The garden was small, not
many steps and only a few moments until she
could retreat to the privacy of her room.

'How shall we start?' he asked.

She barely registered the question, so thick
was the congestion of her thoughts and emotions. She drew a deep, steadying breath. Forced
herself to focus. 'I've had several notes and
cards from various connections in antiquities
since I came to Town. I told them all I was only

here for a short time and on other business. Except one.'

He waited.

'An old acquaintance that I must see.' She drew a deep breath. 'As luck would have it, he'll also be the one we should start with.'

'When?' He was all impatience.

She understood. They had reached Ashton House again and she felt a similar need for peace and the time to reflect on all that she had just got herself into—and everything further that she had yet to consider.

'Tomorrow,' she answered. 'Your sister will be at home to visitors in the afternoon. Call then and we will begin.' She started up towards the door, but paused, suddenly struck by inspiration. 'Lord Marland,' she called as she turned back. 'Do you, by chance, own a phaeton?'

He frowned. 'I do.'

'Then please do drive it tomorrow when you come to fetch me.' She smiled confidingly at him. 'I do love a fast phaeton.'

Chapter Six

Striding away from Cavendish Square, Braedon reached for a fleeting sense of anticipation, lost hold of contentment, failed to keep a grip on even a feeling of satisfaction at eliciting Hardwick's promise of assistance.

It made no sense. He'd just greatly increased his chances at obtaining Skanda's Spear, and although she'd declined to come back to Denning, he'd just assumed that he'd have time and opportunity to convince her otherwise. He should be elated. Or pleased, at least.

And he would be, if it were not for the near certainty that he might have traded it all for the chance to touch her. His hands flexed again, remembering the slight span of her waist and the urge to slide higher, to explore lush curves and anchor in her mussed hair.

Hell and damnation. He'd struggled with feelings of betrayal and now they intensified a hundredfold. His old Hardwick had fit so smoothly, easing all the facets of his life. This Hardwick was a danger to his every long-held conviction. She tempted him with soft words and blue eyes shot with gold, until he forgot distance and thought only *nearer.* Until he forgot to be watchful and instead only watched her—and the sweet turn of her smile and the sway of her hips as she walked.

And so every positive feeling faded with each step he took away from her and from Ashton House. They stood on uncharted and uneven ground now. No longer the employer, he was no longer in control.

Oh, he in no way suspected her of angling to compromise him or any such thing. This was Hardwick he was dealing with and she had too much integrity for him to even entertain such a thought. But she was human—and female. It was conceivable—probable—that she might come to expect something in return for her assistance. Something universally mundane, but singularly unsafe, such as conversation. His fists curled. The chance to ask *questions.*

He abhorred questions. Hated to be poked at or prodded. For such a thing as a truly innocent question did not exist, did it? Like her seemingly innocuous query about sunsets. There was no answer that did not reveal some ugliness, dredge up a memory that he'd laboured to bury deep. Was he supposed to tell her that he met the sunset with a ritual that had begun as a boy? That he marked the moment as a victory that he'd survived another day—not always intact, but eager for the respite of a few hours when his brother and father would be occupied with food and drink and women?

Denial and frustration roiled in his gut. He glanced about, eager for an excuse to release it. He'd reached Piccadilly and its more raucous evening crowds, but his size had always decreased the chances of being accosted, even in London's most dismal neighbourhoods. Tonight, though—he shook out his arms and stamped his foot to feel the reassuring press of the blade hidden in his boot—tonight he would welcome the chance to take his frustrations out on a few unsuspecting thugs.

He continued, heading east. The fog had thickened here, closer to the river. Images shifted in the mists, seemingly as real as the night-time revellers winking in and out of the vapour. He saw the surprise in Hardwick's wide eyes when she'd first glimpsed him, the rapid flutter of her pulse, visible in the soft curve of her neck when he'd lifted her from the ground.

Damn it all to hell and back. Braedon stopped short. A diversion, that was what he needed.

And if one wouldn't present itself, then he would seek it out. He stopped at the next street to gain his bearings—and smiled. A minute's quick walk and he slipped down a darkened side street, before ducking into a thoroughly disreputable hole aptly named the Tangled Arms.

The place retained all the gloom, smoke and low-ceilinged glory that he recalled, but the inhabitants proved disappointingly lacklustre. He did his best. He stomped in, snarled his order and cleared a booth of a couple of rough dockworkers with only a look.

An hour's worth of glaring challenges had yielded only wary glances, a tired offer from the barmaid and a start of a raging headache. Disgusted, he gave it up as a bad job and headed for home, his priorities shifting to a good brandy capable of wiping away the taste of homebrewed rotgut and the oblivion of sleep.

It was not to be. He'd barely dragged himself into the little-used town house in Bury Street when Dobbs, his creaky London butler, stepped forwards into the dimly lit entry hall.

'There's been a…delivery, of sorts.' The old man sketched a short bow and managed to catch the hat that Braedon tossed in his direction.

'It can't pertain to me,' he answered on his way to the stairs. 'Nobody even knows I'm in Town and, frankly, I prefer to keep it that way.'

He waved a hand. 'Just handle things as you normally would. I won't be here long enough to disrupt your routine.'

'A moment, sir. Perhaps I should rephrase.' Dobbs cleared his throat. 'You have visitors, my lord.'

'Visitors?' Braedon stopped with his foot on the first stair and glanced towards the darkened transom window. 'At this hour?'

'Well, and it wasn't this late hour when first we arrived, was it?' The gravelled voice emerged from a small antechamber, a stout form accompanying it. 'And a long wait it's been, too, hasn't it, with naught but a couple o' straight-backed chairs and a pot o' tea?'

He raised a brow in Dobbs's direction.

The butler looked as discomfited as he'd ever seen him. 'Forgive me, my lord.' He shifted his stance and stole a glance toward the figure planted on the other side of the hall. 'I wasn't sure how you… That is, what I should do.'

Figures, Braedon corrected himself. The short, comfortably round woman who had ad-dressed him had not come alone. She had a child pressed to her hip. He lolled against her, his face turned into her skirts as if he were asleep on his feet.

'I won't be leavin' either, until I've had my say,' she warned.

She gulped as Braedon approached her, running a nervous eye up the length of him.

'What can I do for you, madam?'

She clutched the boy with both hands. 'Are ye the marquess, then?'

'I am.'

'Ah, good.' She heaved a sigh. 'I'm Essie Nichols. I've brought ye your nevvie.'

Having no idea what a nevvie might be, Braedon glanced over his shoulder at Dobbs. The butler remained supremely unhelpful, however. He had fixed unblinking eyes on the child.

He turned back. 'I'm sorry, Mrs Nichols, but I do not understand.'

'Your nevvie,' she said firmly. 'And I can't be taking no for an answer, either.'

'Dobbs?' He shot the butler a searing demand for translation.

'Sir. I believe the lady means to say…your nephew.'

The truth didn't register at first. Braedon frowned and rotated again, ready to inform the woman that she had clearly entrenched herself in the house of the wrong marquess. But she was patting the lad on the back, jostling him awake and urging him to stand straight and greet his uncle.

A massive yawn emerged from folds of her skirt. Time slowed as the boy turned his head to stare at Braedon out of sleepy eyes.

Connor's eyes. And Connor's nose, slightly elongated. And unmistakably, Connor's square, solid jaw.

Nausea and a horrid, instant revulsion nearly staggered him. It took an extreme force of will to hold his position. His instinctive reaction was to step backwards, away from that all-too-familiar regard.

The woman appeared oblivious. 'I've kept him these two years, lettin' him do odd jobs about the inn, just as Maggie asked, afore she died.' She flushed. 'But business has been off. We missed one too many mortgage payments. The place belongs to the bank now.'

Braedon tore his gaze from the boy. He had a horrid suspicion where this was leading. He shook his head. 'Mrs Nichols—'

'We board ship tomorrow evenin', bound for America,' she interrupted. 'My man, my youngest and me. My oldest got herself betrothed and means to stay.' She gave the boy a nudge. 'There's no money for his passage, my lord. Ye'll have to take him now. It's time he was back with family.'

'No.' Braedon did step back now. 'I'm afraid not.'

'Well, and who else is to take him, then?' She stuck her hands on her hips. 'Yer his only kin. Ye can't think to be denyin' that, will ye?'

He stared again at the boy. It was like looking through a window into his past.

'He's the very picture of yer brother. Anybody that ever met him would say the same.' She glared. 'And any number of folk knows about the time he spent with Maggie. Yer brother hisself claimed the boy and dandled him on his knee, right there in the taproom.'

'Wait.' The boy spoke for the first time, his voice heavy with fatigue, but eager none the less. 'I've something...' He fished about in his pocket, withdrew his fist and thrust it at Braedon. 'I'm to show you this. My da gave it to me when I was but small. He always said I was to show it to you, should I meet you and you doubt me.'

All three adults held their breath as the grubby hand opened. It held a small, carved dog.

The pain was intense, made worse by the unexpected nature of it. Braedon closed his eyes. How very like Connor to choose an object that would awaken the cruellest memories.

'It's yours, isn't it?' The boy sounded awake now.

Braedon fervently wished that *he* was not awake, that this was all a gin-induced nightmare. 'It was, once.'

'Well, then, my lord?' The woman's voice was laced with expectation.

He opened his eyes to meet hers. 'Of course

he must be Connor's son. But he cannot stay. I don't even live here.' He gestured at the dimly lit hall, at the parlour adjacent with the covers still over the furniture. 'The house is half-closed up. It's no place for a child.'

'It's a better place than the streets. Better than the poorhouse back home or what passes for an orphanage here in Town, too. In any case, he's yours now, to do with as you please.' Mrs Nichols belied the casual cruelty of her words as she stepped up beside the boy. She straightened his jacket and gave him an awkward smile. 'Remember the manners ye been taught. Be a help to his lordship as ye were to us and don't give him no trouble.'

His face pinched, the boy nodded.

With a last squeeze of his thin shoulders, the woman stepped away. She nodded to Braedon and headed for the door.

'My lord?' Dobbs's eyes showed nearly white with dread.

Braedon was in complete sympathy with him. His gaze was locked with the boy's now. The lad's remained steady, neither sliding away nor narrowing with threat—so completely unlike his father's. Still, unwelcome memories flooded him. But so, too, did old knowledge and habits grown rusty. Very deliberately, he drew a breath, closed a door on his feelings of alarm and let familiar numbness creep in.

'Dobbs, get the address of Mrs Nichols's lodgings, please,' he ordered woodenly. 'I'll arrange for something to be sent for your trouble, ma'am.'

'I do thank ye,' she said with some relief. 'We could use it.'

'What is your name?' he asked the boy.

'Rob.'

'To the kitchens with you, then, Rob. I expect you are hungry. Dobbs will take you.'

'And then?' The lad raised a belligerent chin. Now that was pure Connor.

'And then I will make arrangements for you. You will stay here until then.'

Braedon turned away. Turmoil died away as he mounted the steps, roiling emotion calmed. He'd forgotten the relief that came of embracing the numbness. He did more than that now. He opened himself wide and welcomed it, sucked it in with each deeply drawn breath. It was only a matter of time, he knew, before its work would be done and he'd find himself as dead and hollow on the inside as the ring of his boots on the stairs.

He could scarcely wait.

Chapter Seven

H e was being watched. Braedon felt it the next afternoon, as he pulled on his driving coat and accepted his gloves. There. From the corner of his eye he caught sight of the small form huddled at the base of the rail two storeys up. He didn't acknowledge the child's steady regard, but neither did he mind it. Sometime during the long night he had come to realise that the boy's arrival was serendipitous—and not the disaster he had first feared.

He had been unbalanced of late, off-kilter, and it had begun the moment he'd first glimpsed Hardwick in a gown of ocean-blue. At last he'd realised how ridiculous—insupportable, really—it was to allow the shock of her transformation to affect him. And it must have been the shock. For in the end, what had truly changed?

So Hardwick was now a pretty girl. Well, he was a marquess with a great deal of experience with pretty girls—and with keeping his balance. All he needed to do was accept her help and hold her at a distance. He'd done it for months at Denning. This need be no different.

Yes, the boy's arrival—indeed, the discovery of his existence—was just the shock he'd needed to restore his equilibrium. It had shaken him awake and reminded him who he really was.

'Check the post carefully, Dobbs,' he instructed now, taking up his hat. 'Watch for any missives from my stewards and set them aside. We have, what, six estates attached to the marquisate?'

'Seven, if you include the hunting box, my lord.'

'As you say. Surely one of them will have a nice couple or comfortable family willing to take on our unexpected guest.' He darted his eyes upwards. The slight figure promptly disappeared.

'Yes, sir. Of course.' Dobbs brightened at the mere mention of the boy's imminent departure.

The observation gave Braedon pause. 'And instruct Mrs Grady to take him shopping. Did he arrive with any clothes other than those on his back?'

'No, sir,' the butler replied. 'But there is no

need. Mrs Grady and the maids have already raided the attics for a suitable wardrobe.'

'Excellent. Well, then. Order up something special for him, will you? Some tin soldiers, perhaps? Don't lads enjoy that sort of thing?' He had no idea. He wondered if he'd ever been a lad at all.

'Of course, sir. I'll see to it.'

Braedon took his leave then, feeling lighter than he had in weeks. He went so far as to whistle his way across Mayfair, causing his team's ears to twitch back at him, and managed to hold on to his good humour even when he saw that Mairi's parlour was full of chattering women.

'Braedon!' Mairi called as he paused on the threshold. 'Here you are at last. Come in.' She beckoned. 'I'll pour you a dish of tea.'

'No, thank you,' he answered. 'I cannot stay. My horses are standing.'

His demurral was no hindrance to his sister's guests. He'd had no idea his sister's airy front room could even hold this many women, but fully half of them rose to gather around. Some seemed genuinely happy to greet him. Others were likely only happy to be able to say they'd been present at one of his few forays into polite society. Several eyed him with predatory gleams and offered him welcomes full of mischief—and promise.

Unfazed, Braedon smiled at them all. He was

himself again. Contained. Aloof. He gave them the flirtatious greetings that they craved, keeping the atmosphere light, his manner charming and impersonal. They tittered and fluttered and adored him for it.

Several minutes passed before he was able to disengage himself enough to peer about the room. Surely Hardwick was here somewhere. He craned his neck, peering around Mairi's bosom friend, the bold widow, Mrs Edmunds. Ah, he caught a glimpse of Hardwick's dark head bent over a ledger at a tiny desk, slightly removed from the throng of guests.

'Good God, Mairi,' he exclaimed. 'I have more cause than most to know of Hardwick's skills—not to mention her discretion—but surely you haven't set her to tallying up your household accounts?'

'Don't be absurd,' Mairi answered with a roll of her eyes. 'Come, ladies, do return to your seats so that I may at least see my brother to speak to him. Indeed,' she continued, 'you cannot lay Chloe's peculiarities to my door. Someone said something to set the dear girl off and she could not rest until she got her latest notion down in her ever-present notebook.'

Her remark struck a chord. Braedon peered at the ledger Hardwick laboured over and recalled seeing her bent over a similar book at Denning.

'It's all Miss Margary's fault,' Hardwick

called with a wave of her hand. 'She raved about her florist and I had to get the particulars down!'

'I've learned not to argue with her.' Mairi grinned. 'Not when her odd kicks return such amazing results.' She smirked at the lady closest to her. 'So much we've accomplished in a few weeks, and such surprises we've cooked up for our ball!' The smile she cast in Hardwick's direction shone with affection. 'And I've begun to suspect that that notebook is the secret to her success!'

'Don't tease us about the birthday ball, Lady Ashton,' someone scolded. 'Not when you refuse to give us even a hint about the delights you've planned.'

'Well, I shall give you quite a large hint,' Hardwick said, closing the ledger and rising from her chair. 'For just this morning I finished putting down my notes about Le Cygne, the most fabulous confectionery. Do any of you know of it?' She paused for a chorus of conflicting answers. 'I highly recommend the place. Madame Hobert is an amazing talent and most accommodating. Just wait until you see what she's come up with for us.'

Twitters of excitement broke out. Braedon noticed none of it. His stare was fixed on Hardwick.

She was new again. Another transformation. The woman across the room, smiling and prattling along with the rest, was not the Hardwick he'd known at Denning. Neither was she the carefully covered, tightly contained lady he'd encountered yesterday.

This time Hardwick was clad in a deceptively simple day gown. Her skin glowed porcelain against soft chintz in the palest pink. Someone had drawn her heavy ebony hair high, then gathered it into a loose twist allowed to drape along the elegant sweep of her neck. Her square bodice was cut low, the simple waistline high. She looked soft, natural, winsome—and he could not look away.

What was she doing? For surely this was not a random alteration. Of all women, Hardwick would comprehend the significance that accompanied the garments she wore. Who better would understand the power of suggestion, the role of perception that came with appearances?

What was she about? Gradually he did come to himself enough to spare a look around. She was dressed largely like the other ladies, if with less adornment. Was that it? Was she only trying to fit in? Or was she trying a new persona with each costume change, hoping to discover where she belonged?

His jaw clenched. In all likelihood she was merely trying to drive him insane.

Next to him, Mrs Edmunds was not partaking of the conversation like the rest of the ladies. He felt the weight of her regard, told himself to wake up, to break his gaze away as her head swivelled repeatedly between him and Hardwick.

Too late. The widow straightened suddenly. 'Miss Hardwick, I would suppose that notebook of yours holds many secrets,' she called. 'Things every society hostess would dearly love to know.'

Hardwick shrugged in their direction. 'No secrets, Mrs Edmunds, but a few useful titbits, I'm sure.'

The older woman's smile grew, more calculating than pleasant. 'Then perhaps you'll share a bit more?'

'Gladly, ma'am, but not today.' She gestured in his direction. 'For Lord Marland has kindly agreed to drive me to the printers this afternoon.' She turned to address his sister. 'I'm sure I'll be able to answer his questions, my lady.' And then she grinned.

Braedon blinked.

'Your brother drives a phaeton, I've discovered.' She actually *winked* at his sister.

'Oh, you and your phaetons.' Mairi laughed. 'Thank you, dear. And thank you, Braedon, for escorting her. But do be careful? Don't listen to her when she urges you to drive like the wind.'

Braedon stepped back, retreating from what might be the most disturbing reincarnation of

Hardwick yet. *Aloof,* he reminded himself. *Contained.*

Numb.

'Don't keep her too long,' Mairi warned. 'We have much work to do. I must investigate the back parlour, where I'm told the wallpaper has begun to bubble.' She thrust her lip out in a pout.

'Oh, but that paper is practically new, is it not?' someone asked. A chorus of advice gained in volume.

Braedon nodded at his sister, and then addressed Hardwick without looking directly at her. 'I don't wish to keep my team standing. I'll drive them around while you fetch your wrap.'

He gave a short, general bow of leave-taking—and fled.

They were done at the stationer's in record time. Now the Carlton House colonnade whizzed past, a dizzying pattern of gleaming stone and dark shadow that dazzled Chloe as they moved down Pall Mall at a clip.

She slapped a hand to her dainty straw hat and laughed in exhilaration. 'It's like flying, is it not?' she called out.

A quick glance down and a tightening of the tension around the marquess's eyes served as her only answer. She sighed, but refused to lose heart. The day shone bright, the wind was a marvel against her face and she was perched perilously close to the marquess on the phaeton's bench. His large form loomed over her and occupied more than his fair share of the space. She didn't mind. She pretended not to notice his thick-hewn thigh marching alongside hers, trapping the fringed end of her colourful shawl, and tried not to stare at his large and shining boot dwarfing her own small, slippered foot.

He held his silence, even when their shoulders brushed on the leaning turn onto Haymarket, and still Chloe refused to despair. He'd had ease and charm enough for Lady Ashton's friends this morning—and she still held tight to the fading glory of yesterday's smile.

No denying—that smile had thrown her into a state of confusion. She'd been unable to recover last night, with the marquess so compellingly near. A night alone in her room had been no help; she'd spent hours tossing and turning and recalling the feel of his large hands on her waist, remembering the heat coming off him and how she'd yearned for him to pull her close.

But she'd spent the morning getting more than just her notebook in order. She'd seized a few quiet hours to consider her role here and re-evaluate her rash response to Lord Marland's request.

And she'd decided that her pledge to help the marquess did not negate the promises that she had made to herself. The realisation was such a relief that she'd repeated it again. And again. Until it became a quiet, reassuring refrain.

She'd vowed to experiment, had she not? She'd made a conscious decision to embrace life and all the possibilities it might offer. Surely the marquess's request slid neatly into that category? She flushed. Lord Marland had been a fantasy for Hardwick, never a true option. Perhaps for Chloe, things might be different.

'There we are.' She directed the marquess towards a small, unassuming shopfront, perched between a hosier's and a coffee shop. They waited while a wagon, loaded with fragrant hay, lumbered on and out of their way, and then Lord Marland slid his vehicle in close to the pavement. His groom jumped down to handle the horses and the marquess crossed over to help her alight. This time his hands did not linger on her.

She quashed a swell of disappointment. He stood so close she was forced to look up and up to meet his gaze. 'When we enter,' she directed, 'please allow me to do the talking.'

Ah. It took annoyance to break through that carefully blank facade. Chloe watched his quick struggle to quell it and revelled in her small victory. She'd spent time enough masking her emotional reactions to him; his turn was past due.

She looked forwards to making the task more difficult for him.

He glared at her. 'May I ask why?'

She couldn't answer for a moment. All of her disparate thoughts were colliding as she stared at him. She talked to herself of possibilities, but practicality was a trait that would always be part of her nature. The chances of her having any sort of relationship with the marquess after their objective was obtained were so slim to be almost incalculable. All he wanted was the Spear. But would it truly satisfy him? It was just another object, another prize for his collection. After that, she feared, he would need another. And another. There would never be enough of them to ease his isolation.

She would do as he asked. She would help him track down this mysterious weapon. But perhaps it would be a greater gift if she *did* make it more difficult to stifle his emotions.

Still waiting, he raised a brow.

She widened her eyes. 'You are a man of many talents, my lord. I had no idea it was even possible for one to frown and to raise a quizzical brow at the same time.' She tilted her head. 'Did it take much practice for you to master the skill?'

'None at all,' he returned easily. 'You may count it as one of my many natural gifts.' He leaned in closer yet and the very air tightened between them. 'Would you care to chance a guess at what another one might be?'

Oh, she knew the answer, with no need to guess. Even if she hadn't heard the tales about his many European paramours, she had plenty of insight into the matter. As her lurching heartbeat and ragged breath attested.

'I am a master of...' His breath tickled her as he put his mouth right next to her ear. Shivers ran like water up and down her spine.

'...easy conversation.' He stood straight suddenly and stepped back. His tone switched from seductive to sardonic. 'So why should I not indulge in it with your shopkeeper friend?'

Did he think this was a game? The fact that he played at all was a victory—for him as much as for her. She laughed. 'Look further if you are seeking a testimonial, my lord. I'm sure that in over a year *we* have not had a conversation that did not revolve around a construction schedule, rusty blade or mouldy scabbard.'

'Then I should be brilliantly prepared for today's interview,' he said with a scowl.

'I fear it won't be so easy.'

'Why ever not?'

She smiled. 'Because the keeper of this shop is Signor Pisano.'

'And?'

Chloe allowed her gaze to run a leisurely course along the appealing length of him. 'And the *signor* does not approve of arrogant noblemen. He does not approve of anyone who keeps a private collection and refuses to grant access to scholars or other interested parties.' She placed a hand square upon the centre of his chest, ignoring the thrilling sparks that stiffened her fingers and coursed along her arm. 'Most especially, my lord, the *signor* does not approve of you.'

Without waiting for a response, she whirled and entered the shop.

The bell over the door tinkled softly. Chloe paused to take a deep breath and gather herself. The front room glowed warm in the afternoon light. She stepped further in, ran her hand along one of the many wood cases and allowed herself to be transported. Beeswax and ammonia, a hint of harsh chemicals and lush, heavy notes of *café au lait*—the scents in this room never failed to make her feel like a girl again.

A girl reassured by the constant nature of the place. The configuration of handsome shelves and cabinets along the wall and glass-topped display cases marching through the centre never changed, and neither did her welcome here.

A soft step from the back, the ring of a curtain being pulled, and then the familiar cry. 'Chloe, my dear, come in, come in!' Signor Pisano beckoned. 'I began to fear you had forgotten me.'

Remorse seized her, and dread, to see her old

friend so frail and bent over. 'Never, dear sir,' she said. She obeyed his summons, infusing all the warmth she could into her words and the press of her hand on his.

The bell rang again. The *signor* gazed over her shoulder with pleased expectation—and then he recognised the marquess. His expression grew sour as he glanced back to her. 'You've brought your employer along this time, I see.'

'Indeed.' She waved at the marquess. 'Do come over, my lord, and allow me to present Signor Pisano, the proprietor of this establishment. He is the only man I have ever met who might surpass even your knowledge of ancient weapons.'

He came, taking his time and taking everything in with clear interest. Chloe saw the moment that his eye fell on the display of blades in the specially designed long case, but he did not pause. He reached them, made a smart bow and said with every evidence of sincerity, 'It is indeed a pleasure, *signor.* May I compliment you on the neatness and organisation of the premises? It feels as if each of your treasures is celebrated and not merely available for purchase.'

Chloe's mouth dropped. Never had she seen Signor Pisano flush with pleasure over a bit of flattery, but the marquess had clearly caught him off guard.

'Indeed,' Lord Marland continued, 'this feels more like a museum than any shop I've ever been in.'

'An astute observation, my lord,' Chloe said. 'Signor Pisano was once head curator of a very fine museum in Padua.'

'*Si,* before French troops came and stripped it bare.' The *signor* sighed. 'It was all long ago.'

'And may I ask how you came to be acquainted with our Hardwick?' the marquess asked.

Now it was Chloe's turn to colour up. 'Signor Pisano was a great friend of my father's,' she answered quickly.

'Of *both* your fathers,' the old man said sharply. 'And your dear mother as well.' He sighed. 'Ah, Chloe, though proud they all would surely be of the way you've managed, I know they would each agree that it is time for you to give up this nonsensical position, working for *him*.' He gestured toward the marquess. 'It's time you found a man, *cara mia,* and made some babies for me to spoil. It is not to much to ask, is it, before I go to my reward?'

Coloured up? Chloe knew her face had gone a deeper scarlet than the brightly painted rims on his lordship's phaeton. 'Please, *signor*. Now is not the time for that old argument.'

'*Si,*' he agreed with a sigh. 'With you it is never the time. But, *cara,* do you think I do not know why you have come? And brought him along with you?' The old man rolled his eyes. 'You will forgive the bluntness of old age, my lord, but I feel I must tell you the truth. Chloe must, of course, always be welcome here. But I am not so pleased to see you on my doorstep.'

'I will readily forgive you, sir, if you will but tell me why you feel this way.'

'It is because I am no fool, sir! I know why you are here and I want no part in it. Do you think it has been easy, staying out of this mess so far? No! It has been a trial—and now, your very presence here has made it all for naught.'

Chloe exchanged a glance with the marquess. 'Come, *signor.*' She pulled over a stool. 'Come and sit. And please, tell us.'

'Tell you what?' the old man demanded, easing onto the seat and waving an irritable hand in the air. 'Tell you what a circus it has become, the search for this cursed item? How every collector in England is here in London and in a frenzy? Night and day they come, pestering, questioning, searching for some titbit about Skanda's Spear. And you are no different, my lord. Are you not here for the same purpose?'

His face darkening, the marquess nodded. For the first time, Chloe began to wonder if this had been a mistake.

Signor Pisano was eyeing Lord Marland's tall form in patent disgust. His wavering fin-

ger pointed dismissively to the marquess's wide
shoulders. 'Pah,' he spat. 'So you might well be
the biggest hound in this hunt, but you are not
the most experienced, nor even the richest, if
rumour is to be believed. And the Spear is no
ordinary artefact. It's going to take more than a
title and a heavy purse to bag the prize.'

She moved to help as the old man slid off the
stool, but he waved her irritably away. 'Well,
come along, then,' he ordered as he stalked to
a dark corner in the rear of the shopfront. 'For
Chloe's sake I will not order you from my establishment, but I will be damned if I will leave
you in plain sight for all the world to see. One
hint of you spending the afternoon and my life,
it will not be worth the living.' He made his way
to an elaborately carved wardrobe near the back.
Yanking open the door, he stabbed a finger into
the shadowed space behind it. 'Back here!' he
ordered.

Lord Marland hesitated.

'It won't do you any good to tip your hand too
early, either,' the older man said crossly. 'There
is a great deal of talk about your collection and
even more bitterness over some of your triumphant acquisitions.' He shrugged. 'The rest of
them are likely to close ranks against you, but
if you are willing to take the chance...'

The marquess stared at her. Chloe lifted a
shoulder. 'Can we not go along with it?' she

asked in a whisper. 'He's likely right about building resentment. And while he may be old and eccentric, he's also our best chance for obtaining solid information on the status of the Spear.'

After a long moment of scrutiny, he nodded. 'If we are to keep this meeting clandestine,' Lord Marland called to the *signor*, 'then leaving my phaeton to wait outside is counterproductive. I'll send my groom on.' He looked to Chloe again. 'If you will not mind the walk back.'

'Of course not.' She nodded and raised her voice. 'The *signor* is right and we must do what we can to protect his peace of mind.'

It took but a moment for the marquess to speak to his man. He re-entered the shop to the tinkling accompaniment of the bells and made his way to the back.

'*Dio mio,*' the *signor* groaned as Lord Marland slid into the dark corner. 'Even this is not enough to disguise your bulk.' He reached out and pinched the marquess on the arm. 'What do they feed the boys in the north?'

'Why do we not just retire to the back room, *signor*?' Chloe asked.

'No, no,' he grumped in answer. 'There is a window on to the alley. It is one of the reasons I took these rooms—for the light. So many delicate pieces—I must have light to work. And these foolish treasure seekers grow desperate.

The shop is closed and they sneak around to the back and pound upon the glass. The shop is open and they sneak around, hoping to find something that I do not have. It is a misery, I tell you.'

'I have no wish to inconvenience you. Nor do I have time to waste. Perhaps we had best go then, if you have nothing to say about the Spear. Hardwick?' The marquess gestured towards the door. 'Traffic is growing thick outside. We might still catch my groom.'

'I did not say I had nothing to say!' The old man rolled his eyes. 'I said I had nothing to say to them.'

Chloe bit back a grin. Lord Marland merely crossed his arms and waited.

'The first thing I must tell you is that your wisest course would be to abandon your quest right now.' Signor Pisano gave a shudder. 'For many years I have heard tales of this Spear. Quiet rumblings and rumours, mostly. In all that time I have only heard of despair coming to those that possess it.'

'Is it the curse that you speak of?' Chloe asked. 'I confess, I do not know the details, but I am surprised that you would lend it credence.'

The old man nodded. 'Anyone with experience will tell you that most of these tales—curses or hauntings or ill omens—are nonsense, often invented to drive up the value of a piece.'

'Most?' Lord Marland prodded.

'*Si.*' The *signor* drew a deep breath. 'I have met every sort of character in my long years in this field. Now I speak of one man in particular. He was not a good man,' he said bleakly. For a moment he held silent. 'He came from the East. He knew the value of fear. He inspired it often and easily—and he never failed to make a profit from it.' He raised his gaze and met her own. 'And yet, the only thing I ever knew *him* to be afraid of was Skanda's Spear.'

Silence hung heavy after his pronouncement, but Signor Pisano was speaking volumes with his gaze. Chloe started when the shop bell rang out again, sharp and impatient.

'Pisano!' a new voice called. 'Come out here at once! I would speak with you!'

The *signor* shot Lord Marland a look of accusation and disgust, then his visage wiped clean, he stepped around the opened wardrobe door and turned to greet his customer. 'Ah, Mr Laxton, such a surprise, to see you again so soon. I shall be pleased to help you, just as soon as I have finished with this lovely couple.'

Laxton! Chloe took a step deeper into the shadows, closer to the marquess. She lifted a finger to her lips and Lord Marland, understanding, nodded. Laxton was another collector, rich as Croesus, due to his father's luck with diamonds in South Africa, and ruthless in his pursuit of a piece. He and Hardwick had clashed several times in the past, and he was still smarting furiously over her victory in obtaining the Japanese pole arm for the marquess.

'I won't be put off, Pisano,' Laxton snarled. 'Word is racing through the streets that Marland was seen entering your shop this morning. I hope you have not forgotten who your best customer might be. I've dropped a damned good amount of money here. You had better not be holding out on me, in favour of him.'

Chloe bit her lip. The man could not see her or the marquess, she was certain, due to the wardrobe door and the dim light, but she turned and began to examine the stacked paintings leaning against the wall. If she needed to, she could lift one to cover her face, or Lord Marland's.

'You wound me, sir, believing sordid rumour over my own word. I told you, I know nothing of Skanda's Spear. And so I should tell the Marauding Marquess, should he ever grace my humble establishment with his patronage. Now, if you will excuse me, this young lady and her husband are searching for some artwork for their new home.' The *signor* turned his back on the man. He waggled his eyebrows dramatically in Chloe's direction and pointed towards the curtain leading to the back.

'They can damned well look over your stacks

of musty paintings on their own,' Laxton demanded. 'I want you to go over this list with me. It is a reckoning of all the previous owners of the Spear that I have been able to track down. See if you can add to the tally.'

Signor Pisano sighed. 'Do forgive me, my fine lady,' he said turning to face Chloe. 'Perhaps it would be best if I see to Mr Laxton. I believe he will not be staying long.' He started to turn away, but then stopped, his face brightening. 'Ah, but I have been struck with an idea. It grieves me that you have found nothing to please you, but I have been assembling a collection that might interest you. I have been working on them in the back room, preparing them for display, but I would not mind if you stepped back there to have a look. Yes—right through that curtain. First door on the right.' In front of him, where Laxton could not see, he made shooing motions with his hands.

Chloe looked to Lord Marland. A storm brewed over his brow. His fists were clenched and he looked in no way inclined to go along with the *signor*'s ruse. She bit her lip. She'd seen a boxing match once, at the village fair. And right now the marquess resembled nothing so much as a pugilist ready to step from his corner and pummel his opponent.

She scowled and shook her head at him. Greatly daring, she reached out and put her hand on his arm. She murmured a faint assent to Signor Pisano and tugged the marquess through the curtain.

His coat was of the softest superfine, but the arm beneath was rock-hard and radiating tension. He yanked away from her as they stepped along a narrow corridor and into the more brightly lit workroom.

Chloe closed the door and pressed her ear to it. Only the faintest murmur of the men's voices was audible from here. Inside, the marquess began to pace with the restless grace of a caged tiger. She leaned against the door for a moment, waiting for the strength of the hard wood beneath her fingers to replace the echoing feel of his flesh.

At last she turned to him. 'Shall we go out the back, do you think?'

Chapter Eight

Braedon was feeling neither calm nor aloof. Laxton's effrontery had got his blood up, triggering his competitive spirit and stirring up a maddening surge of anger at the thought of the man getting his hands on the Spear that was meant for him.

He deliberately embraced the turbulent emotions. They made such a welcome distraction from his unnerving reaction to Hardwick. A *blushing* Hardwick, who had gone nearly the same charming shade of pink as her gown when Signor Pisano urged her to leave him behind for a husband and babies.

Babies. Hardwick. The mind boggled.

Though his mind—and various other parts of him as well—could readily imagine the process of getting children on her. Especially in her latest incarnation. Those softly abundant curves, that falling twist of ebony hair. This was what she'd hidden from him all of these months, damn her. The thought pricked like needles of frustration under his skin and sent him pacing around the surprisingly spacious workroom.

'Shall we go out the back, do you think?' she asked from the door.

The question brought him back, forced him to focus on their predicament. He spun about. 'I was under the impression that the *signor* had more to tell us about the Spear, before we were interrupted.' He frowned. 'But you know him best. Did you come away with the same idea?'

Silent, she nodded.

'Then we stay.' He allowed all the turmoil inside of him to be expressed as harsh severity. 'I have no wish to bring trouble to your friend, but we cannot fail at this, Hardwick. I don't care if Laxton and a hundred others are after the Spear. I have to have it.'

She breathed deeply. 'Why?'

Braedon's breath began to come faster. The question flummoxed him—and he was damned well getting tired of being flummoxed by Hardwick. 'Because it belongs in the collection.'

Her gaze remained steady. 'Yes, so you've said. But why?'

His fists tightened. His torso began to vibrate with the force of his irritation. He wished, suddenly and intently, for the feel of a blade in his hand. For a skilled opponent and the chance to spend his frustration in blood and sweat and the clash of steel. 'I would vastly prefer not to discuss the reasons why. It is a family matter.'

'I see.' She nodded and moved away from the door. A long worktable occupied the centre of the room. She paused in front of it and kept her gaze fixed on the items scattered across it. 'Families can be so polarising, can they not? You and I are perfect examples of both ends of the spectrum. My family is gone now, but I spent my life trying to stay close to them. Yours is gone, too, but even still you try to push them away.'

Braedon gaped at her. This was it. Exactly what he'd feared when he'd been forced to ask for her help rather than command it. Prying questions. Conjectures. The fact that hers were remarkably accurate conjectures only made everything worse.

She stilled, her fingers gripping the table before her. He thought at first that the objects in front of her had captured her attention. He moved closer. Spread over the table lay a collection of Lover's Eye's—those miniature portraits of just the eye of a loved one that had been so popular at the end of the last century.

'What is it?' he asked.

She made a cutting gesture with her hand. 'Listen,' she breathed.

He lifted his chin. There. Male voices approaching the door, one of them unmistakably Signor Pisano's, raised in protest.

Braedon did not hesitate. A low, plush seat occupied the corner next to the fire. He gripped Hardwick's hand and dragged her bodily over to it. He seated himself and positioned her standing before the chair, facing him and blocking his view of the door.

She went willingly. Her head was cocked, her attention focused on the *signor*'s suddenly audible words. He must be right outside.

'Your paranoia is getting the better of you, Mr Laxton,' the old man complained. 'That is a perfectly ordinary couple in there. Valued customers. I won't have you disturbing them.'

'And I won't have you deceiving me. I don't know what prompted me to remember that Marland's much-vaunted assistant is a woman, but if I find you've concealed the pair of them I will ruin you, Pisano. I'll blacken your name so thoroughly that collectors will dig through rubbish heaps themselves before buying anything from you.' The door rattled. 'Now move out of my way, old man, before you are hurt.'

Hardwick, panic in her eyes, began to step away.

Braedon grasped her, held her in place. 'Bend down,' he ordered.

'What?'

'Bend. Down. Now.' He tugged on her arm until she was forced to move closer and her knees touched his. He kept pulling until she was bent over at the waist, forced to brace her hands on either side of the chair. Her face was positioned mere inches from his.

Behind them, the door opened.

'Of course I wish you to be happy, dear heart.' Braedon stared into Hardwick's dark eyes and pitched his voice seductive and low. 'But why on earth should I pay for a pretty portrait of some stranger's eye when my wife has such a lovely pair of her own?' He ran his hand slowly up the length of her arm. Lightly, he circled her shoulder before spreading his hand across the top of her back. 'Instead, if you are fond of the notion, why do we not hire someone to paint me your beautiful eye as a keepsake?'

Comprehension dawned on Hardwick's face. Only silence echoed in the room behind her.

He couldn't see Laxton, but Braedon guessed that the man was indulging in a prime view of Hardwick's behind. Let him. It couldn't compare to his own vantage, so close to her flushed expression—or the peek at her lush bosom afforded by her gaping bodice.

'Or better yet,' he purred, 'we might commission a portrait of a more…interesting portion of your anatomy?'

She had the heart for it. She tried to play

along. But her colour was high and her pupils had gone wide and dark with excitement, nerves…and something that looked alarmingly like yearning. She opened her mouth, but nothing emerged but a breathless sound of agreement.

He felt breathless himself. But he forged on and did what he'd spent weeks trying not to envision, what he'd been lying to himself about, what he'd wanted to do since she first waltzed down his stairs in a shifting gown of green-blue. He reached up, wound his other arm around her waist and pulled her in for a kiss—long, demanding and deep.

For just a moment, she forgot herself, forgot their audience and stiffened in shock. He didn't let up. He tugged her again, urged her to settle astride his lap and enfolded her in his arms.

Abruptly, she thawed. Her small hands left his shoulders to curl around his neck. She settled herself more thoroughly against his pounding groin and opened her mouth before the onslaught of his.

What utter madness. This was *Hardwick* hovering over him, trapped in the weight of his embrace, capturing him with her irresistible mix of innocence and devastating sensuality. His brain scrambled to get the message through, but it seemed the rest of him refused to listen.

Contained? Aloof? Surely Braedon had never

heard of such concepts. He was thoroughly anchored in this moment, on fire, alight with passion and with the need to burrow closer, feel more. He deepened the kiss, sent his tongue seeking hers. She made a sound at the back of her throat, a low growl of surprise and approval. And then she responded. Willingly, she entwined her tongue with his. Her fingers trailed up the front of him until she cupped his jaw with her dainty hand. The lightest touch, the most innocent caress, yet a slow twist began inside him, a tangle of something deep and insistent.

Something treacherous. Something completely unwise and even more dangerous. And yet he was helpless against it.

A throat cleared behind her. 'As you see, Mr Laxton, there is no conspiracy. Merely a young and happy newlywed couple.'

Laxton grumbled his answer, but the door closed.

They were left alone once more. With an extreme force of will, Braedon broke the kiss.

Hardwick blinked down at him, unfocused. Her gaze fixed on his lips. He returned the favour; she looked mussed and adorable—and terrifyingly—like she wanted more.

'Well, then,' she said shakily, 'I think we showed Mr Laxton.'

He grimaced. 'Not yet.' He gripped her arms,

lifted and set her back on unsteady feet. 'But we will. It is only a matter of time.'

'It is only a matter of time,' Signor Pisano said on a sigh, easing the door closed behind him again, 'before they all discover that you are here and that you are also after the Spear.'

Chloe, huddling across the room at the window, held silent. Let the marquess answer. He'd done something to her with that kiss, broken her like Pandora's box. She was occupied enough trying to piece herself back together. Refocusing on the reasons why they were here was beyond her—as was stuffing a torrent of dangerous emotions back under lock and key.

'True, of course,' the marquess admitted. 'But it would be to our advantage if we could delay their discovery.' He pushed away from the far edge of the mantel, where he had retreated—and stayed—after their…encounter.

She gripped the windowsill and frantically held back a peal of ironic, slightly unhinged laughter. *He* had no difficulty moving past that kiss, while she still shook with the aftermath of so much blazing passion. She had lost herself completely to it. But for him it had been no more than a means to an end.

That wasn't the worst of it. She'd come apart, and heady and addictive—if unrequited—desire was not the only evil to be released through the cracks in her soul. Shards of her new-found confidence lay scattered at her feet. The fear that she'd tried so hard to subdue swelled suddenly with new life.

She pressed her lips together. How arrogant she had been, hoping to change his behaviour. How blind she had been to consequences of changing hers. She'd convinced herself to embrace opportunity—even persuaded herself that it might exist between the two of them. Yet foolishly, only now did she consider another possibility: that Lord Marland could hurt her. Terribly. If she allowed it.

Perhaps some of her resentment had escaped only to find a home with Signor Pisano. Her old friend was favouring the marquess with a hard look. 'It will only be a matter of time before you find yourself slit from stem to stern with one of your own blades, my lord, should I ever see you touch Chloe in that manner again.'

'*Signor!*' Chloe gasped. 'Please!' The shock of his temper was what she needed. She had changed her behaviour, indeed, her entire approach to life. She had already made the decision not to be ruled by fear—she could not go back now.

Reaching for him, she left her retreat near the window and crossed to her old friend. 'It was a simple kiss, nothing more. A ruse, concocted to protect you and your reputation, you must remember. Of course it will not happen again.'

'Simple? Bah! It looked quite complicated from where I was standing.'

'Well, it was not,' she insisted. 'It is not. I have left the marquess's employ, do you not recall? Once we have obtained the Spear our association will end and we will be going our separate ways.' She ignored the stab of pain the words brought on. She'd already conquered this hurt once. She could do it again. She need only be sure there was no repeat of today's performance to knock her from her path.

'From the looks of things, that day cannot come quickly enough,' the *signor* grumbled.

'It is entirely in your power to speed it along,' the marquess spoke up.

'Almost, you convince me not to counsel you as I should.' He grimaced and gave way, moving to take a seat at the worktable. 'But I am duty-bound to ask you again if you won't give up this quest?' He shivered. 'I have the strongest feeling that you should not pursue this.'

Lord Marland shook his head. Chloe merely gave a quick shrug.

The *signor* gave a heavy sigh. 'Very well.' He fiddled disconsolately with one of the small portraits.

They waited. The silence stretched out. At

last, Chloe spoke up. '*Signor*, what can you
tell us?'

He gave her a bleak look. 'It is not much.'

'Is Skanda's Spear in London?' Lord Marland
asked. 'Can you confirm that much, at least?'

The *signor* nodded.

'Have you seen it for yourself?' the marquess
quickly continued.

'No.' The older man met Lord Marland's
gaze. 'But I know someone who has.'

'Who is it, *signor*?' Chloe asked gently.

He straightened. 'Now there is someone I
should like to introduce you to, *cara*. Arthur
Claibourne, the Earl of Conover. A young man,
but quite knowledgeable.' He grinned. 'Fa-
mously good-looking—and reputed to be the
biggest catch on the marriage mart.'

'He might be an Adonis walking among us,'
the marquess said sourly. 'But what matters is
if he is trustworthy—and if he knows enough
to be of any use. Can you depend on his word?'

The *signor* nodded. 'We have worked together in the past, authenticating certain pieces.
The Saxons are his area of particular interest
and expertise, but the Society of Antiquaries
has tapped him to handle a very delicate matter
regarding the Spear.'

'The Society has?' the marquess said with
surprise. 'But what have they to do with it?'

'Wait a moment.' The older man rose from

his stool and shuffled over to a bookcase standing on the other side of the window. He withdrew a battered tome and retrieved something from inside. Crossing slowly back, he stopped at Chloe's seat and handed her two thick sheets of heavy vellum.

'But what is it?' she asked.

'The tickets you will need if you truly wish to enter this game.' He tapped them. 'Oh, it's bad enough now. But this is where the real mayhem will begin.' He shook his head in disapproval.

Chloe scanned the top-most sheet. 'Invitations?'

'The Society is hosting a lecture on legendary ancient weapons. Skanda's Spear is to be one of the pieces featured. The event is open only by invitation—and everyone invited has shown an interest in obtaining that Spear.' He patted her hand. 'I asked the Earl of Conover specifically to tender you an invitation.' He sent a sour glance in Lord Marland's direction. 'I suppose that you can have mine.'

Chloe watched for his reaction, but the marquess only bowed his thanks. 'When is it to be held?' he asked.

'In four days' time,' the *signor* answered. 'There might be some posturing and jockeying for position in the meantime, but the race for the Spear will really begin at that lecture.'

Chloe jumped as he suddenly gripped her

forearm tightly. 'You must be careful, my dear. There is an air of something…desperation, perhaps, surrounding this object. I do not understand it.' He gestured toward the door. 'Laxton was merely rude. Others will likely be worse.' His dearly familiar face had gone anxious and sad. 'Promise me that you will take care.'

'I do promise,' she said, gripping his arm in return.

'And you, my lord,' the *signor* said to the marquess. 'You must vow to protect her.'

Together they turned to regard her with solemn gazes.

'I promise it.' Lord Marland spoke to her friend, but his eyes were locked on hers as he spoke. 'I will keep her safe from harm.'

Again, she was forced to bite back a laugh. The greatest danger to her well-being stood right before her, in shining Hessian boots. She suffered the most incredible urge to say it out loud.

But she did not. She dropped her gaze instead. This was all turning out to be so much more difficult than she had expected. Somewhere lay a path between paralysing fear and unacceptable risk. All she had to do was to find it.

Chapter Nine

Tighten. Release. Tighten. Release.

Braedon's right hand flexed continuously until he stretched his fingers wide to put an end to it. He ached for a blade, could not wait to get to the practice area he had set up in the gallery at Marland House. His gut roiled with irritation and longing, anger and want. Too many conflicting emotions. He needed to purge them with lunges and stabs, with a pounding heart and sweating pores.

Instead, he struggled to keep his step light and his pace steady as they made their way towards Mayfair. Even more difficult was the effort to keep his eyes from straying to the woman at his side.

It felt like an impossibility—that he'd actually kissed Hardwick. Yet it had been a logical course of action, considering the circumstances, Signor Pisano's fears and his own reluctance to tip his hand to Laxton.

Improbable, then—not impossible. And even more unlikely had been his incredible enjoyment of the thing. By all the saints in heaven, he'd been enticed, entranced and more than ready to take down her bodice, tuck up her skirts and immerse them both in a rising swell of pleasure.

She'd been ready, too. So sweetly she'd melted into him. Years he'd spent erecting the armour about him, and in a moment's time, she'd moulded all of her soft curves against him, found every nick and chink, and started to erode it all away.

And now he had to work out just what the hell to do with her. That had not been *his* Hardwick, thrusting her tongue against his. He could not take home to Denning the girl who'd settled herself so snugly against his engorged manhood.

God help him, but he wanted to. He did not want to go back to a home without her quiet presence, her steady, managing ways or her unfailing support. He was going to have to find a way to persuade her back into her buttoned-up persona—or he was going to have to give her up.

The very thought called up another desperate swirl of emotion in his gut.

'Four days,' he said abruptly, just to chase

those desolate thoughts away. 'We've started behind the game in this chase for the Spear— and now we must wait four days to catch up? Surely there is something we can do. More we can learn.'

'I'll make a few enquiries,' Hardwick answered. 'But I confess, I'll be glad of the delay. I will use the time to get a good deal accomplished for your sister.'

He took her elbow as they crossed the intersection at Coventry Street. 'A little over a week away, is it not? Mairi said that Ashton is pushing to make it back in time.' He grimaced. 'Good Lord, but the man had best make it. I don't wish to even contemplate the furor that would ensue, did he not.'

'Oh, he will make it.' Nimbly, she stepped out of the way of a footman carting a pile of bandboxes into a house. 'He'll arrive in time to see and appreciate the incredible amount of care and thought that the countess has put into this event.' She gave a self-conscious little laugh. 'I believe your sister means to bare her heart—and then, of course, they will live happily ever after.'

Braedon fervently hoped she was right. 'And what of you, then, Hardwick? What will you do when Mairi's event is over? She will be wrapped up in her husband. You will have no more planning or errands or many little details to keep on top of.'

'I will be all right,' she answered without looking at him.

'How? Why? You say you won't come back to Denning. Then just what is next for you?'

She held her silence as they continued to walk.

Her stubbornness combined with every other emotion surging inside of him and prodded forth a rush of anger. 'Come now, Hardwick,' he insisted. 'Tell me. What will you do?'

'Why?' She whirled on him. 'Why should I tell you? You, who shares nothing? What gives you the right to demand answers of me?'

Stunned, he could not answer. Likely because a good answer didn't exist.

'For the life of me, I cannot understand why you would care, in any case,' she fumed. But then her eyes widened and her mouth dropped and she rounded on him. 'Unless you fear I mean to take advantage of your sister? Is that what you think, Lord Marland?'

'What? No, of course not.'

'What is it, then?' She shot him a look of scorn. 'Are you afraid I'll go husband hunting among Lady Ashton's male acquaintances?'

The thought almost physically repulsed him. 'Is that what you are after, then?' he asked, biting back bile. 'A husband?'

Her entire face pinched inwards with fury. 'Oh, I did play my role well, did I not, Lord

Marland? Why is it so preposterous to you that I should dream of such things—marriage and children? Someone of my own?'

Now he was the one to hold silent, because, again, there was no answer to such a question.

Abruptly all the anger drained from her. Only sadness remained. 'It is the sort of life most women expect, is it not?'

'Is it what you wish for yourself?' he asked roughly. He watched her closely, not sure what he hoped her response would be.

It was only because he was paying such close attention that he saw it—something dark moving behind her eyes. Something more bleak and obscure than the fury that had lived there moments before. But her tone gave him no clue as to what it might be.

'I...I don't know,' she answered, sounding only wistful. 'Sometimes I think that it is all that I wish for, and yet...I cannot quite see it.' She sighed and glanced askance at him. She was hugging the low iron fence set before the buildings on this block with each step, as if it gave her a sense of security. 'I know I am not a choice for the men who live in your sister's world.'

In his world. The words resonated between them, for all that they had been left unsaid.

'Yet, I don't know the sort of man that *I* would choose,' she continued. 'Largely because I'm not quite sure where it is that I belong.' She heaved a sigh. 'And so, when your sister's ball is over…I shall keep looking, I suppose.'

Braedon shook his head. Here it was. Exactly the sort of conversation that he wished never to have. Far from light and superficial, it was everything that he knew to be dangerous. Too personal, too intimate, too *much* of everything. He should cut it off, push her away. She'd already made one assault on his line of defences. He needed to repulse her before she succeeded in weakening them further.

It was common sense. Basic strategy. He knew the truth of it—and yet he turned his head sharply towards her. 'Looking for what, exactly?'

She shrugged. 'For myself.'

She was maddening. Infinitely appealing, mysterious, vulnerable and utterly maddening. And he was a colossal fool. She had him confused and conflicted, and in his state of complete exasperation, he rounded on her. 'I confess, I can perfectly understand your confusion. For over a year you lived under my roof, the ideal assistant, the very picture of efficiency and reliability. Yet in the past two days I've seen you adopt the role of a baker's kitchen assistant, my sister's extremely competent secretary, and now…' he gestured '…this.'

A lovely young woman. Warm. And, oh, so eminently kissable.

He pushed the traitorous thoughts away. 'Which of them is the real you?'

She increased her pace. 'Perhaps all of them,' she said defensively. 'Do you not understand?' Coming to a sudden halt, she turned to him. 'You are the Marquess of Marland. The infamous Marauding Marquess! Does that mean that you are the master of Castle Denning, its land and people—and nothing else?'

He frowned.

'Of course not. You are many things. A peer of the realm, with political reach and influence. A diplomat, who has worked with kings and ministers and leaders of governments. You are a war hero. A warrior. A man with a passion for the past and for the tools used before you, by men like you.' She crossed her arms and raised a brow. 'An experienced and accomplished lover, as well, if rumour is to be believed.'

My God, she had him blushing like a schoolgirl. 'I don't think—'

'Exactly!' she exclaimed. She started walking again, and her words tumbled from her nearly as fast as her feet carried her. 'You don't think. You know who you are. You have been given many chances to explore all the many different facets that make you the man you are. It has been different for me. The image is unfinished, the puzzle incomplete.' She sighed. 'My role was cast at Denning. I wasn't going to learn anything more. I agreed to come to London with your sister because I was hoping for the opportunity—for numerous opportunities—to find pieces of me.'

Her words rang true; the pictures she painted loomed clear and vivid. But he did not want to accept them, for they meant that he had no chance of recovering his Hardwick—the one he was coming to realise that he so desperately wanted back.

'Do you know what I believe?' he demanded, speeding up to catch her. 'I think that *my* Hardwick is the woman you truly are. How else could you live the role and perform so well, were it not so? You do know who you are. I know it, too, but for some reason I cannot understand, you are afraid to admit it.'

She increased the distance between them, stepping closer to the busy traffic travelling up and down King Street. 'I would only be afraid, my lord, if I thought you were correct.'

'Come, Hardwick,' he chided. 'Listen to reason—'

'No! It is your turn to listen.' Anguish twisted her expression. 'Do you think that I was born that way? That I was a cold, sober child who suppressed her needs, her wants, her every emotion? Who turned it all into fuel so that she could work and work and work to fulfil some-one else's dream?'

His heart gave a great thump, then stilled along with the rest of him.

She stopped, too. 'Do you think that I sprang from the womb hiding behind a row of military-precise buttons and yards of bombazine?'

He swallowed. 'Of course not.'

She walked on. 'How do you suppose that I came to have so much knowledge about history? Did you not think it odd that I so quickly came to understand all that I needed to know about a collection like yours?'

'I assumed that your father taught you,' he said stiffly.

'You are partly right,' she nodded. 'My father—my real father—was a curator at the British museum. He loved history and his work. He would take me there at times, to show me treasures and tell many wonderful tales. I listened and I enjoyed his attention, of course, but history was *his* passion.'

They had reached Princes Street. Ahead, a narrow lane lay tucked between the houses. Hardwick paused at the mouth of it. 'Come,' she beckoned. 'There is privacy here and this time it is I who would prefer no audience for what I mean to say.'

A warning prickle ran up his spine. With a final cautionary throb it reached his neck, raising all the fine hairs there. Braedon cast a quick glance north towards Cavendish Square and considered leaving Hardwick where she was. It wasn't far to Mairi's house now. And he greatly feared that the woman he'd hoped to bring back home was already past his reach. Disappointment swamped him, but dread surged even higher. They had shared enough confidences for the day—or for a lifetime.

For long seconds he wavered. Hardwick waited a moment, limned beautifully in the afternoon sun, before, without warning, she reached up and removed her confection of a bonnet. Before the light could gather itself to do battle with the inky darkness of her hair, she turned and disappeared.

It was a foregone conclusion, then. Without further hesitation he admitted defeat and followed her until the lane opened into a small, cobbled yard.

'My father died,' Hardwick continued as if there had been no interlude. The bonnet swung from her hand. She didn't turn to face him as she stepped into the yard. 'Just as autumn was turning to winter he caught a fever. He lingered nearly until Christmas.'

Because the sun had begun its travels west, only one wall of the courtyard was still bright and warm. Hardwick moved to the bench placed against the brick and sat.

'Things were…difficult for my mother and me after that. The situation had become dire when she unexpectedly encountered George Hardwick. He had been a friend to my father and seemed overjoyed to see her. A quick courtship, then they were married.'

Braedon did not join her on the bench. The intimacies she communicated were risk enough for him. He kept to his feet, leaned against the sun-drenched warmth of the wall and listened.

'She didn't love him,' Hardwick whispered. 'I could see it. But she tried her best to make him happy. She never smiled, during all those months when we were alone. But for him…' She swallowed the rest of the sentence. 'She was never very strong, but she cooked his favourite meals, tried to brighten his rooms and listened as he recounted his frustration with the political aspects of his work.' For a long moment she sat quietly, her head resting against the back of the bench.

'But he must have spoken of his work to you as well?' Braedon asked.

She nodded. 'I watched her—and I learned.' She shivered despite the heat baking into the wall behind her. 'Those long, difficult months that Mama and I were alone… The cold and the hunger, they were bad. Losing our little house was horribly difficult. But the fear…'

She carried a voluminous Indian shawl of many colours, each rich shade complementary to the delicate pink of her gown. Draped artfully at her elbows before, now she shook it out and wrapped it tight around her. He might have told her from experience that nothing so external could protect her from the seeping cold of difficult memories, but he merely watched and waited for her to continue.

'The constant uncertainty was the worst. Never knowing when our next meal would come, if we would scrape together enough funds for rent or be forced to move on to a new set of cramped and dirty rooms.' She drew a deep, restoring breath. 'And the loneliness. For my mama was never the same after his death. She just…disappeared into herself. There were days on end when I could not coax her out of bed.' Her voice had dipped lower as she spoke, but now she looked up to meet Braedon's gaze directly. 'I did not want to go back to that, you see. I would have done anything to keep us from going back.

'So I did as she did. More than anything, I wished to keep George Hardwick happy. I was the most amiable child the world had ever seen. I was quiet and polite. I showed an interest in his work, began to ask him questions about the artefacts he obtained, asked him to describe his projects and his displays.' She straightened. 'As a strategy, it proved highly successful. I quickly learned to share his interests. We became close. His approval and friendship and regard were so important to me—after that long difficult spell, they meant as much as the warm home and full larder he provided.'

He frowned. 'But Hardwick was in Europe when I met him.'

'Yes.' She sighed. 'Despite her inability to match his level of regard, he really did love my mother. Three years they were married and he treated her so gently, as if she was made of spun sugar. He would do anything to make her laugh. It became a game. He loved to bring her little treats to make her smile. We were mostly happy, the three of us together.' She blinked back tears. 'But there came one of those springs in which you barely see the sun for all of the continuous rain. Mama caught a chill and declined to linger like my father. One day she began to cough and within a week she was gone. George was devastated.'

'He left you at school,' Braedon said. 'He mentioned it when I met him in Brussels. We were both hoping to purchase the same Roman legionary's dagger.'

'Yes. He couldn't bear to stay at home with the memories of my mother.' Her eyes closed. 'I suppose I was the worst reminder.' She sighed. 'So he assured me that he loved me. He asked me to take his name, before he left, as the situation abroad was still unsettled. And he made me officially his heir.' She paused, and grief nearly emanated from her pores. 'And then he, too, was gone.'

He'd lost control, allowed the conversation to slip into territory more dangerous than any he'd faced in the wars. Braedon drew a deep breath and reached out to pull them both back from the brink. 'But the buttons and the bombazine? Where did that come in?' He straightened. 'Surely you did not concoct that get-up for my sake?'

She shook her head to answer his question. 'No. It came about at school. It was such a misery. I was the pupil with no parents to come along on visits, no family to go home to on holidays. It made me the nuisance that someone had to stay back and be responsible for when the rest of the school had gone home. I was an easy target, for other students and for discontented teachers. I had hopes, but it didn't get any better after I finished and took a position as a teacher.'

Appalled, he protested, 'But why do such a thing? Stay where you were unhappy?'

'I was young. Alone. I had nowhere else to go,' she said simply. 'Father wouldn't hear of me joining him on his travels. They were more restricted and grew more dangerous as the wars progressed.'

Braedon felt like a fool—a guilty, culpable fool—because by that time he had surely hired away her stepfather and made him his factor.

'I was the youngest teacher and already unpopular, but I grew tired of being the scapegoat for the entire school. So I decided to repeat the lesson I had learned after my mother's second marriage. I watched the headmistress of the school, asked questions and listened to her likes and complaints. She had been educated in a convent herself and bemoaned the fact that English parents would not consider nuns as instructors. She longed for the structure and order of her youth. She despaired of teachers more interested in dresses and beaus than their students. She tired of dismissing them for flirting with the dancing master or losing them to marriage.'

He gave a horrified laugh. 'So you thought to fit them up in a modified nun's costume?'

She bit back a laugh. 'Well, yes. Sifting through all of her complaints, it seemed a good idea.'

'To the headmistress, perhaps. I cannot imagine the rest of them were happy with your ideas—or your sense of fashion.'

'And that's exactly why it worked. The teachers who cared for such things rebelled—and eventually left.'

'And you became the headmistress's pet?' he asked with sarcasm.

'No, even better, I became invisible. I blended right in with those who couldn't have cared less about the uniform. I kept quiet and became anonymous. I was more function—arithmetic and elocution for the youngest pupils—than a person. It was bliss. I wasn't a target any longer. I felt swaddled behind my row of buttons and yards of fabric. Safe.'

Braedon stared at her. He understood. And he was at once imagining her donning her clothes like her own armour and watching the sunlight disappear into the ebony of her hair, when the realisation hit him. No glancing blow, either. It thumped him with the force of a cannon, scattering fury and shock like so much shrapnel.

'Damn it all to hell and back,' he said in a voice throbbing with anger. 'You did it again at Denning, didn't you? You watched me with the same purpose, studied my ways and adjusted your behaviour, your very *self*—to become what I needed most?'

She didn't answer, only stubbornly met his gaze. But he already knew the truth. Rage boiled in his belly and constricted his airways. His fists clenched impotently at his sides.

Until he took in her apprehension, felt the unease she tried to wring away with twisting hands. He reached for calm. Breathed deep. 'Well, it was asinine behaviour, without a doubt.' He managed to maintain a tone of civil disdain. 'And it's landed you in the predicament you find yourself in now.' He nodded. 'But it certainly made you one damned fine assistant.'

She straightened. 'Then you are not angry?'

'I'm angry as hell. And I'm disgusted with you, with myself and with nearly everyone else in your misbegotten life.' He pushed away from the wall and began to pace in the enclosed space, from one unremarkable brick wall to the next. 'You do know that your stepfather truly cared for you? He spoke of you often.'

'Of course,' she said, startled. 'As I did for him.'

'I can't help but feel that there are other observations that you have failed to make—and that they leave more than one hole in your theories.'

Polite disbelief coloured her cool glance.

'It's true. I still do not believe that it is possible for anyone—even you—to live a lie or play a part for twenty-four hours a day. Do you think that it was all part of the charade, that you never incorporated anything personal or true into your role?'

Still she didn't answer, though she glanced his way and then quickly ducked her head.

He regarded her a moment in silence before he understood. 'Ah, now I can see the wheels turning in your mind. You think even if you had let something slip in, that I would not have noticed.'

She pressed her lips together. 'I think that if I had revealed something, you would not have noticed even if I had given it to you in a song and dance.'

'How do I take my coffee?' he asked abruptly.

'With one sugar only,' she replied easily. Her brow rose. 'How do I take mine?'

He regarded her with disdain. 'I am not so easily fooled. I've never seen you take coffee, only tea. Plain tea.' He thought a moment. 'Although I can recall you adding a bit of honey in the winter months.'

She looked reluctantly impressed.

'We were colleagues,' he said. 'We worked together for months. I would be the worst sort of cad if I did not know a bit about you.'

'Yes, well I dare say even Mrs Goodmond might recall how I take my tea.'

'How painful it is to discover what a villain you find me. Well, you are wrong and I can prove it. For I recall one incident, not so far past either, when you let your guard down a bit. I vividly remember when you mentioned that you enjoy the seashore.'

Both eyebrows rose. 'I believe what I said was that I would some day like to live at the seashore.'

'There. You see. I was paying attention.'

She smiled at his jest, but it was a look of condescension. As if his inadequacy merely proved her point. And abruptly the smouldering embers of his rage roared back to life. He closed his eyes against that look and the echoes of ancient fury that it summoned. But it was no good. The memories were there, awake in his head and sending anger flickering along his veins. How many times had he seen such a smile—full of pity and disappointed resignation—on his father's face? How many countless more instances had his brother's face echoed that expression, just before it melted into the crafty promise of malevolence?

This. This was exactly why he disdained this sort of personal alliance. Why it was safer to stick to clearly defined roles: master and servant, employer and employee. Why emotional distance and armour and even symbolic rows of buttons were such utterly brilliant ideas.

But the buttons were gone and his insulating armour showed signs of the battering she'd given it. He had to put a stop to it before the cracks grew any wider. So he snapped open his eyes and let loose with a torrent of angry words.

'Damn it, Hardwick! Don't look at me in that way. I am not a monster, nor did I ever act as one. And you were never the saint in this cautionary tale either—so pray do not fault me for failing to discover that which you were trying so hard to keep hidden.'

The offensive smile faded. Stricken, she took a step back. But this was Hardwick, so it was merely a matter of seconds before her chin lifted. 'Very well, my lord. I do apologise. It was not my intention to find fault, but merely to explain why I must follow a path that you so obviously disapprove.'

She turned away, her lips pressed tight, and Braedon cursed to see her bravado fail. Her shoulders drooping, she stepped towards the narrow alley.

He let her go. Cursing inwardly, he watched her pause in the last bit of shadow before the mouth of the narrow lane. Breathing deeply, she straightened her spine and stepped into the sun.

'Hardwick.'

He was a fool. Why stop her? She was firm in her purpose, which meant that he must be firm in his. She would move on—and he must allow it.

'It can't have been easy for you, catering to my every whim for so long. I am a harsh task-master. A difficult man. Everything in my life has conspired to mould me into a cold and re-mote form.' For once, as a gift to her, he allowed true remorse to enter his tone. 'I do not pine over it. In fact, I nearly always appreciate the benefits of my nature, but if it has in some way harmed you, then I do apologise.' He gestured toward the street. 'Why do you not go on alone? The garden is visible from here. You are nearly home. It should be perfectly safe.' He gave her a nod and turned back, allowing the cool darkness of the alley to soothe his inflamed nerves.

He never heard her approach. Yet somehow he was not surprised when her hand lightly brushed his shoulder.

'I am the one who must apologise,' she whispered. 'I feel so…fractured. Lost.'

Her hand slipped down to lightly grip his arm. Such a soft touch from a tiny hand, yet it set his heart to racing and held him completely in thrall. She tugged and he allowed her to pull him about to face her.

'It is confusing enough inside my heart and my mind.' She ducked her head a moment. Her gaze rested on her fingers, now resting lightly above his heart. Undoubtedly she could feel the rapid rise and fall of his chest. 'I can only imagine how erratic I must appear from the outside.'

He should go. The wisest course of action would be to step back, to keep away, to lead her firmly to Mairi's door and to leave her there. For good.

He reached out instead, ignored his every natural impulse and ran a finger along the pure ivory curve of her jaw. 'Just because you are looking does not mean that you are lost,' he said roughly.

And just because he touched her did not mean he didn't have to put her away from him.

'Tea with honey,' he said, his voice low. 'Hard

work. A shining blade. An organised desk. A fast ride in an open vehicle. All things that you do well or enjoy. It seems to me that you have more pieces to your puzzle than you might think.'

She swallowed. His heart pounded. He was cupping her cheek now and she leaned into the caress. Her soft skin rubbed into his calloused palm.

'And just today we've discovered another. Something else I know you to enjoy.'

She gazed up at him through a fan of thick lashes.

Every instinct shouted frantically for him to stop. The very same gut feelings that had saved his life on the battlefield and steered him safely through diplomatic arenas and social minefields.

He ignored them all.

He paid heed to her artlessly beckoning gaze instead. God, how could she combine innocence and allure into such a heady mix? There was no thought of or desire for numbness now. She called and an answering thrum coursed through him. Excitement and desire sparked to life where they touched and spiralled outwards. It sped though his veins and he felt high and wild and more alive than at any other moment in his life.

He followed her call with his hand, allowing it to travel along her jaw and down the white and slender column of his throat. She arched into the caress and he answered again, sliding up and burying his fingers into the ebony sheen of her hair. He pulled her close. Her eyes slid closed as he leaned in to cover her mouth with his.

Chapter Ten

Courage. Their kiss tasted of it—glorious heat and climbing passion and the incredible blaze of courage that it took for each of them to lose themselves in the dangerous give and take of this moment.

Risk lived here. Chloe understood it—she knew that exploration went hand in hand with jeopardy. That she was making herself vulnerable to the one person left on earth with the ability to do her true harm.

She didn't care.

His kiss burned hotter, coaxed harder than it had done earlier and she responded in kind. Her arms crept higher. Up and up again, she allowed her fingers to wander, over the broad expanse of his chest and along the strong and solid column of his neck. She fulfilled the fantasies of a thousand nights when she slid her fingers home—into the thick, silken strands of his hair.

Unreal. Almost unbelievable, that this was happening at last. She was consumed with want, transformed by joy and wild, fierce need into an unfamiliar, untamed, and demanding version of herself. With a moan climbing from deep within, she pulled him closer and tighter against her.

He heard her, knew better than she what she needed. She gasped in protest when he tore his mouth from hers. But he wasn't leaving her.

'We are a pair of damned fools,' he growled.

She nodded—and tugged on his shoulders, urging him back. Instead he wrapped thick, strong arms around her and lifted her as if she were nothing more than a rag doll. Feeling warm and incredibly safe, she burrowed into his embrace.

Until he set her down and pressed her hard against the fading warmth of the brick wall.

Yes. A hundred times, yes. Only him. No one else held the power to lure her from safety into the far more hazardous territory of desire. He leaned down to her again and she parted her lips to the insistent pressure of his. Thrust for thrust, she met his tongue and gave back the same searing passion that he poured into her.

Her shawl had disappeared, lost somewhere

on the cobbled stones. She had no need of it, in any case. The solid wall behind her gave up its heat, but it was as nothing compared to the inferno left in the wake of the marquess's hands. Huge and powerful, calloused from swordplay, they encompassed her waist. Heat raged from every point of contact. The flames soared even higher as one hand crept upwards, blazing a trail along her ribs. Ever so slowly his fingers teased, breaching the swell of her breast, circling with tantalising slowness—before abruptly cupping her entirely.

Delicacy was abandoned. She tore her mouth away and groaned deeply. Breath exploded from her as he rubbed a palm across the engorged peak of her nipple. Her back arched, pressing her into the caress, asking for more. He answered with a quick, hard pass of his thumb and then he pinched her right through all the thin layers of intervening fabric.

Her legs nearly gave way beneath her. With gratitude she pressed her shoulders against the brick behind her and asked again.

'More,' she whispered. 'Again.'

He opened his mouth, but the small sound of a delicately clearing throat did not come from him.

He froze. She stiffened.

'Sorry, guv, but I figgered it'd be better to interrupt sooner, 'stead o' later.'

Chloe couldn't see. The marquess had moved instinctively to shield her. One instant they were locked in an embrace, the next he had spun about to face the threat, one large hand reached back to hold her safe. He was pressed so close that she felt the rumble of his chest as he spoke.

'I'm hard pressed to think why you would interrupt us at all,' he said harshly. 'Especially as we do not know each other.' His arm moved away from her. She stepped a bit to the side and caught her first glimpse of the new arrival.

Not a boy, nor yet a man, he stood, feet braced wide, in the narrow entrance to the alley. As she watched, he crossed his arms and allowed a cheeky smile to spread across his face. 'Was paid ter do it,' he said casually. 'Leastaways, I was paid ter follow ye and report back where the pair o' ye landed when ye left the old man's shop.' He lifted a shoulder. 'Thought I'd give ye the chance ter make me a better offer.'

'Who hired you for such a foolish errand?'

The young man shrugged. 'Don't know. Some gentry cove. Don't rightly care who he is, long as his coin is good.'

'Surely you can come up with a more thorough description.' The marquess sounded distinctly annoyed.

Chloe took another step and emerged fully from behind him. 'Just tell us how you are to deliver your information.'

The young man's grin stretched into a smile. 'I'm to meet the cove at Somerset House.'

She exchanged a glance with Lord Marland. 'Definitely Laxton,' she said.

'He keeps offices there?'

She nodded.

The marquess's expression shifted from annoyed into calculating. 'Repeat this,' he demanded abruptly of the boy. He rattled off an address.

Clearly sensing an opportunity, the young man stood taller and gave him back the same words.

'Again.'

He repeated the information.

'I'll triple the scoundrel's original offer, should you agree to give him that address—and nothing else.'

'Done!'

The marquess tossed him a purse. 'That should meet the price.'

'Aye.' The young man hefted it once, then tucked it away. He nodded. 'I'd work with ye again, guv. In a heartbeat.'

'You'll regret it, should I ever again catch you working against me,' Lord Marland answered with dark promise.

The scamp's eyes darkened. The pair of them squared off across the small cobbled yard for a long moment. Then with a quick nod of acknowledgement, the young rogue turned and sauntered away.

Her shawl lay in a heap by the bench. Chloe stepped over to fetch it. She refused to look directly at the marquess—or the wall she had just been pressed so ecstatically against. 'Whose address was that?' she asked as she pulled the soft material across her shoulders.

'A certain cabinet minister's,' the marquess answered. 'He was recently married.'

She sighed. 'You do think of everything.' The sun had gone from the small space, and so had the fleeting passion. 'We had best return to your sister.'

Braedon had come within inches of being captured by the enemy once, in a raid on a French pay wagon that had helped to cement his nickname. He had indeed been caught with a nobleman's wife in Prussia and had once come very close to being tripped up by an extremely savvy Russian spy during the talks in Vienna. Though each situation had held its own perils, he'd kept a cool head, held alarm at bay and prevailed with the utter implacability that he had learned at his father's knee.

He fervently wished he could say the same about today. How lowering to be brought to the brink of panic by a slip of a girl in a pink dress.

Yet Hardwick had done it. She'd broken him.

Tempted him past a line that he never should have allowed either of them to approach. It was the boundary that only now he realised he had feared all along—the line in that sand that had made him ignore the thousands of little ways she had always called to him. The one that had made him, like Ulysses, stuff his ears with pitch to ignore the siren's call.

But he'd heard the call today—and he'd answered. Now they were over the line and had left it behind them in the distance. And he had no idea where to go from here.

He eyed her cautiously as they made their way towards the north side of the Cavendish Square. He might be lost, but she looked entirely unaffected by their encounter. She walked quite normally at his side—and Braedon didn't know whether to be insulted or relieved. Finally they made it far enough to glimpse Ashton House past the trees in the garden…and Hardwick began to trot ahead.

'Lady Ashton,' she called. 'What is it?'

He looked up to find Mairi perched on the steps of her town house, directing a steady stream of servants carrying furniture out to an open wagon. He hurried on Hardwick's heels.

'No, no! I want the wagon full before you place the tarpaulin over it,' Mairi was scolding a footman. 'We should be able to send it all in one trip. Oh!' she exclaimed as Hardwick grasped her arm. 'There you are—the two of you! I expected you back long before this.' She spoke cheerfully enough, but Braedon caught the signs of tension at the corners of her mouth and in the tight grip she kept on Hardwick.

'But what has happened?' Hardwick asked.

'Damp!' Mairi exclaimed with drama. 'Damp has happened, with all the resulting disastrous results! You recall the bubbling wallpaper in the back parlour? Well, the answer became painfully clear this morning. There's a spot on the roof that must have been leaking for months, and every inch of paper is backed with a carpet of mould.'

'Oh, good heavens,' gasped Hardwick.

'And the smell! We began pulling paper and it's horrible. It's spreading, too. The timber is starting to rot and it's already reaching into the other rooms along the west wall. We have to clear the entire side of the house and replace a large section of the wall.' She bit her trembling lip. 'There can be no question of holding the ball here, now.' She squeezed Hardwick's arm. 'In fact, there's some debate on whether we should be allowed to stay at all.'

'Oh, no!' Hardwick gripped her with her other hand, too. 'And after all of your lovely ideas and hard work.' Braedon watched her brow lower and her face take on a familiar, mulish expression—and he knew that Mairi had gained herself a champion. 'But you are not to worry,' Hardwick assured his sister. 'I refuse to let all of our effort go to waste. A place to stay shouldn't be hard to find and as for the ball—well, there must be assembly rooms we could rent. I'll start today—'

'Just a moment, dear,' Mairi said with a pat of her hand. 'I said we could not hold the ball *here*, but you are correct. There are alternatives.'

His sister was staring at him, now, with an unmistakably expectant gleam in her eye.

'What?' he asked, defensively. 'I'm sorry to hear the bad news, my dear. But I don't know the first thing about mould.'

'Nor would I expect you to.' She tilted her head and cocked an eyebrow at him. 'But I would expect you to offer to house me and mine in my time of need.'

Braedon fought back a surge of anxiety. Matters with Hardwick were unsettled at best. He'd failed to coax her back to her old persona, and surely the last thing he needed was to suffer her new one running tame in his household. 'Well, I suppose you can stay with me,' he said reluctantly, unable to see a way out. 'It won't be comfortable, I warn you. The place has been closed up for a score of years and is dusty and deserted as a tomb.'

She arched a brow. 'I should also expect you to allow me to host my party in the perfectly charming and free-of-mould ballroom in Marland House.' She smiled. 'You have the lovely long gallery, too. Indeed, I don't know why I didn't think to have the thing there in the first place.'

'Now, hold on a moment. You are forging too far ahead.' He frowned. 'I can count the staff of the place on one hand. They have no experience in pulling something like this off.' He concealed his anxiety behind a sharp tone. 'Come now, Mairi. You know Father had no interest in the place. There hasn't been so much as a card party there in a score of years.'

'Those are just excuses, Braedon.'

'It's logic, my dear. Dobbs is old and set in his ways. I doubt he could manage the frenzy and confusion of putting together an event of this scale. Nor am I confident in his ability to see the thing done to your satisfaction.'

'Don't be ridiculous.' Mairi's voice had taken on a definite edge of hysteria. 'Chloe and I shall handle everything. I'll bring along all of my servants. Why, I'm sure I shan't even be around to be in your hair. Chloe can see to the cleaning and preparation of your place while I am here during the day, overseeing the reconstruction.' She sent an apologetic glance in Hardwick's direction. 'I can do the orders and purchasing from here, too, and just have everything delivered to you at Marland House.'

She shot him a trembling smile. 'So you see, Braedon, you will hardly be inconvenienced a whit. Neither you nor Dobbs will have to do a thing except dress appropriately and show up the night of the ball.' She drew a deep breath. 'Please, Braedon. My marriage is at stake.'

He cursed long and hard under his breath. He sneaked a peek at Hardwick and had to hold back a snort. Of course she would be of no help. Her face set, she stared steadfastly at the pavement. But he could sense that she was waiting. As were the passing servants. Suddenly it seemed as if all of Mayfair hung, breath bated, for his answer.

'Oh, very well,' he ground out.

'Thank you, dear!' Mairi cried. She reached out and hugged him tight. Hardwick let out a long, pent-up breath. Even the damned servants were smiling.

'Oh, this will work out wonderfully well!' Mairi let him go and reached out to Hardwick instead. 'But there will have to be changes! Braedon's dining room has twice the seating as ours. We shall have to go to round tables. And the invitations!' she gasped. 'Oh, I know you've only just been to the stationers, but, darling, won't you go back and notify them of the new address?'

He sighed and nodded his acquiescence.

'You are an angel. But you will have to go

quickly, before he closes up for the day.' Mairi had already mentally dismissed him. She turned to go back to the house and beckoned Hardwick after her. 'Oh! But I've forgotten!' she said, pausing. 'Your friend, Sir Thomas Cobbe, is looking for you! He stopped by earlier.'

'Thom? Looking for me—here?'

'Yes. I thought it must be urgent, for him to come searching here. Perhaps he left a message for you at Marland House.'

'I'll head home, then.' He flung up a hand to stall his sister's protest. *'After* stopping at the stationers. Again.' He tried to catch Hardwick's eye, to say farewell or even gauge some sort of reaction from her after the extremities of the day, but she only gave him a quick nod before passing through the doorway.

Hmmph. Well. He stared after her a moment before shaking himself awake. She was right, of course. Correct in every way—to act as if nothing had changed. Because nothing had. They were at an impasse. There was no need to stand here like some lovesick swain. He clambered down the stairs and stalked his way back toward the Strand.

It wasn't until after the stationers, when he was halfway home again, that he remembered the boy.

Braedon found him—Rob, he'd said his name was—in the nursery at the top of the house.

Even in the dim light, the place looked musty and unused. The boy knelt at the window, his breath fogging the panes as he watched the twilight blanketing the city.

He shifted back, his arm moving, and Braedon caught sight of the carved dog in his hand. He ran it back and forth along the windowsill and up the frame. Casting about the nursery, Braedon noticed a table along the wall. Upon it, the feeble light picked up the bright colours of the set of new tin soldiers, laid out in neat lines.

For the briefest of instants, Braedon reconsidered what he'd come to do. But the boy turned and the sight of that profile against the flaming colour of the sky convinced him. He recalled his own shocked reaction at his first glimpse of the child and thought of how much worse it would likely be for Mairi—and he strode into the room.

'Dobbs said that you didn't enjoy the soldiers?' he asked as he crossed to the small table.

Showing no alarm, Rob glanced over his shoulder. 'I don't know what to do with them.' The dog continued to frolic before the window.

Braedon breathed deeply. Mairi had never dealt well with Connor. Far more volatile than he and more easily roused to a temper, she had made an ideal target for their brother's cruelty. He'd done all that he could to shelter her, but there was no absolute protection against Connor's sort of malice. He'd been spiteful, hateful—and infinitely patient. Mairi had always been a little highly strung, but much of her instability could be laid at Connor's door.

He couldn't predict her reaction to Connor's son. The resemblance was chilling. She could be slightly upset to discover the boy's existence, or she could plunge into an overwrought spiral of dark emotions.

He sensed that his sister was at a crossroads now. If she healed this rift with Ashton, if they spoke freely at last about their obvious affection for each other, Braedon could see Mairi settling down to a calmer, happier life. Braedon wanted that for her—and would not allow anything to get in the way of it.

'Rob, would you come over here for a moment? I have something I would like to discuss with you.'

The boy climbed down from the window seat. Braedon took one of the small chairs at the table and slowly he approached and took the other.

'Do you want your dog back?' the boy asked stoically.

He noticed that he held it clutched tightly in his hand. 'No. Of course not. Your father gave it to you. It is yours to keep.'

The child noticeably relaxed. Braedon picked up a tiny infantryman and tested his finger against the small, shining bayonet. He set him down again, aimed him carefully at an opposing Frenchman, and mimicked the sound of gunfire. The toy obligingly fell down at the flick of his finger, but the boy didn't rise to the bait.

'Why don't you cut your hair?' the child asked abruptly.

He blinked. 'Because I don't wish to.'

The boy fingered his own short hair and waited.

Braedon forged ahead. 'You like dogs, do you?'

Ah. An involuntary smile—the first sign of enthusiasm—or any emotion—he'd seen. 'Oh, yes.'

'Do you know how to care for them?'

Rob nodded. 'We had them at the inn. One at the kitchen spit and another in the stable, to help guard the horses. I fed them every day. I kept them brushed.' He paused a moment before sticking his chin out in stubborn fashion. 'My da liked dogs. He hunted with them.'

'That he did,' Braedon said with an easiness that nearly choked him. 'Nearly every day, in fact.' He waited a beat and then continued. 'I wanted you to know that I've written to several very nice places in the country. I told them about you. I'm certain we can find a comfortable home for you soon, but it is going to take a fortnight or so, at the least. You'll stay here in the meantime.'

The boy's face remained blank. Carefully so. Braedon suspected that he was suppressing some strong emotion.

'There is one problem,' he continued. 'The number of people in the house is about to double.' He lowered his voice confidingly. 'Worse, there is to be a ball held here, in this house, very soon. It will mean a dreadful lot of work. There will be a hustle and bustle as preparations are made.'

Still no reaction. It was new and unsettling, seeing calm on that familiar face. He kept waiting for the child to explode into violent action.

'Servants will be moving in here.' He paused. 'And there will be two ladies. They will be in and out, working to make everything ready. One of them has hair as dark as night. The other's hair is a lighter brown.' He swallowed. 'It would be best if they did not know that you were here.' Leaning in, he caught the boy's eye. 'Especially the brown-haired one.'

That stirred the boy to life. 'Why?'

Braedon breathed deep. 'Because it will upset her to see you.'

Rob bit his lip. 'Because I look like my da?'

Braedon nodded. Seeing a crestfallen expression on that face was like something out of a dream. Yet the boy could not help how he looked. 'Rob, I think that you are old enough. I shall strike a bargain with you.' He leaned forwards. 'You keep hidden when the ladies are near—'

'Especially the one with brown hair?' Rob reiterated.

'Especially her. You keep hidden…and I will get you a dog of your own.'

Rob frowned. 'You mean—a real dog?'

'A real dog.'

The boy's eyes lit with joy, and then narrowed. 'Mine to keep, you mean?' He looked wary. 'You won't take him away. Later?'

Braedon sighed. This would possibly complicate matters as he sought a place for the boy, but it was little enough to do for the child. 'I'll make sure that, wherever you go from here, you will be allowed to take the dog with you.'

The boy beamed. 'I should like a dog with short hair, 'stead o' long. Brown hair is better'n black. And not too big, please.'

'Shall we shake hands on the pact, then? As gentlemen?'

Resolute, Rob stuck out a small hand. 'I do promise, sir. That brown-haired lady won't never know that I'm here.'

Braedon left the nursery feeling as low as a snake. He'd been reduced to bribery—with a child. The boy shouldn't be punished for the circumstances of his birth. Yet Braedon had to think of Mairi's welfare first.

God, what had happened to his simple, tidy life? The vast, safe distance that he normally kept between him and the rest of the world had suddenly become cluttered. His plans to obtain the Spear of Skanda had certainly become complicated. And Hardwick? There was no end to the difficulties there.

He needed a long, hot soak to cleanse away the troubles of the day. But first—first he needed to lose himself in thrust and stab and parry, to forget everything in the clean swipe of a blade through air.

He barreled down the stairs, two at a time.

Chapter Eleven

Chloe was feeling unsettled. Unbalanced. And the uneasy feeling was not due to her current position, perched upon a ladder, cleaning a crystal chandelier in Lord Marland's dusty passageway.

The din of constant, cheerful chatter sounded faintly through the wall behind her. Lady Ashton's household had settled into Marland House as if they belonged here. The servants set to scrubbing the ballroom were going about the job with good heart. She sighed, wishing she could share in their contentment. Instead, an odd feeling of trepidation had grown over the last two days. She tried to tell herself it was only an overreaction to Laxton's hired spy, but she'd felt strangely as if eyes were on her at times. The sensation was strongest in the streets, when she was out and about on errands, but it plagued her here in Lord Marland's home, too. Several times she had glanced up and caught sight of a boy peering out at her. He always disappeared quickly, and no one else ever seemed to notice him.

A servant's child, surely. Yet still, it was oddly unsettling.

Although, if she was going to be strictly honest with herself, then she must admit that there was also a healthy amount of pique in the swirl of her mixed emotions. Pique—because the gaze that she *wished* to catch was nowhere to be found.

Chloe strongly suspected that the marquess was feeling just as disconcerted as she. She'd barely caught a glimpse of him, even though she'd spent long hours overseeing an army of servants in the massive undertaking of readying his home for the ball. He appeared to be avoiding the muss and fuss, but she rather thought that he was avoiding her. No doubt he hadn't decided how to act with her. He'd given up his pursuit of Hardwick—and he didn't seem to have any idea what to do with Chloe.

She knew what she wanted him to do. She'd snatched up every chore that allowed her to sit—even atop a ladder—because her knees still intermittently failed her. Two days after a succession of scorching kisses and she still felt a puddle of unresolved lust. She directed servants, moved furniture, polished every sort of surface—and every moment she longed for his mouth over hers. She dreamed of the stroke of his hand—and the hot, pulsing feelings that they provoked in her. She wanted it all again—and she wanted it with an intensity that amazed her.

She—the very soul of organisation—suddenly found it impossible to concentrate. She kept finding herself paused in mid-task, unsure of how long she'd been standing motionless while she tried to convince herself to take matters into her own hands. To live up to the promises that she'd made herself and approach him. To ask clearly for what she wanted.

More than once she had rallied to the point of action—and then she'd caught a glimpse of his distracted, nearly haunted face from a distance. And then it would start. She would imagine the various heart-rending responses he might make to such a request: shock, distaste, or worse, pity—and she would know that she could never do it.

A quiet step nearby woke her from another reverie. She picked up her cloth and began polishing again—until Lord Marland came into view below. He stepped carefully from the back of the house, as if hoping to go undetected. In his hands he lugged a large basket hinged in the middle.

He picked up his pace without looking up.

Clearly he wasn't expecting her to be perched up here. For a brief, cowardly moment Chloe considered letting him go by.

No. She had not come to London to be chicken-hearted. She drew a deep breath. 'Good afternoon, my lord,' she called. 'Might I have a word with you?'

He froze. Turning, he fixed on the ladder and looked up. 'Hardwick.' He frowned. 'What are you doing up there?'

'Fighting what looks to be a couple of decades' worth of dust and cobwebs,' she said cheerfully.

He lifted a shoulder. 'Well, I did warn the pair of you. Come down, before you harm yourself.' With careful precision he walked the few steps to set the basket in a corner. Turning back, he reached up for her.

A small, high-pitched noise from that direction startled her. But she forgot it in the heat and quivering excitement of his hands on her again. He gripped her tightly about the waist, she dropped her hands on his shoulders, and without effort he set her on the floor.

Neither moved. Chloe stood, helpless, while dust drifted from above to settle in his hair and over the expanse of brown superfine across his shoulders. Her insides were drifting, falling just as aimlessly. Her heart raced even as heat bubbled up inside of her again, pooling under the touch of his hands and spreading like a molten river through the rest of her.

Surely he felt it, too, for he pulled his hands abruptly away and stepped back. 'I've been finding what I could about the Spear,' he said quickly. 'Signor Pisano was right—the whole antiquarian community is in an uproar. Have you been in touch with your contacts?'

'Yes,' she said, swallowing back surging need. 'I've had a word or exchanged notes with nearly everyone I know. Still, I've had no luck discovering who the mysterious nabob in possession of the Spear might be. Have you fared any better?'

'Nothing concrete. The wildest rumours are threading through the city.'

'Yes,' she agreed. 'I've heard the strangest reports about the artefact itself. One of my contacts heard it was fashioned of gilded wood and already rotting. Another postulates it to be taller than a man while still another swears that it is no bigger than a hand span.'

He snorted. 'Laxton is putting it about that the thing was brought to English shores with the intent to assassinate the Prince Regent. He is classifying his determination to obtain it as patriotic duty.'

Chloe rolled her eyes. 'Since you mentioned Laxton, I stopped you because I wished to ask if you have been experiencing anything unusual?'

He frowned. 'Unusual in what way?'

She described her sensation of being watched. 'It was particularly strong in the street yesterday afternoon. I was on my way to Ashton House, to fetch some things left behind in my room. But there something was…off. It all looked normal enough, but it felt wrong, as if nothing was exactly as I had left it.'

'I haven't noticed anything.' He grimaced. 'All of our nerves are stretched. And you have the added burden of the preparation for Mairi's event. It's likely nothing.' After a moment, he grinned. 'Although I do recall Mrs Edmunds's interest in your notebook. Perhaps she is trying to steal all of your best hostess secrets.'

He'd shocked her into a laugh. 'You may be right.' Suddenly, she was tired of endless waiting, of skirting the edge of a precipice. Determined to jump, or at least to gain some of her answers now, she looked up at him through her lashes. 'I have been under an unfamiliar… strain.'

He didn't respond. And she forgot her own opening salvo when her attention was drawn sharply elsewhere. She stared at the basket in the corner. There. It happened again.

The basket *moved*.

In the blink of an eye, so did she. She reached the corner, knelt down and peered inside.

And her heart melted. Inside curled a delectable bit of rich chestnut and pearly white fur. The puppy coiled, shining black nose to fluffy tail. When she gasped in delight, he opened an eye, heaved a great sigh and promptly went back to sleep.

'Oh, how *adorable*,' she whispered. She looked up as the marquess followed her over. 'Do you mean to give her to the boy?'

'Him,' he corrected automatically. Then he flushed just the smallest bit. 'What boy?'

Chloe laughed and, spreading her skirts, settled down on the floor against the wall. 'That's just what I was going to ask you. He's quick— nobody else ever seems to be able to catch a glimpse of him. Who is he?'

Lord Marland sighed and sank down beside her. 'He's my…tenant. An orphaned boy from one of the villages near Denning. I'm searching for a good home for him.' He shrugged. 'It's foolish, I suppose. The dog. It might complicate matters as I look.'

Perhaps it was the rumble of the marquess's voice that woke the pup. He yawned, stood and stretched. And then he put his tiny paws on the edge of the basket and watched her expectantly.

'Good day to you, you delicious little piece of fluff,' Chloe crooned. She looked to the marquess. 'May I?'

He only raised a brow, which she took as assent. She lifted the warm, wriggling body into her arms and giggled as the sweet baby reached for her face and began to slather her jaw with doggy kisses. Laughing helplessly, she looked over the pup at Lord Marland—and felt her temperature begin to climb.

He stared at her with a hot gaze that set her stomach to fluttering.

'It's not foolish,' she whispered.

'It's a risk,' he replied.

The weight of his attention felt nearly palpable against her skin. It felt so intimate, sitting here, shoulder to shoulder with the faded noise of the servants echoing in the distance. Incredibly intimate, as if the sharing of whispers held the same importance as the kisses they'd exchanged days ago.

It was she who broke first. She glanced away from the intensity of his gaze and looked down into the puppy's big eyes. 'Did you have a dog, then? When you were small?' She brushed the silky ears.

'Yes.' One syllable, but it came out as rough as gravel.

'I did, too, but I was very young. I don't recall much, but I do remember the joy and the mischief and the contentment that comes with such as these.' She smiled at him. 'It's very thoughtful of you to wish to share the experience with this boy. He must feel very alone.'

He didn't answer.

'They can keep each other busy, be bosom companions. It will likely be just the thing for a displaced boy—having someone to take care of.'

The sound he made was pained. 'That's likely the last thing he needs.'

She buried her face in the puppy's soft fur. 'Perhaps not,' she said softly. 'Everyone needs that warm feeling—someone to love or something to give love back.' She paused a moment, eyes unfocused, lost in the past. 'Sometimes taking care of someone or something—it can be the best way to feel safe.'

She blinked away memories to find him staring at her with a mix of concern and horror on his face.

Chloe shivered. 'Why do you look at me like that?'

'Because you scare the hell out of me.'

She rather liked the sound of that.

He closed his eyes and she had the sudden thought that he was dealing with memories of his own. 'You asked if I had a dog?' He huffed, a sound that was too bleak to be called laughter. 'Well, I started out with a small, carved dog. I was very young when a groom gave it to me. It was just a toy, but he had carved it himself and it was very important to me.' He opened his eyes, but shifted position so that he focused on the ladder rather than her—as if he could not speak and look at her at the same time. 'My brother took it.'

Her mouth rounded. 'I'm so sorry.'

He exhaled. 'Lord, but I carried on as if the thing had been real. I mourned it as if it had been so. Finally my father tired of the fracas and decided that if I felt so strongly then I was ready for the responsibility of a real pet.' He smiled, but it quickly turned to a grimace as he eyed the animal snuggled in her arms. 'He was a great-footed beast of a pup. Ugly as the day was long—not at all like this fine gentleman. Needless to say, I was enraptured.'

Chloe bit her lip, suddenly afraid of where this story might be headed.

'How did you put it? Bosom companions? That we were. Night and day, inside and out, that pup spent every minute with me. God's teeth, but I had never been so content.' He grinned. 'Mairi grew insanely jealous, of course. Though she was barely toddling around the nursery she demanded a dog of her own.'

She waited, lips pressed tight. Afraid to ask the question.

'And Connor…Connor only voiced an objection once, when he said that animals belonged outside. Dogs belonged in the kennel, he argued, and should only be brought out to hunt. I ignored him, of course. And my father sided with me, for once.'

They sat in silence for a while. Chloe did not press him. She only wondered if he would be able to continue and tried to steel herself for the possibility.

'I've never spoken of it,' he said, low.

'You don't have to—'

'Just listen,' he snapped. He sucked in a breath and nodded. 'He was in that awkward, almost-grown stage, when they are forever tripping over their own feet. That day I was reading in the library by the fire. He lay at my feet. Connor arrived. Father had summoned us to the stables, where his prized mare was foaling. We were to be on hand to celebrate and to help, if necessary. Of course, the dog could not come, as he might upset the mare.'

He shrugged. 'I was glad to go. The impending birth had been the talk of the stables for months. I was caught up in the beauty of it, in my father's excitement, in the general holiday air. I don't know when Connor slipped out. I only know that when it was done, my father had his colt, my brother was gone and so was my dog.'

Chloe could only make a small, questioning sound.

He nodded. 'I knew. Everyone knew. Connor returned late that night and never said a word about where he had been. Father, as usual, did not press the issue, did not ask what he did not want to know for certain. I was directing the servants, searching the cellars and attics, the forests and the swamps.' He sighed. 'Years later I found canine bones deep in a cave in the limestone cliffs. I suppose predators might have scattered them, but some of the breaks were so clean...'

She could not hold back a sob.

He turned to her then, his expression hard. 'You were right to leave Denning, Hardwick. And I have been right to stay away from you for the last days.'

'I—'

He stopped her when he gripped her arm, hard. 'Don't you see? Our philosophies are so far opposite as to be irreconcilable. Do you understand the revulsion I feel when you speak of caring for someone in order to feel safe? It is the antithesis of safe. It leaves you open to harm, vulnerable to attack.'

He took her hand. 'It makes me fear for you, Hardwick. I am afraid that in your quest for self-discovery you are going to be hurt.' He pressed a quick kiss to her hand and climbed to his feet. He collected the pup from her arms and placed him back in the basket.

Standing and looking down at her in that way, it suddenly felt as if he were very far away from her.

'But the thing I fear the most—' he visibly

shuddered '—I am deathly afraid that I am going to be the one to do it.'

He spun on his heel and fled down the dimly lit hall. Chloe watched him go, mourning as the emptiness of her arms echoed the hollowness she felt inside.

Chapter Twelve

For the day and a half following his talk with Hardwick, Braedon had found ways to keep relentlessly busy.

He had spent hours sparring with Thom.

'I don't feel slighted, you know,' his friend had said, wiping his brow as they paused during one session. 'Because you are using me to work out your frustrations, I mean.' He grinned. 'Though I wouldn't mind knowing if it's frustration over that old spear or if it's over your old assistant?'

Braedon hadn't answered. He'd just motioned Thom back into position and lunged with deadly intent.

'Both, I'd say,' Thom had wheezed, later.

He had also carved time for a couple of sessions with the boy and his pup, after being summoned by cries of alarm and anger to a scene of mayhem. Climbing to the top floor, he had found the spaniel growling in ecstasy while winning a tug of war with an exasperated maid's skirts.

She was kneeling, trying to fend off the dog while gathering up broken crockery and fighting a spreading jam stain. Rob had come running from the nursery as Braedon made his way from the landing.

'Get your dog, Rob,' he ordered as he bent to help the maid to her feet.

It took the boy a while to detach the pup from her skirts; as soon as he did, the scamp charged into the midst of the mess and began to lap up jam.

'Oh, no, you don't,' Braedon said. He scooped the wriggling pup up and tucked him under his arm. Placing a hand over his muzzle, he said, 'No, sir.' He held on until the wiggling ceased and the pup calmed.

'Did you hurt him?' the boy asked, troubled as he took his friend from Braedon's outstretched arm.

'No. I merely sent him a message, asking him to settle down a bit.' He beckoned the pair of them. 'Come. Let's go outside and I'll give you some pointers.'

They set the dog free to ramble about the small patch of turf behind the kitchen gardens.

'He's a pack animal, Rob,' Braedon explained. 'He needs you to let him know that you are in charge. It's your job to teach him what is acceptable and what isn't. He'll be happier once he's learned what's expected of him.' He shot the boy a wry grin as the dog rolled ecstatically in the grass at their feet. 'I dare say we all will.'

He instructed the boy on some gentle ways to discipline his friend. To his relief, Rob was attentive rather than defensive and eager to learn. He and the pup had obviously bonded, which went a long way to reassuring Braedon about the boy's nature.

'And don't forget to praise him when he's done well,' he said, ruffling the dog's ears. 'That's just as important as letting him know when he's done wrong.'

Rob gave a start. Climbing to his feet, he looked at Braedon with a clear, green gaze. 'What if he's done something wrong, but he doesn't know what it is?'

Braedon stopped short. With a sigh, he crossed to the low garden wall. Perched upon it, he invited the boy to join him with a nod and a jerk of his head.

'You haven't done anything wrong, Rob. I can tell how hard you've worked to keep your end of the bargain. The brown-haired lady seems completely unaware. I know it's hard, but I appreciate how you've kept your word.'

The boy merely waited, sad and expectant.

Braedon scrubbed a hand in his hair. 'It's just…things are complicated right now. But look, I'm trying to find you a home you'll love. Growing up in the country is best for a boy and his dog. There will be good food, nice people and plenty of room to roam.'

'Will you come and visit us? Some time?'

For the first time it wasn't painful to look into that hopeful face. 'Yes, I will.' And he meant it. 'Now let's see if Mrs Grady can find us a bone for this fine fellow. And perhaps a biscuit for you?'

When he hadn't been pounding his frustrations out or schooling young boys and animals, Braedon had trolled through his clubs and through every gallery, market and shop, listening to the *Sturm und Drang* surrounding the Spear rise to a fever pitch.

'How do you do it, Marland?' Lord Sykes had asked him. 'The rest of us are balancing on a knife's edge of tension and you just sit back, the very image of calm.'

Braedon had merely smiled.

'I do wonder if perhaps you know more than the rest of us,' the baron had said bitterly. 'I would have thought you'd be taking this more seriously than anyone.'

'I'm just biding my time,' he had told the

baron. 'When the right moment comes, you'll see how serious I am.'

All of that had taken up a great deal of time—yet somehow Braedon had still found plenty of opportunity to worry endlessly over his last meeting with Hardwick. Most of it he had spent alternating between berating himself for a fool and congratulating himself on the performance of a selfless act.

God, what a risk he'd taken, telling that story, and to Hardwick of all people. More familiar with his personal life and work habits than anyone, she'd already proved herself capable of frighteningly accurate insight into his soul. And now he'd ripped off his protective armour and given her a good long look at the ugliness beneath.

The worst part was—it hadn't even been difficult. He'd felt so profoundly connected to her in that damned passageway. Connected on an elemental, deeply dangerous level—in a way that felt far more risky than a few, paltry kisses.

And that was exactly why he'd had to tell her. Their affinity was undeniable—but it could have no future, and it was better if that was made clear now.

It was also why his preparation for this evening had become so important. Finally, the time had come. Tonight was the Antiquarian Society's lecture. Besides dressing appropriately for the evening—which meant those damned, pinching shoes—Braedon must also gird himself for the true beginning of the race for Skanda's Spear, and, most important, he had to find his distance again. He had to summon all of his defences to shield against Hardwick's magnetic pull.

He knew it was good planning, sound strategy. He had worked on it as he readied himself for the evening. He sought out the old, familiar numbness as Dobbs helped him into his coat. He descended the stairs feeling strong and ready.

All of this, and still he suffered a tremendous blow at the first sight of her.

She stood waiting for him in the front parlour, a vision of ebony hair and flawless, pale skin. Obviously he had missed a spot as he'd donned his armour, because her first glance pierced his chest and stirred up something low and wicked in his belly.

Mairi had been at work again. He knew even before he saw his sister's proud expression. Hardwick was dressed in an elaborate gown of deepest blue, shot with black. Tiny diamonds twinkled like stars in her hair. She looked decadent and delicious, like she'd been wrapped in midnight—and all Braedon wished to do was lose himself in the dark.

'Oh, dear,' Mairi chirped. 'I know I've been caught up in plans for the ball. I hadn't really thought of this evening as anything but a business gathering. But now...' Her gaze travelled back and forth between the two of them. 'I wonder if you really ought to have a chaperon?'

Hardwick frowned. 'No, you were right, my lady. It is a lecture more than a social gathering and our focus tonight is solely on your brother's collection. There is no need to worry yourself.'

Mairi pulled on her gloves. 'Well, I cannot go myself, unfortunately. I am promised to the Edmunds' ball and Eugenia would be furious with me, did I not attend.' She frowned. 'Let me think a moment...'

But Braedon had recalled himself and his mission. He was the Marauding Marquess, was he not? Hiding until the advantage lay in revealing himself was his expertise. And tonight he intended to do what he did best.

'Hardwick is right,' he interrupted. 'There is no need to worry. In any case, I obtained my own ticket and returned Signor Pisano's to him. I've sent a separate vehicle to collect him. He will be waiting for us outside the Hanover Square Rooms.'

'He's agreed to attend?' Hardwick asked in surprise.

'I convinced him that it might be best for you to be accompanied by a...companion.'

Her eyes widened. 'Why? Have you heard about my notebook?'

Braedon frowned. 'No. What of it?'

'It's gone missing.' She raised her chin. 'At first I thought it had only been left behind in the confusion of the move, but it is gone. And I do not believe its disappearance to be the work of a rival hostess, either. Yesterday I caught a glimpse of Laxton's lackey...' She flushed. 'Our friend from the courtyard. He was loitering outside when Lady Ashton and I returned here yesterday.'

'It could have been anyone,' fretted Mairi. 'Between the construction in my home and the preparations for the ball here, there has been a regular parade of strangers in and out of both houses.'

'Damn it all!' Braedon was stricken. He'd been worrying so hard about protecting Hardwick's tender feelings that he'd left her open to a far more physical danger. He paced to the far end of the room, then returned rapidly to loom over her. 'We will have to step carefully tonight. I want you to stay by my side at every second. Do you understand?'

'Oh, dear.' Mairi wrung her hands. 'Perhaps you should go alone tonight, Braedon.'

'No!' protested Hardwick.

'I don't believe it is anything except rival collectors hoping to get a leg up on me, my dear,' he said to reassure his sister. Glancing at Hardwick, he hardened his tone. 'And we don't want them to think they've rattled us.' He frowned. 'But stick close. I want that damned Spear and I mean to have it—but I won't have you harmed in the getting of it.'

She nodded agreement.

'Good.' Braedon bade his sister goodnight and handed Hardwick into her wrap. 'Are you ready?' he asked.

She breathed deeply and nodded again.

'Then let's go.'

Lord, but she was a fool several times over. Purposefully, she avoided glancing at the marquess, seated across from her in the carriage, rigid and stiff. She hadn't seen him since yesterday afternoon. He'd told her that tragic tale—perhaps not the only one he might have chosen, she suspected—and he'd done it with purpose. It had been meant to illustrate his point and warn her off.

She understood that—but still a hot current of want swept along her veins. He looked so handsome in his formal dress, every woman's fantasy of a warrior leashed. She wanted to hop across the small space separating them and burrow on to his lap. She longed to tug the narrow cord that held back his hair, dig her fingers in and shake his dark locks free. Most of all, she wanted to press her lips to his hard, unsmiling mouth and make him forget that anything had ever happened to make him hide away from the rest of the world.

Yet it had—and she was not free to do any of those things. She watched the passing streets instead and cast about for any other subject on which to focus her attention.

The strange occurrences over the last few days proved a distraction. And surprisingly, after only a few minutes she had to cover her mouth to stifle a laugh.

'What is it?' asked the marquess.

She took her hand away and grinned at him. 'I was only wondering, if Laxton was the one behind the theft of my notebook, what he thought about my detailed notes on menus, entertainment and flowers.'

He didn't return her smile, but she noticed the tension fade from around his eyes a bit.

She sighed. 'I've seen your tenant boy around the house. He and the pup seem happy together. I even lured the pup to me once, by way of a pocketful of scraps, but the boy stayed hidden around the corner.' She chuckled. 'And once the scraps were gone, I grew less interesting.'

Lord Marland did not respond.

Her smile softened. 'I've seen them romping out in the back garden, too. I don't think that dog has ever met a delivery person he didn't adore.'

'Was Mairi with you?' He asked the question of the darkened window.

'No. As she said, she's spending most of her days at Ashton House. I've been the one in charge of setting your house to rights.'

He leaned forwards. 'Here we are.' Lowering the window, he peered out. 'Just a few carriages ahead of us. And the *signor* is waiting at the corner.'

Chloe took her turn. 'Oh, heavens. He doesn't look happy.'

He wasn't.

'Dio Mio,' the older man said by way of greeting as they descended to meet him. 'I feel like a pig trussed for the spit.'

'Oh, I am sorry, *signor*,' Chloe said, gripping his hand. 'I know you had no wish to come this evening.'

'Bah,' he said, pulling away. 'There was no escaping it in the end. This matter has grown beyond all normal expectations.' He frowned. 'I only hope it ends well.'

Chloe took his arm, then accepted Lord Marland's on her other side. She held the same hope. But she was beginning to have her doubts.

Together the three of them entered the brightly lit assembly rooms.

Chapter Thirteen

'Surely it's nothing but a rumour,' Lord Sykes repeated again. 'It's too absurd to be true.'

Footmen passed through the crowd, carrying trays of sparkling wines. Braedon grabbed a flute as it passed by and drained it in one long swallow.

'Who in their right mind, in possession of such an object, would choose to *give* it away, rather than sell it?' Sykes demanded.

'I'm sure I don't know.'

'No one would!' the baron exclaimed. 'It's absurd. And what nonsense this scuttlebutt is…that this unknown nabob intends to give the thing away—but only to the right person? What constitutes the right person then? I ask you, Marland?'

'I'm sure I don't know,' Braedon repeated. He

exchanged a glance with Hardwick, who stood nearby. She raised a brow in his direction before Signor Pisano called her attention away. With flair and a great deal of pleasure, the *signor* introduced her to the Earl of Conover, their host for the evening and the only scholar reputed to have actually seen the Spear of Skanda.

'I'll tell you,' Sykes said with passion. 'The right person is the one with the deepest pockets!'

'So says the man with very deep pockets indeed,' answered Braedon with a grin.

'*Damned* deep, I tell you.' The baron gestured out over the sea of gentlemen shifting and chattering with excitement as they waited to be called to the lecture in the main room. 'Just look at them all…every one of them here for the same purpose. I deserve a chance at the Spear just as much as any one of them.'

Braedon merely shrugged, but he did gaze over the crowd. Here and there in the expanse of dark formal wear he could spot a burst of colour—the few women attending gathered in languid groups. Hardwick, close at his side, stood apart from the other women—in every way possible.

They'd been mobbed when they entered, by scholars welcoming him back to Town, by enthusiasts wanting to hear of his collection, and by Laxton, clearly hoping to discover what they might know of the Spear. Braedon had worried a moment, as some of the men obviously dismissed Hardwick and still others thought to manipulate her for information.

He needn't have bothered to worry. Hardwick handled the situation magnificently. She spoke with some of the foremost experts on ancient weapons with knowledge and authority. Her enthusiasm blazed through and he knew he wasn't the only man affected by her shining eyes and animated expression.

He wasn't the only one admiring her generous figure in that incredible blue dress, either. She was drawing attention from all over the room—and he was constantly reaching for a non-existent blade. Bad enough the others were ogling the low-cut silk of her bodice, but somehow word had got around that she had resigned as his assistant. He heard her receive two serious requests for an interview and at least one sly innuendo about a new position. Signor Pisano defused that situation by smacking his walking stick across the offender's shins—and thus neatly preventing Braedon from throttling him with his bare hands.

He glanced over at her again, still deeply engaged with the earl. The man could stand as a model for the quintessential English nobleman: he was all shining teeth and curling blond hair and freshly scrubbed good looks. The man didn't even have the grace to look as if his shoes pinched. No, the Earl of Conover was in his element—and he looked elementally interested in Hardwick.

They were debating something, the pair of them. Braedon knew that mulish look of Hardwick's. Her face was alight and she spoke low and fast, just the way she always did when she was trying to convince him of some small, vitally important point. Conover did not look overly upset about it. He did not look offended that a mere woman sought to tell him something he didn't know. He nodded and gave every indication that he was listening intently.

Until—there it was. The earl's gaze travelled slightly, moving admiringly over Hardwick's elaborate coiffure. He said something in reply to a question—and dropped his attention briefly to her bosom.

Suddenly Braedon was envisioning the man at the functional end of his Japanese pole arm.

He moved quickly to interrupt them, telling himself that Hardwick was bound to steer the conversation to the Spear if she possibly could. She didn't realise it, but there were a few bits of information about the piece that he hadn't shared with her. Things he'd rather she heard as late as he could manage it, if at all.

He stepped close and took her arm. 'Hardwick. Conover.' He bowed and gestured toward the top of the stairs where a porter had just emerged. 'It appears that it is time to begin.'

Fascinating. Chloe found the lecture to be utterly riveting. Several speakers took part, each presenting a thorough report on an ancient weapon of legendary status. The stuff of dreams, most of them sounded, possessing magical properties or granting extraordinary skills. The evening began to take on an air of myth and fantasy.

Until the Earl of Conover took the stage. Matter of factly, he spoke of Skanda, a war god of Hindu mythology. He described the earliest origins and versions of the figure and the characteristics that came to be associated with him. And then he brought out his illustrations, large diagrams and charts with detailed depictions, even measurements, of the weapon. A burnished wood shaft, he mentioned. A wide point in the shape of a spade. Precious metals and inlaid jewels.

Now she was no longer the only one spellbound. The entire hall full of men was held rapt. Next to her, the marquess had ceased to breathe.

She glanced askance at him again. A warrior in thrall. So much energy, purpose and power, focused with such singular intent. He was the most striking man in the room and she was mad for him.

It was truth—and it called forth a great, shivering gutful of fear. How had she let this happen? She'd known better, even all the way back at Denning. And yet she'd allowed him to sneak in on her. She'd gone and fallen hard and deep and irrevocably in love with a man who could not—or possibly would not—allow himself to love her back.

The crowd was applauding, climbing to their feet to show their appreciation as the lecture ended, but she found that she could not rise.

This was the beginning of the end. A matter of days and Lady Ashton's ball would be over. Perhaps a few days past that, she predicted, and someone was going to gain possession of that spear.

'Now that was nearly everything I could have wished for,' the marquess said, leaning down towards her. 'Nearly. I have several questions I'd like to put to Conover before he leaves.'

Still, she had not risen.

'Hardwick?' He frowned at her. 'Are you ready?'

She bit back a slightly hysterical laugh. Oh, Lord, yes, she was ready. But she doubted that he ever would be.

'Let's go,' he said, impatient. 'I'm going to have to fight my way through to speak to the earl.'

Signor Pisano leaned heavily on his walking

stick as he stood. 'My feet hurt,' he complained. 'I'm not fighting anyone to get anywhere. I'm going to find a corner with a seat in it.'

But the crowd was large and excited. Progress was slow as the audience flowed out of the hall, toward the stairs and the reception rooms. The *signor*'s steps grew slower, his legs stiffer. When they finally filed out of the main hall, they found a wide space at one side, between the doors and the landing of the stairs, set up with comfortable chairs and a sideboard. The *signor*'s face lit up.

'Ah, here we are. I'll sit here and rest before I tackle those stairs.'

Chloe took his arm and avoided the marquess's eye. 'I'll sit with him.'

'No, no,' the *signor* protested. 'I'm not the only old man in this crowd. There will be others.' He grinned. 'We shall have a fine time picking that programme apart.'

She could feel Lord Marland's speculative gaze upon her. 'No,' he said slowly. 'Hardwick should stay with one of us. I would appreciate it if you would keep an eye on her.'

She cast him a hard look and moved off with the *signor*. Gentlemen were already gathering in the little antechamber, and, as promised, they launched into an exhaustive rehash of the speakers, their topics and various members of the audience.

Chloe could not focus enough to follow. She couldn't even bring herself to regret the chance to hear more of Skanda and his spear from the knowledgeable Earl of Conover. She was entirely caught up in the irony of her situation. Hadn't she left Denning to avoid just such a scenario—where she felt more for the marquess than he did for her? Granted, some things had changed. He saw *her* now. Knew more about her than anyone, in fact. But still, the message he'd sent was painfully clear. And the realisation was painful; she'd run all this way just to end up in the place that frightened her most.

How incredibly lowering. Her spirits had sunk, so much so that she hadn't noticed as the hour grew later and the group thinner. She was startled when the *signor* tapped her with his stick, to discover that nearly everyone had gone and even the sounds of raucous discussion from downstairs had faded.

'I'm for home, my dear,' Signor Pisano announced. 'But first I shall step into the gentlemen's retiring room.'

'Oh!' Chloe stood. 'I'll just go find the marquess.'

'No, no. He doesn't want you wandering about on your own. I shall be just down there, do you see?' He gestured towards a passage across the wide aisle, at the other side of the landing. 'Wait here and we'll find him together.'

The *signor* moved off, leaving her alone, save for one gentleman asleep in the corner. His head was tilted back, resting against the wall. A gentle snore rumbled from his open mouth. She took her seat again.

The stranger snorted suddenly and came awake, sputtering. A stout, nearly round man, he had a bald head, a bulbous nose and a pair of brilliant blue eyes. He wiped his mouth and grinned at her, exposing a set of crooked teeth. Sitting up straight, he caught sight of the *signor*'s retreating figure.

'Know Pisano, do you?' he asked.

'Yes, very well.' His grin was infectious; she couldn't help but return it. 'Since I was a little girl.'

'Me, too. A long time, that is, not since I was a girl.' He let loose a hard laugh at his own joke. He looked her over carefully. 'You're the girl that works for Lord Marland, ain't you?'

She hesitated, but nodded.

'How did you like the lecture, then?'

She smiled. 'Very well, indeed. So many wonderful legends! I was particularly struck by the story of Sun Wu Kong, the Monkey King. So clever to have a staff that can change from the size of a needle all the way up to a mighty pillar!'

'Useful, too,' the stranger agreed. 'But not as useful as Freyja's Cloak, I'd wager. Would be nice to be able to change to a falcon and fly away.'

They discussed all the presented weapons for a few minutes before he eyed her cagily. 'How about that bit on Skanda's Spear, eh? Conover had them drooling, he did. I have to say, I enjoyed the audience as much as the information.'

'It was fascinating. I especially enjoyed hearing all of the background information on Skanda.' Chloe pursed her lips. 'Who would have thought a Hindu war god would ride a peacock?'

The odd little man laughed. 'Maybe it's a distraction as he rides into battle? Ah, but how should one such as I know? For all that I have the body of a god—a Buddha, that is!' He rubbed his substantial belly and laughed again.

She laughed with him, but he sobered quickly and then frowned. 'I've heard of your Lord Marland's collection. I'll wager he's more than a bit interested in getting his hands on that Spear.'

'It would be in good hands, if he did,' Hardwick said stoutly. 'The marquess is extremely passionate about all of his pieces.' She tried to keep her expression neutral. 'Are you hoping to obtain the weapon, too?'

'Lord, no!' he scoffed. 'I've no interest in the damned thing.' He dismissed the topic with a wave of his hand. 'So, it does sound as if you enjoy working for Marland.'

'I…I did. Though I've recently left my position.' She couldn't force anything further past the lump in her throat.

'Ah, I see.' He frowned. 'Well, I've heard that he's a cold and solitary man, with no love even for his own family. No doubt you are better off away from him.'

'The marquess's only family is his sister and I can assure you that he loves her very much,' Chloe said sternly. 'No doubt you are better off not listening to idle gossip.'

'Perhaps I should not,' he agreed with a smile. He pushed heavily to his feet. 'Well, I'm off. I'd heard there was to be champagne at the reception. I hope there is some left.' He bowed over her hand. 'Good evening, my dear. I'm happy to have met you.'

She nodded a goodbye and watched him head downstairs. Bemused, she realised suddenly that she had not learned his name. Alone in the small antechamber now, she waited.

Around her the building grew quieter. Porters had put out the lights in the main lecture hall. The reception downstairs must surely be over, although she suspected many of the attendees would only move their discussions to their clubs. She waited, rooted to the chair by the heavy weight of her thoughts. Minutes passed. What could be keeping the *signor*? She had just decided to rise and move in the direction of the retiring room when she heard a soft scrape behind her.

Her hackles rose and she stood. It had come from the direction of the main room. Surely it was a servant, come to put the place to rights? She drifted toward the entrance, but there was nothing to see in the darkened room. And why was there no further noise? No quiet talk as the porters went about their business? Growing nervous, she strained her ears. Nothing. Perhaps she had only imagined it.

There came the soft, unmistakable sound of a heavy footstep, quite near.

Spooked, she retreated, stepping backwards. She struck a chair leg and stumbled. Spinning about, she launched herself towards the stairs—and fell into a pair of sturdy arms.

'*Oof,*' a gentleman said. 'Miss Hardwick? Are you quite all right?'

She tried to pull away, but found herself held tight. She stared wildly up—into the pleasant blue gaze of the Earl of Conover.

'Yes. Good heavens.' She struggled for composure. 'Thank you, my lord. I was frightened, I thought I heard someone…' She gestured over her shoulder into the main hall.

He smiled down at her and, setting her steadily on her feet, let her go. 'Yes, the event is nearly over, it would seem. The servants are likely clearing up.' He looked into her face.

'Gracious, you really were frightened.' His expression grew serious. 'This matter with the Spear has put everyone in the antiquities community on edge, has it not?'

'Yes, of course. That must be it.' She couldn't resist another glance behind her.

He took her hand and placed it on his arm. 'You're trembling! Come, I'll take you downstairs.'

'Thank you, but I am waiting for a friend.' She pulled her hand away. 'Lord Marland was looking for you, however. He was hoping for a word with you.'

'As I was hoping for a word with you.' A slight grin spread over his face as he sent an appraising glance travelling all about her form. 'I admit, it is most interesting—and intriguing—to find a woman involved in a business like this.' He watched her closely. 'Tell me, if you wouldn't mind—was there something specific about the Spear of Skanda that drew you here tonight?'

Chloe managed a chuckle. 'Only Lord Marland's emphatic desire to make the thing the centrepiece of his collection.'

'Ah, yes. I had heard that you have managed his collection magnificently.'

She flushed a bit. 'Thank you.' She grinned up at him. 'It's all true, of course. Until now, that is. I'm afraid I've failed the marquess, regarding this particular weapon. The only certain facts I've heard at all have come tonight, from you.'

He gave her a mock frown. 'And is that a note of doubt I detect?' He dropped his tone to a near-whisper, requiring her to lean closer. 'I assure you, Miss Hardwick, that I told only the truth tonight.' He paused. 'Though, perhaps not all of the truth.' His gaze swept down her again, as if he were considering something. 'Your reputation is such, I felt sure that you might have uncovered some further information regarding the piece. There are certain facts that I'm sure you would find interesting.'

In her eagerness she shifted nearer. 'I'm sure I would, should you care to share.'

'I think perhaps I do care,' the earl mused. He shocked her then by taking her hand in his. 'For example, had you heard that, throughout the ages, the Spear has been owned by a singularly large number of women?'

'Truly?' Chloe looked up at him, her eyes wide. 'Unusual, wouldn't you think? Seeing as it is a weapon of war?'

Intent, he stepped closer, still holding her gaze. 'Unusual, yes,' he said low, 'but understandable, when you consider—'

'Hardwick?' From the passage on the other side of the stairs, her name echoed. 'Hardwick!' The door to the retiring room opened and the

marquess peered out. Chloe and the earl both
turned in his direction.

'There you are.' He stepped out and crossed
over to them, a black look sketching over his
face. 'And Conover. What are the two of you up
to?'

The earl dropped her hand, and only then did
Chloe realise how close they had been standing.
Too close for true propriety, she suspected, but
she felt certain that Conover had been on the
verge of disclosing something important.

'Up to?' the earl echoed smoothly. 'Why,
nothing but what you might expect.' His smile
was for her. 'More antiquities talk. You are
very fortunate in your lovely young assistant,
Marland.'

'You do not have to tell me so, Conover,' the
marquess snapped. 'And I know enough to understand that neither her youth nor her beauty
have anything to do with it.'

His tone echoed harshly and Chloe noted
that he did not correct the earl regarding her
status. But then, she hadn't either. 'Where is
the *signor*?' she asked. 'And how did you get in
there? I've been here with an eye on the passage
all along.'

'There's another exit,' he explained tightly,
still keeping an eye on Conover. 'The *signor*
went out that one and got confused. I found him

wandering about downstairs, quite put out and looking for you.'

'Oh, the poor dear! Where is he now?'

'The evening tired him out,' the marquess answered. 'I didn't like his colour, so I summoned the carriage.'

'And I should do the same,' the earl said. He bowed over Chloe's hand. 'Miss Hardwick, it has been a very great pleasure. I hope that we might continue our talk again, soon.' He eyed the marquess. 'Perhaps I might call on you?'

She smiled. 'I would certainly enjoy hearing more, my lord. Good evening.'

With a nod to Lord Marland, he took his leave, whistling cheerfully as he headed down the stairs. Chloe looked to the marquess, excited to tell him the little she'd learned, but was surprised at the glare he sent in her direction.

'The wily bastard,' he said in a low voice. 'I vow, he was avoiding me deliberately downstairs. And then to find him so cosily ensconced up here with you!'

She recoiled at the accusation in his tone. And then she began to grow angry herself. 'Yes,' she said coolly. 'I do believe he sought me out deliberately.'

'For what reason?' he demanded. 'So he could hold your hand and look deeply into your eyes?'

'Don't be ridiculous.' She shrugged. 'Perhaps he sought me out because he enjoyed our earlier discussion. I rather thought he meant to tell me something important.'

'Oh, I don't doubt that for a moment,' the marquess gritted out. The sarcasm in his tone infuriated her. 'Perhaps the address of the house where he conducts his *affaires*?'

Chloe gasped.

'I suppose he could have been trying to annoy me.' He folded his arms, looking as belligerent as she'd ever seen him. 'But, no, I dare say my first instinct was right. He just wanted a chance to get under your skirts.'

'How *dare* you?' She whirled away from him. Holding tight to the rail, she rushed down the steps.

He was right behind her. When she reached the bottom, he gripped her arm.

She pulled away. 'The *signor* is waiting,' she said icily. With her head held high, she sailed across the reception area toward the doors. Only a few stragglers were left down here. The earl was nowhere to be seen, but the portly, bald gentleman from upstairs sat at a deserted bar. He raised a glass in her direction. She nodded in return.

Neither she nor Lord Marland spoke while a porter fetched her wrap. Chin elevated, she accepted the marquess's help into it, then stepped on to the pavement and paused, confused. 'I do not see your carriage.'

'I told you, the *signor* did not look well. I sent him home.' He indicated another vehicle. 'I procured us a hack.'

Chloe climbed in and sat down, making herself as small as possible in the tiny space. The marquess took the other seat. The carriage jerked to a start and they rode in icy silence for several minutes.

Eventually, Lord Marland sighed. 'I am sorry, Hardwick.'

Her chin went up again. 'As well you should be. The earl behaved as a perfect gentleman. Our discussion was purely professional.'

He wasn't looking at her, but staring at the darkness outside the window. 'I don't even know why I said such a thing.'

'Nor do I,' she said sharply, refusing to relent. 'You have made it perfectly clear that you have no interest in me as a woman. Yet the first time you take a notion that someone else might, you grow as cranky as a dog with a bone.'

He made no response. Bleakly, she realised it was because he could not refute the truth. Shocking, really, how much it hurt.

It had been a quick ride across Mayfair. She'd hardly had time to catch her breath before the carriage rolled to a stop. His hands were gentle as he helped her descend, but there was still a sense of raw emotion in the air between them.

The house was dark. Most of the household was likely in bed—she had been working them hard. And it was too early to expect the countess back from her social revels. It was an awkward, in-between time, she supposed. It felt fitting, somehow.

The marquess sent the hackney off, then fumbled with a key with surprising awkwardness. Chloe watched his shaking hand and decided to give way, just a little. Looking up, she sighed. 'I miss the stars,' she said, unthinking. 'The night sky in London is just a darker version of the daytime haze.'

The door swung open. 'There are stars aplenty in your hair, tonight.' The low timbre of his voice echoed in the dark and vibrated deep in the pit of her belly. Uncertain, she turned and raised a shaking hand to her coiffure.

He stared, and heat began to rise inside, growing sweeter and deeper the longer his gaze roved over her. After a moment, he took her other hand and led her inside. One lone candle burned in a marble niche, but there was no one posted at the door.

They should go their separate ways now, she thought. She should head immediately for her bed. But instead, with unspoken accord, they both made their way to the front parlour.

He went immediately to resurrect the dying fire. Feeling perfectly wicked and equally determined, Chloe took a moment to close the door and lock it, before she sat. She waited.

And waited. A long time, indeed. The fire flared to life, but still the marquess crouched before it, staring into the flames as if looking for the answers to their dilemma.

She was patient. Yet the minutes ticked by. The tension in the room ratcheted higher. Coals faded and fell. And Chloe warred with herself. She hoped and despaired in turn. He was obviously conflicted. Or perhaps he'd just forgotten her.

She stood suddenly. She'd waited long enough. Her heart ached, but for one last time, she would make things easier for him.

'I met the most interesting man tonight,' Chloe said, striving for a casual tone. She would make her report on what she had learned and then she would retreat to her room to bind all the many painful wounds he had inflicted on her.

But it was if the sound of her voice catapulted him into action. 'Don't!' he ordered, launching away from the fireplace. He shot her a pained look. 'We are close to wrapping this up, one way or another, and I am damned grateful, for this is so much more difficult that I had anticipated.'

Chloe's jaw hardened. She reconsidered, suddenly, her earlier, charitable notion. 'What is difficult, Lord Marland?'

'This!' He glared at her and gestured between them. 'You and me. My God, do you know what you have done to me? How tempting you are tonight?' he demanded. 'All I want to do is touch you. Every man in that room wanted to touch you, too, and if I had had a blade, I might have run them all through.'

She blinked in amazement. 'I—'

'No.' Despair thickened his voice. 'I know you are not mine. I know it in my heart and in my mind and down to my very core, but I don't give a damn. I have to fight to keep myself from pushing you up against a wall and running my hands all over you.' He heaved a great sigh and fastened his gaze on her coiffure. 'I've dreamt all night of plucking those shining bits of light from your hair and losing myself in the midnight shadows of it.'

Triumph bloomed in Chloe's chest, along with a great tidal sweep of desire. She stood, staring at the marquess, taking in his enormous strength, drinking in his glorious height and width. She caught sight of her reflection in the window behind him. Her earrings winked at her from just beyond his broad shoulders. Her breath caught and her fingers flew to touch one—and she knew suddenly that she was a warrior, too.

'Then why don't you?' she asked softly.

'Because I cannot!' he said harshly. 'I will

not—not when there can be no future in it.' He gave her a scathing glance. 'Do you think I want to hear of the men you met tonight? You met scores of them and every man-jack one of them had the sense to find you more than *interesting*.' He barked a short, ironic laugh. 'They've barely scratched your surface and they instantly recognised your incredible value.' He dropped his gaze. 'They made me feel like a fool.'

Her heart softened. 'You are not a fool.'

'I feel like one.' In a blur of motion he turned suddenly and slammed his fist into the wall. 'We are both fools, Hardwick! What are we doing? Why do we torture ourselves? This ground has been covered. You won't go back and I cannot move forwards. So where does that leave us?'

She went to him and laid her hands on his strong, solid arm. 'Here,' she answered. 'It leaves us right here.'

'I don't know where "here" is.' His tone was flat.

'I don't either. But I know what I want it to be.' She leaned her head against him. 'I only know…that I don't want to live in fear any more. For too long I've feared the hurt that lives in my past. For the past weeks I have been recoiling from the pain that might lie in my future.' She shook her head and frowned at him. 'But tonight, it struck me anyway.'

He made a sound of denial, but she cut him

off. 'Do you understand how horribly difficult you are? My feelings for you are not simple or even pretty. They come with burdens, too. And the worst one is fear.' She swallowed. 'When I left Denning, I vowed I would stop hiding. I promised myself I would leave fear behind— and here you are, with a great bundle of it attached.'

She drew a deep breath. 'Good God, do you understand that every significant person in my life has found a new and painful way to leave me behind? I'm only just beginning to understand how it has warped me. Look at the way I twisted myself at Denning—I created a shell of a person to hide behind. It took a long time to realise that I might be safe behind there, but I was still alone. And being lonely is just as painful as being left.'

Mute, he shook his head.

'I know you don't agree. But I am speaking for me.' She stiffened her spine. 'I left because I didn't want to live without at least the chance for happiness, adventure, contentment and love.' She glanced down at her hands. Breathing deeply, she gathered strength. When she looked back at him, she allowed the ring of conviction to colour her words. 'I care for you. I know you don't wish to hear it, but I do. And I am not going to hide from it. I know that nothing about this is going to be easy. I know there are enormous risks. But if I have to choose between a chance for happiness and pain or continued loneliness and pain, then I'm going to take the chance at happiness.'

She stepped around him until she stood pressed against his hard chest. 'Your sister's ball is nearly upon us. She'll be moving back to Ashton House soon and when she does, I'll be leaving, too.'

He glared at her. 'To go where?'

She shrugged. 'To my own rooms. To my own life. But there is time left before then. I want to spend it with you. I choose you, and I choose to let go of the fear in my past and worry for the future.' Her hands slipped to his waist. She stepped close and gazed directly into his eyes. 'Why do we not just try living for right now?'

'You make it sound easy.' He groaned. 'But my past has a stranglehold on my every breath—and I've never questioned the wisdom of it.'

She snorted and could not keep the bitterness from her voice. 'Good heavens, we are so alike, it's laughable.'

His arms tightened suddenly and pulled her in against him. Chloe's heart thrilled and she gave a great shiver. He was warmth and might—and uncertainty. She lifted her hands and wrapped them around his neck. 'For once in my life I want to fully embrace the moment I am in. In the present moment I could be happy,' she whispered, 'because you are in it, too.' She had to blink back sudden tears. 'This is it—one of the most important pieces that I have been missing. I know I shouldn't ask you for it.'

He bent towards her. 'Hardwick…'

She pushed abruptly away. 'No!' she said sharply.

He blinked. 'No?'

'No. Hardwick is in my past and yours as well. If we are going to be together, I want it to be *now*.'

He reached to pull her back.

She crossed her arms and waited.

He scrubbed a hand at his neck in confusion. 'Hard—'

Her expression must have shone as fierce as her frustration.

'Oh.' His brow lifted. He growled. 'Come here—*Chloe*.'

She went.

Chapter Fourteen

God, but he was the worst sort of filthy cad.

And Hardwick—no, *Chloe*—was his complete opposite. Unbelievable, how she'd changed. Grown. If you had stood this shining, sparkling girl before him several weeks ago, he never would have placed her as the same woman. She was courage and fire. She brimmed with life and every wonderful thing in it. She had always given him her best, dating back from even before he'd met her face to face. But now she had reached deep inside herself and found she had so much more to give.

And he was going to take it, he acknowledged with a groan. Because that's who he was: a selfish, rutting bastard. He was powerless to refuse her, even though there was nothing inside of him to match her. Nothing that he could offer her in return.

She was matchless tonight, in any case. Gorgeous in that blue-black gown. The creamy tops of her breasts glowed above it. His gaze drifted over the ivory skin of her shoulders, the shining pink of her mouth. His attention was drawn, suddenly, to her shining, golden earrings.

'My God, are those—?' Braedon stepped closer for a better look. 'Chloe, are those your *buttons*?'

She grinned, suddenly shy. 'I had them made,' she said on a whisper. 'To remind me— never to hide again.'

He trailed his fingers lightly down over her arms. He traced teasing circles around her wrists and flattened his hands beneath hers. So small and soft, her palms rested, light as a feather on his. Slowly he began to step back, moving unerringly to the sofa behind him. Unwilling to break their contact, she followed. The lightest, simplest touch, yet heat flared at that only point of contact—their barely touching palms and the tiny flutter of her fingers atop his.

Fine words she gave him. Lovely, courageous words that set his soul afire and sent waves of desire rippling through his body. The old dread hovered over his heart, the fear of damaging the thing he wanted most. And he was going to hurt her, even though she didn't deserve it.

She had tempted him like the very devil; now he was returning the favour—and together they had edged past some vague point of no return.

The back of his knees struck the sofa. He sank down on the cushions and sighed in resignation and relief as she stepped into the circle of his embrace. She was his now. He reached for her at last.

Their lips touched and he was gentle with her. Slow. He gripped her waist, then ran his hands further, up along the supple strength of her back. In turn, she lifted her hands to his face. Her fingers traced his hairline and then followed the curve of his jaw.

'I will never regret this,' she whispered.

He dragged her down to him and kissed her hard. Mad, swift passion, it had been hovering, waiting in the wings for the moment he let down his guard. Wild and sweet and abandoned. He lost himself in her courage and her yearning and her tender care. A hundred kisses, a thousand he gave her, until his chest was heaving like a bellows and she was gasping for air.

Pulling back, he rested his forehead on her chin. 'Turn around,' he said softly.

She did. Taking his time, he began to undress her. Slowly, buttons slid loose. With a whisper of sound, ties slipped from their tangles. He made a sensuous dance of it, torturing and thrilling them both as her clothes peeled away, layer by layer.

At last she was bare to the waist. Fabric lay in discarded heaps about them, but he did not turn her. Instead he reached up. One by one he plucked the bright jewels from her hair. Pin by pin, lock by lock, he loosened her hair, until it fell like black water over her shoulders and down her back.

He buried his face in the thick, rich abundance of it. He breathed it in. Marvelling at the softness against his cheek, he reached around and cupped her full breasts in both hands.

She groaned and arched into his caress.

He squeezed again and explored her curves. He rubbed his thumbs over the straining peaks of her nipples until she squirmed against him.

Then he turned her. And looked his fill. 'God, but you are beautiful,' he said on a whisper. 'I can't understand how you hid it from me for so long. It seems impossible.' He glanced up at her. 'And cruel.'

Keeping his gaze locked with hers, he leaned in and licked his tongue over a taut bud.

She gave a great shudder all over.

'Well, then,' he said, 'perhaps I've found a way to repay your unkindness.' He licked her again and suckled her. His fingers found her other nipple and rolled it as she curled into him and moaned. Before long her hips were moving against him as she shifted from one leg to the other.

'Yes,' she breathed. *'Yes.'*

He let her slide free with a slick pop.

She protested, arching into him again. 'My l—'

'No!' He said it as sharply as she had done to him, earlier. *'Chloe,'* he rasped.

She shivered.

'As I call your name, so must you use mine. I want to hear it.'

She nodded.

'Now. Say it now.'

'Braedon,' she moaned.

In one swift movement he swept her off of her feet and laid her back along the sofa. Breathing hard, she gazed up at him. Candlelight danced over her skin and glowed in her dark eyes. All of the fine lines of her face—cheek, jaw and chin—stood out in relief.

Leaning back, he began to remove his clothes. He smiled when she propped up on one elbow to assist. Soon he was bare to the waist as well. Grinning with satisfaction, Chloe trailed a caress across his shoulders, along his ribs and down to his breeches. Anticipation shone in her eyes as she drifted back to the cushions.

He returned her grin and reached for—

'My feet?' she said in surprise, rising up again. Braedon laughed. 'Just lay back and trust me.'

Lovingly, he picked up her foot. Her skin flowed like silk in his hands. Her bones were so fragile. Carefully, he pushed his thumbs up and over the pad of her foot. She gasped in pleasure. He dug a knuckle into the arch of her foot and she melted. Tenderly, he laboured over both of her feet and then he began to run soft fingers up the length of her legs.

His own skin tightened. Chloe lay languid and warm beneath his hands as he quickly finished undressing her, but he was growing more taut and hard by the second. He bent to her breast again and teased her thighs apart.

Chloe allowed it, if only because she had become a void in the very air around her, an empty space of need that existed only to be filled. She longed to touch him, to make him feel the wonder with which he gifted her, but she was helpless. Held in thrall to the sensations he created inside her.

His fingers worked magic between her legs and his mouth did amazing things to her breast. Gradually the universe shrank, condensing to the scant few inches between them. He stroked, she writhed, until nothing existed save the two of them and the pleasure that lived between them.

It shifted, their pleasure. It grew, changed, becoming a wave that reached for the moon, lifting her higher and higher. She rode it willingly.

Stretching for him, she tugged relentlessly, pulling him towards her.

'Please,' she whispered. 'Please, now.'

'There is no need…' he began.

She gripped his shoulders hard. 'No,' she said urgently. 'We've come so far together, I won't go on alone.'

He hesitated, perhaps because he knew she spoke of so much more than merely physical things. 'The risk—'

'Have you ever known me to be a fool?' she demanded. 'I put on a pretty gown, but I didn't leave my brain behind on the dressing table. My courses are just over.' She said it without a trace of the shyness she felt. She knew it would doom her. 'There could be no better time for this.' She moved against his hand. 'And there are some things in life that are worth the risk.'

'Chloe, I—'

His words ended in a hiss as she reached out and cupped his manhood. He throbbed in her hand, warm and heavy, thoroughly and wonderfully male.

And he was convinced. With a growl he surged against her. In a matter of seconds the remainder of his clothes landed beside hers on the floor. He pushed her back, drew her hands over her head and knelt between her thighs.

'Yes,' she said as she sighed.

And he was inside her. Deep and wide, he

stretched her. She gasped, but he moved again, demanding more. She gave in, gave way, with most satisfying results.

Again he moved, but carefully. Slow and steady, he stroked. Tenderly, he touched her face. Immense power, held in check. For her sake. Such glorious, heady stuff. Massive, he loomed everywhere. In and above, around and over. All the power of an avalanche to crush and destroy her, yet she'd never felt safer.

Joy infused her. Pleasure seized her. Faster they moved and Chloe found herself reduced to simple need once again. More and more and more, she wanted. And then she was there, thrust with him into a place of frenzied happiness. A space where distinctions such as you and me ceased to existed, leaving only a perfect blend of *us*, *together*.

And together they drifted, entwined and yet free, until they were recalled to earth. They followed paths beat out by the gradually settling pounding of their hearts.

Replete. Content.

But separate again.

Chapter Fifteen

The following day—the last before Lady Ashton's ball—was a full one. Chloe had a list a mile long, columns of last-stage planning, decorating and setting up to accomplish. Of all days, today she needed a clear head and every one of her abilities to organise matters and inspire people.

What she had instead was a dreamy sense of satiety and fledgling hope—and a tendency to find that she'd been standing still and staring off into the distance for an undetermined amount of time.

It was foolish. It was impractical. And it happened again as she was tenting exotic fabrics from the ceiling, transforming the morning room into a Middle Eastern fantasy—and taking twice as long as needed to do it.

'Miss Hardwick? Miss? Miss Hardwick!'

Startled, she turned to find a scowling footman trying to gain her attention. He held the glass-based bottom of an elegant Egyptian hookah in one hand and the tall metal stem of the water pipe in another. 'Have you any idea how these go together?' he asked, clearly frustrated.

Chloe grimaced. 'No, I'm afraid I don't. But we'd best work it out quickly. There are two more of those to be unpacked still. It won't be a decent smoking room without a hookah or three, or so the countess insists.' She dug in her apron pocket for a pencil and in another for a slip of paper. 'Here. This is the address of the tobacconist in Haymarket where I obtained them. Run down there and ask for his assistance—but do it quickly, if you please.'

'Aye,' he agreed. He left and Chloe took a handful of tacks from a maid and went back to attaching fabric to the wainscoting. The footman had left the door open, but it took a few minutes for a series of distant, rhythmic thuds to penetrate her concentration. Once she noticed the noise, however, her head came up. Her heart rate ratcheted and a slow smile spread over her face.

'Trudy, there are only a few lengths left,' she said to the maid. 'Can you finish here?' Within moments she was gone from the room and heading for the stairs.

The long gallery at Marland House stretched

for one entire length of the house. On the floor above it, at either end, corridors ended at a widened, open space, spanned by a railing. It made for a useful spot, to observe the goings on in the long room below, or even to converse with those gathered there.

It was to one of these areas that Chloe headed—the one situated furthest from the marquess's makeshift training area. Grinning, she sank down into a corner. Braedon trained below, alone. She was a good distance away, but the chances of being discovered here were small, and the view...

She shivered. He wore her favourite pair of worn boots and had clearly been at practice for a while. His coat and waistcoat lay over a bench. His linen was soaked with sweat and clung to every muscular hill and valley of his back.

Spellbound, she stared. He moved with deadly, proficient grace, yet she could only view his body as a work of art. It still held the same level of fascination for her—for all that she'd spent last night with her hands all over it.

She stopped that train of thought—because she was flushing, but also because, just as the last time she had spied on the marquess, she was interrupted. She jumped a little and glanced down as a cold, wet nose pushed into the palm of her hand.

'Well, good morning to you,' she whispered

to the spaniel pup. She ruffled his ears and glanced up at the sound of rapid footsteps. The boy came skidding around a corner. She smiled a greeting, but he looked horrified and began a comic attempt to backpedal away from her.

Chloe raised a finger to her lips and pointed down towards the marquess.

He stopped and raised a brow at her. Curiosity obviously got the better of him, for he tiptoed to the railing and peeked over. He looked back at her. Noted the dog in her lap and frowned. 'Black hair,' he whispered.

Chloe had no idea what he meant.

'Are you upset to see me?' he asked quietly.

Puzzled, she shook her head.

His shoulders slumped in relief. 'Good. I thought it must be the other one.'

She merely shrugged and indicated a spot next to her, with a good view of the marquess below. He sat, and for a few minutes they merely held their silence and watched Lord Marland's inadvertent show.

When a short time had passed, Chloe leaned forwards and spoke low in the boy's ear. 'What's your dog's name?'

His sharp little face softened. 'It's Fitzwilliam,' he whispered. 'I saw a gentleman with that name once. It's dignified, don't you think?'

She nodded agreement. 'Though it is a big name for such a little pup.'

'Oh, it's fine. I call him Fitz most of the time. Except when he's in trouble. The way me mam called me Robert, 'stead o' Rob, when I used to empty the whole jar of jam on to my toast.' Obviously struck, he brightened and reached into a pocket. 'Hungry?' he asked. He came up with a grubby fist full of licorice.

Her heart softened. She grinned her thanks, took a piece and bit off a mouthful.

Companionably they chewed and watched the marquess at his work, sharing an occasional comment at a particularly impressive stroke.

'He must go through quite a few training forms,' she whispered at one point, indicating the ragged figure of wood and cloth.

'Must.' Rob frowned. 'He's nicer than I thought.' He glanced over his shoulder at her. 'He's helping me to train Fitz.'

'The marquess?' she asked in surprise. 'How nice.'

'He means to find us a place in the country.' Chloe nodded.

'Fitz listens real good!' he burst out suddenly. 'I do, too.' He looked suddenly guilty. 'I try, anyway. I kept out of the way, like I was asked. And it wasn't easy, either! There are people everywhere now and a bunch of them have brown hair. I did pretty good, though.'

'I'm sure you did,' she soothed.

'And I'm not complicated,' he said, his shoulders drooping. 'At least, I'm trying not to be.'

The little pup, sensitive to the emotion in his friend's voice, rose up in her lap and gave a short bark of encouragement.

They froze.

'Who's up there?' Lord Marland's voice echoed up from below.

In a flash the boy disappeared down the corridor. With a small, startled yelp, the pup leapt from her lap and went chasing after him.

Chloe couldn't stop grinning. Climbing to her knees, she peeked over the railing. 'It's just me.'

The marquess wiped sweat from his brow. 'What are you doing up there?'

There was no suppressing the wicked twist of her mouth. 'Enjoying the view.'

She jumped when he threw his sword aside with a clatter. 'I'll be right up. I've a mind to enjoy the moment.'

He disappeared from view, but Chloe laughed out loud when he came bounding up the stairs two at a time. He rushed towards her, much in the same manner that Rob had rushed away, and swept her up and off her feet.

Eagerly, their lips met. Chloe clutched him tightly, her hands running over his slick back. Without breaking their kiss, he effortlessly carried her to the closest bedchamber, edged the door open with his foot and stepped inside.

He broke away and let her slide down the mountainous front of him. 'If you are of a mind to shirk duties, I can think of a much pleasanter pastime.' It was a small guest chamber that they had invaded, done up in a soothing blue and fitted with a small bed. He nodded towards it and bent down to nuzzle the curve of her neck.

She sighed. 'How you tempt me.' Her head rolled back and a shiver ran through her. 'But the ball is tomorrow! There are at least a hundred things that need to be done today, not the least of which is moving your equipment out of the gallery.'

His hand crept up from her waist and she leaned into the caress. 'I'll help,' he murmured. 'Afterwards.'

Summoning all of her willpower, she pulled away. 'Your sister is here!' she chided. 'Lord Ashton is due to arrive any minute and she is driving her maid insane, trying to make ready for him.'

His head came up. 'Ashton is cutting it close. Thank God he is arriving in time, although if—' A strange expression spread over his face. He drew his hand away from her waist and held it up. As he flexed it into a fist and back open, she noticed that his fingers stuck to his palm. He brought it close to his face and sniffed. And then he stared at her in exasperation. 'I might have known,' he said with a sigh.

Perplexed, she glanced down, only to notice a sticky stained spot on her old gown. Licorice. 'Oh,' she said. 'Yes. I made the acquaintance of your tenant boy.'

He looked back over his shoulder, as if he could see through the closed door and down to the gallery below. Shaking his head, he sighed again and sat down on the edge of the bed. 'Swordplay has long been how I find peace,' he said. 'It has always been my best defence—but it doesn't do a damned bit of good against you.'

She perched herself on his lap. Taking his face in her hands, she kissed him. 'Braedon, I promise you—there is no need to defend against me.'

He made a sound that tore at her heart, a laugh that somehow seemed to originate in despair. Pulling her tight, he buried his face in her hair. 'You don't understand.'

Chloe closed her eyes. 'Then help me to understand. Who was it that you had to defend against? Was it only your brother?' Her heart broke for the boy who had found an old rusted sword and somehow turned it into salvation. 'Your father?' she asked quietly.

He snorted and his breath heated the tender spot behind her ear. She wanted him to find every one of the secret places on her body and make them his.

'No,' he finally answered. 'There was nothing to truly fear from my father. He might have mocked me and expressed his disappointment almost daily, but he largely left me alone.'

'Disappointment?' She pulled back and gave him a teasing grin. 'In a great, strapping son like you?'

He didn't smile in return. 'I'm nothing next to my father or brother. Truly, they were both big as houses—nearly a direct throwback to Viking ancestors, my mother used to say.'

'Vikings, eh?' She looked him over speculatively. Vikings definitely wore boots, did they not?

His desolate expression pulled her back. 'They both had the appetites to go along with the accusation,' he continued. 'For the hunt, for the outdoors. Any kind of sport, really. For food and wine and women.'

He stopped. Briefly, she considered what that might have meant to his mother. He didn't continue, but remembering his previous story, she could hear the words that he didn't say.

'And they had nothing but contempt for any man who didn't enjoy their pleasures with the same gusto,' he said quietly. 'Contempt that could make itself known in any number of ways—especially after they were deep in their cups.'

'And your brother—Connor had darker appetites?' she asked softly.

A shutter fell over his expression. He answered with a slow nod. 'I could never match his height—or his maliciousness—but eventually he knew enough to be frightened when I had a blade in my hand.'

He'd had enough of dismal memories and she had no wish to push him. She smiled at him instead. 'Well, your hands are full of me now. And I'm not frightened.'

'I know.' His bleak expression had not changed. 'And that makes you twice as dangerous as Connor.'

Her eyes filled as she leaned in to claim his mouth with her own. Deeply she kissed him, and without reservation she opened her heart and her soul. With lips and hands and silent caresses she gifted him with all the tender feelings and sweet reassurances she could summon.

He responded, of course, but she could feel desperation in his hold on her.

'Look what just happened,' she said softly, allowing laughter to leak into her words. 'You just shared something of yourself—and the world did not end. Nor did I fall hopelessly at your feet.'

'Why do you bother, then?' he asked hoarsely.

She stroked a hand in his hair. 'Because I want you to know that it is possible.'

She took pity on him then, and kissed him. 'Perhaps I could shirk my duties just a little longer,' she whispered against his mouth. 'But only if you promise to keep your boots on.'

He smiled and, laying her back on the bed, kissed her again. Chloe stretched out beneath him, her happiness tainted, turned bittersweet by the resignation still lurking in his eyes.

Chapter Sixteen

Marland House had been transformed. Braedon, back from an early ride, followed a huge floral display into the entry hall on the morning of Mairi's ball and marvelled at the difference a couple of weeks—and Chloe—had wrought.

No longer a dusty tribute to desertion and neglect, the house glistened with gleaming marble and shining wood. Enticing smells drifted from the kitchens at the back of the house. Pounding and the call of orders echoed from the direction of the ballroom and nearly every room on the first floors were being recruited into service. Servants hustled everywhere, busy, but calm and efficient.

Braedon laid a hand on the banister where a garland twined around the railing. Damned symbolic, that climbing vine of multiple greens and white. The night he'd ascended these stairs and wished for numbness felt a long way away. And he'd got the opposite of it, in any case. Life and energy throbbed through the house, and he didn't just mean the bustling preparation for the ball.

Ashton had arrived yesterday, and the joy and forgiveness with which he and Mairi had reunited had been touching to see. Rob seemed content in the nursery and the bond between him and the pup appeared to be thriving. And then there was Hardwick.

Chloe.

'Lord Marland!' Even Dobbs looked sprightly, although the reason for it was revealed with his words. 'The post has come early today!' He waved a full salver. 'You have a stack of answers from your bailiffs and stewards.' He lowered his voice as he grew closer. 'Surely one of them will have a place for the boy.'

Braedon took up the pile of letters and wondered at the butler's continuing animosity towards the child. Did Dobbs know something that he did not? The boy seemed well behaved. Calm. Not at all like Braedon's brother, to put it bluntly. Perhaps it was only an attitude that spilled over on to the boy from his father. Connor had certainly made the servants' lives as difficult as he'd made everyone else's.

'I'll look them over in the bookroom.' Taking the stack of letters, he climbed the stairs, his thoughts arrowing straight back to Chloe. Good Lord, but she had him flying higher than he had ever allowed himself to go before. When she was near, it was as if she lifted his burdens, leaving him lighter and more carefree. But he could not fail to heed a nagging voice inside of him, recommending caution. Because he knew this…this exultation would be fleeting. It always was. The highs in his life were invariably followed hard by the worst of the lows.

He'd tried to keep to an even keel with her. But he'd failed miserably—and now it was too late. All he could do now was to hold on and try to stay aloft as long as possible. The end would come soon enough. The pain would be hellish, no doubt, but he would embrace it without complaint. It was no more than he deserved, after selfishly accepting what she so sweetly offered.

He'd already felt the first shuddering drop, in fact, after the exquisite session in that bedchamber yesterday. He felt himself harden just thinking about it. She'd been relaxed and happy. Playful. And he had drunk her in through every pore. He'd laid himself open and she had touched him with love and comfort until he swore their souls had touched.

Such ecstasy was never meant to last.

He closed the bookroom door on the noise echoing through the rest of the house and sat down to go through the post. One after another the men in charge of his estates assured him that they knew of no situation for the boy straight off, but each assured him they would look into the matter.

Braedon was surprised to find an easing of the tension around his chest. And then he was annoyed. He had no intention of growing too fond of the boy. He opened the last letter, from Orchard Park, his smallest estate. He read the contents, then let his hand drift to his lap. The caretaker couple at Orchard were childless. They would be thrilled to take the boy in and treat him as their own. With his approval they would groom him to take on the responsibilities of the estate.

The tightness in his chest returned. Letter in hand, he rang for Dobbs and went to the window. He stared down at the traffic without seeing it until the butler arrived.

'My sister, Dobbs. Where is she at present?'

'Lord and Lady Ashton have returned to their home for the morning, sir. I believe the earl wished to assess the damage there.'

Braedon swallowed. 'Miss Hardwick, then. Have her attend me here, if you would.'

Dobbs cleared his throat. 'I fear Miss Hardwick is not here either, sir.'

He frowned, surprised. 'The ball is this evening and it needed both of them to show Ashton some mouldy timber?'

'Miss Hardwick did not accompany them. She received a gentlemen caller a while ago. I believe she agreed to go out with him—for a drive in the park.'

Braedon blinked. 'A gentleman caller?'

Though he obviously disapproved, Dobbs only nodded.

The letter crumpled in his fist. 'Who the hell was it?'

'The Earl of Conover, sir. I admitted him myself, though the hour was unseemly early.'

The drop, though expected, still sickened him. His gut clenched mightily and then fell far and fast and deep, though his feet never moved.

'Conover?' He recalled the marked attention the earl had paid her at the lecture. The sight of them standing close in animated discussion. Her voice echoed in his head, speaking of marriage and children—every woman's dream, she'd called it. He saw her blush once more, in his mind's eye, at Signor Pisano's mention of babies.

She'd sat in the passageway downstairs, buried her nose in that pup's fur and said everyone needed someone to care for—and someone who could give love back.

He nearly vomited on Dobbs's shoes.

'Sir? Lord Marland? Are you well?' The butler's face had paled. 'Shall I fetch you a drink?'

'Yes. No. Of course, I am fine.' He dismissed Dobbs's concern with a wave of his hand. 'The boy, then,' he said, gripping the letter tight. 'Where is the boy?'

'The last I saw, he and his…pet were heading through the kitchens to the garden.'

Blindly, Braedon left the room. His feet moved. His body followed. And yet he felt strangely detached. An overreaction. That's all this was. He told himself so again. She went for a drive in the park. It was nothing. Then why did he feel as if his guts were being torn from him inch by painful inch?

She had promised him nothing. She hadn't even asked for anything beyond a few days. And he sure as hell had not offered her anything more.

The kitchens were a riot of activity. He nearly gave his cook an apoplexy by showing his face there. But he merely nodded to the frantic staff and passed through to the back of the house.

The dog raced around the grassy patch, barking frantically. He darted in and out, growling intermittently at…a form bent over on the ground.

Wretched sobs filled the air. Small shrieks rang out each time the pup dashed close. Rob was bent over the figure—a little girl?—his back to Braedon.

The entire world contracted in an instant.

Braedon's vision went utterly white. Nothing existed, save the few feet between the little trio on the lawn and him—and the multitude of instances that he'd found Connor in just such a situation. Mice trapped only to be tortured to death. Birds with broken wings. The rabbit that had screamed and screamed as his brother skinned it alive. The game warden's adolescent daughter who had thought to tease the heir to the manor and had suffered horribly for it.

The roar exploded out of him. He felt the pop of a vessel bursting in his eye. *'No!'* Braedon launched himself forwards. He reached them in an instant and ruthlessly pushed the boy aside. He only stopped himself from throwing him again by bending over the sobbing girl. 'What the hell do you think you are doing?' he shouted. 'What have you done?'

'Nothing,' the boy answered. He'd rolled easily to the side. He climbed to his feet, wiping dirt from his face. 'I'm all right. It's Pearl that's hurt.'

The girl looked up at him, shocked into silence, perhaps. She was younger than Rob, six years old at the most. Tears and grass streaked her face. Braedon snatched her into his arms and confronted the boy.

'She's just a girl—and smaller than you by half!' Braedon snarled at him in disgust. The dog was still barking with excitement and jumping at his feet. 'I swear by all that is holy—if you have harmed her—'

'What?' Rob looked stunned. 'I didn't do nothing!'

'I saw you…' Braedon stuttered to a stop. He'd only seen him bent over the girl.

Understanding slowly dawned in the boy's eyes. Understanding, and hurt. 'Pearl's the baker's girl. I wouldn't hurt her.' A basket lay on its side nearby. He picked it up. 'She fell because she was afraid of Fitz. Then she was afraid again, too scared to stand up. But he was just playing, chasing her skirts. He didn't mean nothing.' He glanced at the dog, still circling Braedon's legs, and flushed. 'Fitz! Come!' he ordered. He reached out and grabbed his collar as the pup raced past.

Braedon hitched the girl up on to his hip and looked into her face. 'Is that true?'

'I'm sorry about your bread.' She sniffed.

'Damn the bread!' he nearly shouted. Calming his tone, he asked, 'Did you fall? Or did he hurt you?' He nodded toward Rob.

'No, I fell, sir. I'm right sorry.' She glanced at the pup and shuddered. 'I don't like little dogs. Especially them that tug and jump.'

Braedon deflated. All the terror and indignation fled his system, leaving him feeling sick. He set the girl down. Rob handed her the basket.

'Go on, then,' Braedon told her. 'I'm sure Cook is expecting you.'

She managed a little curtsy and ran off.

Rob glared, the perfect image of anger and injury. 'You thought I hurt her? That I would bother a little girl?'

'I…I'm sorry.' Braedon's hand was shaking. 'I apologise. I suppose I must have…jumped to an unwarranted conclusion.'

The boy merely stared at him with reproach before turning and running towards the house. The dog yelped and followed at his heels.

Braedon staggered over to lean on a rough bench near the garden.

Just as he'd thought. The highest highs. And now he'd landed neck-deep in the worst of the lows.

Chapter Seventeen

Chloe breathed deeply, glad for at least a small taste of fresh air and green growing things. She breathed again and tried not to think of all that needed to be done at Marland House. She did love a phaeton, after all. And the pretty morning bid for a fair afternoon and evening.

At this hour the park lay quiet and largely deserted. The very elegant Earl of Conover drove a fine vehicle, pulled by a magnificent team of matched greys. The conversation was easy and light. They spoke of the lecture and of some of the more exotic artefacts they had seen. Everything was perfectly lovely, in short. And yet, she could not summon the same excitement that she'd felt when out riding with Braedon.

She shivered. It felt both odd and exhilarating to use his given name, after all of these months.

She smiled over at the earl. 'This has been a lovely break for me, my lord. But I cannot help but wonder if you had a particular reason for inviting me.' The earl had shown up at Marland House this morning, asking for her. He had been gracious, flattering and at last insistent that she come out for a drive with him. She'd agreed, after a little urging, hoping that he meant to share further information regarding Skanda's Spear.

'Indeed, I did have a particular topic I'd like to discuss.' The carriage path they followed entered a short wooded section. He slowed his team to a walk as they entered the glade. 'I was hoping we could continue the conversation we began the other night.'

'I was hoping you would say so,' she said with a smile. 'I've been thinking over what you said, that Skanda's Spear has known so many woman owners.' She cocked her head at him. 'I can't seem to fathom a reason why it might be so, but I got the impression that you might know something further.'

'I have postulated something, in any case. But in order for it to make sense, I'd like to share a little of the Spear's history.'

'Please,' she nodded for him to continue.

Casually, he flicked his whip, chasing an insect from about his horses' ears. 'There are many stories told of Skanda in the East. Too many to go into today, unfortunately. But the thing you need to know is that many of the tales concern his rivalry with his brother.'

She stilled. 'Is that so?'

'Indeed. They seem to have argued quite incessantly over which of them was held highest in their parents' esteem. One issue in particular begins when the brothers quarrelled over which would be allowed to marry first. It is said that a contest was devised—the brothers would race around the universe to determine the winner. Skanda set off immediately and made the physical trip, but his brother merely stepped a circle around their parents, stating, in essence, that they were the universe. The outcome varies in different tales, but most say that Skanda fell into a fury that still rages to this day.'

A chill swept over Chloe that had nothing to do with the shade. 'Not a sporting chap, then, Skanda.'

The earl chuckled. 'No. I believe, though, that that story is likely the basis for the reputed curse that has come to be associated with the Spear.'

'Are you familiar with the specifics of the curse?' she asked. 'I've been able to find nothing.' She could guess, at least, in which direction it lay and just the hint sent a sickening twist through her stomach.

The boyish, lighthearted Conover had gone. He was all solemnity as he pulled the phaeton to a halt. Without being asked, his groom climbed down and began to walk ahead of the carriage. 'The Spear is said to completely isolate its keepers,' the earl intoned, once his servant had moved beyond earshot. 'A man who owns it will voluntarily cut all the earthly ties that bind him.'

'A superstition,' she whispered.

'Perhaps. It has been recorded, though, by those that pay attention to that sort of thing, that men who have been known to possess the spear have lived cloistered and withdrawn.'

She caught the emphasis in his tone. '*Men* who have possessed it?'

He nodded. 'The curse appears to be ineffective against females.'

Her mind raced. 'There is no nabob, is there?' Her voice grew louder. 'It's been you all along? You've had the Spear?'

'No, no,' he soothed. 'Much of the rumour swirling around Town is true. The Spear only recently arrived here, brought from the East by a man who has lived there for many years. Mr Buckhurst has seen many things there that might defy our imaginations. He says he met an ancient *bhikkhu* on a trip into the mountains. The old man appointed him courier to the Spear, and told him he was meant to be the one to find the weapon's true owner—so that it may go to its final resting place.'

An image of Braedon's grand new wing—the

one that she had helped to build—flashed in her mind. She liked the sound of this less and less. 'It sounds a heavy responsibility. How will this mysterious nabob know the true owner? It would seem his long absence would only make his mission more difficult.'

The earl shook out his reins and urged his team forwards again. Glancing askance at her, he spoke quietly. 'Buckhurst is a shrewd man. He has been watching events unfold very carefully. He feels the weight of his responsibility most keenly.' Conover paused. 'Those men, Miss Hardwick? The ones who lived apart with the Spear? It was not an isolation of contentment. From all accounts, they lived—and died—quite miserably.'

She stared, horrified.

'You have met him, you know.'

'Of course I have not.' She frowned in indignation. 'But I wish I had. Don't you think that I would have had a hundred questions…?' She stopped. Disjointed pieces began to come together to form a whole. 'Oh, good heavens—the man! The man asleep in the antechamber after the lecture?' She recalled his dismissal of the weapon—and his pointed questions about Lord Marland.

She gasped and gripped Conover's arm. 'He's going to give the thing to the marquess! We have to stop him!'

The earl's lips thinned. 'He meant to,' he acknowledged with a nod. 'It would seem that certain facts indicated that the spear might be destined for Lord Marland, including the new wing he's built to house his collection.'

'No,' she breathed.

'But Buckhurst hesitates.'

Chloe seized on the chance. 'Yes. He should. Such a burden is the last thing that Braedon should have to bear.' Frantic, she began to mentally shift through all of the men so passionately interested in obtaining the Spear. A life of isolation and misery? Whom would she condemn? It would indeed be a terrible choice. 'There must be someone else.'

The phaeton eased out of the shaded grove. Warm sunlight washed over them as the earl spoke softly. 'You, Miss Hardwick. Buckhurst is giving the Spear to you. He strongly suspects that the Spear is meant for Marland, but he wishes for you to make the final decision.'

Stunned. She could only blink, so dumb was she struck. 'No,' she whispered. 'I can't... He cannot ask such a thing of me!'

'I agree,' he said flatly. 'But he does. He has.' He paused the phaeton long enough for his groom to remount his seat in the back, then drove on.

Chloe's head was swimming. She didn't want the thing. But with terror and outrage and frustration she suddenly understood why Braedon did. Her fists clenched. She wanted to shout out her feelings of betrayal and anger. Even so long ago, at Denning, she had suspected that he knew more about the Spear than he would admit. She was sure now. Somehow he had discovered the true nature of the weapon.

Even if she dismissed the curse as primitive superstition, it didn't negate his betrayal—not in Chloe's eyes. Still the thing remained a symbol of his detachment, of the emotional distance he laboured to keep between him and the rest of the world.

From her.

'Miss Hardwick?'

With a start, she realised that they had left the park. The earl had pulled to a stop in front of a linen draper's at the corner of Green Street.

'I apologise for the necessity of this deception,' he said, climbing down. 'But we must be careful.' He crossed to the pavement and reached up for her hand. 'Look under the bench as you climb down, he instructed. 'There is a roll of fabric strapped there.'

Startled, she allowed him to assist her and looked where he bid.

'Do you see?'

'Yes.' It looked to be a length of brocade in rich blues and greens.

He thrust his chin towards the shop and gestured for her to precede him. 'In the back corner, to the right,' he said under his breath. 'The same fabric sits there. If you will, admire it and arrange to purchase a length. You will hold it in your lap as we drive you home, afterwards.'

The shopkeeper opened the door to usher them in. Smiling, she acted as casually as she could. She browsed but a minute before following the earl's instructions. It was quickly done. When they were underway again, she spoke up.

'The spear is rolled into the brocade under the bench?' she asked.

'Very good, Miss Hardwick.' He shot her a look of grim approval. 'We'll make the switch when you climb down at Marland House.' They drove in silence for a few moments, before he said quietly, 'I am sorry about all of this.'

She was, too.

'Perhaps you should just keep the Spear yourself. Believe me, I understand the temptation, and you would avoid the risk of anyone getting hurt.'

Anyone except Braedon. A horrifying image of his brother, stealing away that which he cared for the most, invaded her mind. It would be the ultimate betrayal. He would never forgive her. She was doomed to hurt him, either way.

Her heart stilled for a moment. He would be devastated—if he found out.

It was as if Conover read her mind. 'I promise you, I shall never tell a soul you have it.' He shook his head. 'You must realise I'd rather my part in this did not get out, either.'

Her gaze drifted back towards his groom.

The earl saw and understood. 'Joseph is not a risk. Your secret would be safe,' he insisted. 'He's been with me a very long time.' He snorted. 'The keeping of secrets is one of his foremost skills.'

Chloe didn't know what to do. She would never willingly betray Braedon. But she'd worked so hard to draw him out and gain his trust. She desperately wanted him to see that letting someone close could lead to more than just pain. And yet, blithely giving him the Spear felt like a betrayal to her own beliefs, and a deplorable validation of his efforts to keep everyone at bay. Did she dare just hand him such a powerful symbol of his most erroneous tendencies? The last thing she wanted to give him was unspoken permission to distance himself from her.

'Here we go,' Conover said as they stopped in front of Marland House. He kept his face turned forwards, as if watching his horses, and spoke low through his teeth. 'Hand me your bolt of fabric.' A footman was descending the steps, ready to help her from the vehicle. 'Let him assist you down. I'll make the switch as you climb out.'

The footman reached them. 'Let me help you down from there, Miss.'

'Oh, thank you, James,' she said. She did as the earl suggested, even improvising an attempt at a distraction. She pretended that her foot was caught in her skirts and fell heavily into the poor man's arms.

'Oh, dear, I am sorry.' She smiled sheepishly and turned back to Conover.

The earl was grinning as he handed over the brocade.

'Oh, and James?' she said, taking it up again. 'Would you run this straight up to my room for me? I've the perfect use for it in the dining room tonight.'

The footman took it and set off.

Conover nodded in approval.

'I do hope we will see you at the ball this evening, my lord?'

'I would not miss it. In fact, if it is not already claimed, I wonder if you would save the first dance for me?'

She flushed. 'No, I'm not engaged for the first dance. Thank you, I would be happy to stand up with you.'

He gave a short bow from the waist. 'I look forward to it. Good day, Miss Hardwick.' He lifted his reins and drove on.

'Good day,' she called. Trying to keep her tread light, she stepped inside. It was not easy, with her heart so heavy. She went straight to her room. Locking the door, she unrolled the brocade and stared down at the instrument of so much upheaval.

It was in two pieces, as if the craftsman who had made it had known the thing would need to be occasionally tucked and hidden away. When she attached the long bottom shaft into the highly decorated handhold, the Spear stood as high as her shoulder. Otherwise, it was exactly as Conover had described it, and quite a close resemblance to the illustration she'd found in Braedon's library.

The workmanship was lovely. The piece was undoubtedly worth more than she could imagine. Yet Buckhurst had done her no favours, giving it into to her hand.

Now she was fated to betray someone. It only remained to be seen if it would be Braedon, or herself.

Chapter Eighteen

The enormity of everything Mairi and Chloe had accomplished only struck Braedon as he trailed after his sister and her husband, just before the start of the ball. Mairi wished Ashton to be first to see everything. The pair of them had encountered him drinking alone and dragged him along. Now his sister was having a high time showing off the results of so much hard work. She nearly glowed with the pleasure of explaining the significance of each separate stage of the surprise.

They left the masculine extravagance of the smoking room—complete with hookah pipes and every sort of cigar, cheroot and cigarillo a man might wish for—to examine the splendours of the dining room.

'The entire midnight supper has been based

on the traditional food of the Greek Isles,' Mairi effused. She took her husband's arm. 'I know how much you loved them when you toured there. We will have lamb and every sort of fish, and I questioned the cooks of all of our friends until I found one who thought he knew of those grape leaves you adored. Oh,' she fretted, 'I do hope they turn out—'

'Good God, Mairi.' Braedon had been admiring the dining room's fresh decor, done in variegated blues and whites that truly did bring clear oceans and sandy beaches to mind, but now he couldn't stop staring at the large platter being carried in. 'Are those tiny Parthenons carved of *cheese*?'

'One for every table!' She clapped her hands. 'Is it not the most charming thing?'

She rushed off to direct their placement and Braedon took the opportunity to clap Ashton on the back.

'I wanted you to know how very happy she has been, planning this,' he told his brother-in-law. 'It may be a little much.' He waved a hand. 'But every last detail has thrilled her—because she was doing it for you.' He nodded towards his sister and couldn't help but smile. 'She cares for you, man.'

A grin played about Ashton's lips as he gazed after his wife. 'I know.' He looked a little discomfited. 'It's hard to admit, but all of this is more than a little gratifying. She is right—I have felt many times that I have only been valued for my title and position. But seeing all of this...' He stared at Mairi, his expression unabashedly tender. 'It's humbling—and thrilling. She listens. Look at this, Braedon!' His sweeping arm encompassed the whole house. 'She knows me, right down to my favourite sporting rifle. Did you *see* those marzipan Mantons?'

Braedon laughed. 'Frankly, I preferred the target-shaped pastries. They are delicious.' He grew serious. 'About that incident, though, Ashton. That man. I hope you know that it was nothing— She was only trying—'

'I know,' his brother-in-law interrupted. 'I do understand, because I know her as well as she knows me.' He lifted his arm in welcome as Mairi made her way back to them. 'And next time I will remember that and try to keep my stubborn pride in check.'

Braedon watched his sister's face as she slid into her husband's embrace. Privately, he thought the chances were good that there would not be a next time.

'Mairi.' He had to say her name twice before he caught her attention. 'Where is Chloe?'

'She's upstairs, still getting ready for this evening. She's been so busy—' She stopped. Her eyes narrowed, then widened in delight. 'Yes. *Chloe* will be down shortly.'

He shot her a quelling glance and took his leave of them. But truly, it was good to see someone in the house content. He rubbed his brow and set off for his rooms. How his perceptions had changed since this morning! Rob refused to speak with him now. The boy slunk off every time Braedon drew near. Dobbs was cranky as he tried to see to last-minute preparations while at the same time arranging for the boy's early-morning departure. And even from a distance, Hardwick had appeared distressed and distracted this afternoon.

He wondered if it was due to something Conover had said about the Spear. Pisano had sent a note around. The rumours circulating now said that the thing was done. The nabob had handed the weapon off to its new owner and everyone was frantic to discover who it was.

Irritating news, but Braedon had been reluctant to share it with her. Part of him did not want to acknowledge that the hunt was over. And in any case, the tidings hadn't irritated him half so much as the sight of Chloe driving up with Conover. He'd stood at a window, shamelessly spying as the earl dropped her off. He'd seethed with frustration as the damned dandy procured her hand for the first set.

He could still pursue the Spear and its new owner, after all. But he didn't think he could stand in the way of Chloe finding happiness.

He paused at the landing to the third floor, tempted to find an excuse to go to her now. It struck him hard, suddenly, the overwhelming urge to sit at her feet and lay his head in her lap. He would thank her for the incredible help she'd given his sister. He could confess his terrible remorse at the way he'd misjudged Rob. He could crack his soul open a little wider for her and tell her he didn't want to lose her when this was all over. That, like Ashton, he was only just coming to understand the incredible honour she gave him, knowing him so well and caring for him anyway.

He could do all of that, and more. But he didn't.

Because he'd already given her as much as he dared. He'd let her see things that no one else ever had. And still, he sensed, it wasn't enough. Chloe would never be satisfied with only the surface, the most superficial part of him. But that was all he had to give.

This time of frantic activity and overwrought emotion was drawing to an end. Rob's stay, the ball, the quest for the Spear—the doors were closing on all of it. His comforting, empty space was uncomfortably full of people right now, but they would all be gone, soon enough. He would be back at Denning, alone with his new wing and his incredible collection.

Just the way he liked it.

* * *

The gentlemen invited to the Ashtons' ball were delighted with the unique elements of the evening. They happily polluted the smoking room and its immediate surroundings. They flocked in droves to the mock gaming hell, and one by one they derived great pleasure in harassing and teasing Lord Ashton.

Neither were the ladies left out of the fun. Clustered in groups, they endlessly critiqued the food, the decor and the company. Behind their fans they tittered enviously at the earl's besotted regard of his wife, even as they took mental notes for their own future soirées.

Chloe heaved a sigh. A success all around. One she would have taken greater pleasure in, were it not for the accursed Spear hidden in her room.

Where was Braedon? She watched for him as she moved through the house, checking that all progressed smoothly. Not since the previous evening had she seen him. He'd kept his word, after their clandestine encounter, and helped her ready the long gallery. He'd sneaked a surreptitious caress along her backside and tossed her a cocky grin as he'd left. She supposed he could merely be busy, now. Perhaps some of his antiquarian friends were in attendance and he—futilely—sought further news of the Spear. She sighed again. Or perhaps this absence was an attempt at a retreat, as he once again sought to place a distance between them.

She wouldn't know until she found him, and what she longed to do was to track him down and burrow into the reassuring warmth of his embrace.

But she hadn't yet faced him with anything but complete openness and honesty, not since she'd given up Hardwick and left Denning. And she wasn't sure she could meet him with total candour now—not with uncertainty about that damned Spear weighing so heavily on her mind.

Still, she thought she would check on the progress in the dessert room. The countess had mentioned that her brother appeared inordinately fond of the pastries.

She grinned in appreciation when she arrived. Madame Hobert flitted about, putting the finishing touches on a work of genius. The sugar-paste rendition of an English hunt marched across three tables, in brilliant colour and sublime detail.

'The sugar is a nice touch.'

Chloe turned as Mrs Edmunds sidled up alongside her.

'But the really brilliant move was hiring the professional croupiers for the gaming room.' The countess's friend raised a brow. 'Except— how do you expect to lure the men away when it is time for the dancing?'

Chloe laughed. 'I'll leave that up to you la-dies.'

'Mairi says that both were your ideas.' She paused a beat. 'She also says that you won't be staying on with her.'

'No. There's no need, really. Lady Ashton only needed help preparing for this evening.'

'Well, perhaps you are not aware, but I enter-tain both more regularly and more lavishly than Mairi is wont to do.' The other woman glanced at the tables of pretty desserts. 'I could use someone with both your taste and your skills. I would be pleased to have you as my personal secretary.'

Chloe's eyes widened in surprise. 'I don't know what to say! You honour me, Mrs Edmunds.' The temptation was real, the tug on her old mindset palpable, but she stiffened her spine. 'But I mean to take some time for myself. I shall travel a little, I think, and search for a spot that speaks to me while I decide what I'd like to do next.'

The lady blinked in disbelief. 'You are sure? You'd be a fool to leave London now. There at least a score of ladies here who would love to snap you up.'

'I thank you, but I am sure.' Her eyes un-focused and for a moment she lost sight of the gleaming white tables and colourful desserts. 'I've always dreamed of a cottage by the sea.'

'Well then, go to Ramsgate, by all means. Or Brighton. There are plenty of perfectly lovely places to let in those spots. But make it a holiday, for heaven's sake.' She snapped open her fan. 'And when you have had enough of solitude and ocean breezes, then come back to Town and take me up on my offer.'

'Thank you,' Chloe said with a smile. 'Perhaps I will.'

Mrs Edmunds saluted her with her fan and then sauntered away.

Chloe had a quick word with the confectioner, then turned to go herself. Just past the doorway, however, she ran headlong into a masculine form. 'Oh,' she breathed. 'Good evening, Sir Thomas! I hope you are enjoying the ball?'

'I am,' the sword master said. 'I remember what Lady Ashton said, all those weeks ago at Denning. Every masculine delight.' He glanced around. 'You've certainly made good on your promise.'

'Thank you.' She stepped away. 'I should go check on the musicians, it's nearly time for the dancing.'

'Just a moment, if you would.' He glanced down the passageway. 'I'm of the mind that you should perhaps have taken Mrs Edmunds up on her offer.'

Chloe stopped. 'I beg your pardon? Were you eavesdropping, Sir Thomas?'

'No, no,' he assured her. 'Just waiting to have a word with you. I know Braedon came to London because he wanted you back at Denning, but you haven't exactly lived up to your promises to him, have you?' He ran a measuring look down the front of her. 'I doubt he'll have you back now.'

'I don't understand.' Sir Thomas's usual expression had changed. He stared at her, crafty and knowing. He looked like a stranger.

'I mean Skanda's Spear, of course.'

Chloe froze.

'Or hadn't you heard? The word is out that it has been given over to a new owner.'

'Already?' she breathed, shocked.

One side of his mouth curled into a smile. 'I've always found bad news to travel twice as fast as good.'

She was struck, suddenly, by his manner. It was almost as if her was enjoying her discomfort. Her eyes narrowed. 'I didn't know you were interested in antiquities.'

'Anyone who knows Braedon knows of his interest in that particular item.'

'Truly?' She raised a doubting brow. 'Because I've always found Lord Marland to be intensely private regarding his collection.'

'Keeps you in his counsel and no one else, eh?' The sword master looked calculatingly about him at the glittering crowd moving through the corridor. 'Well, you haven't exactly been available lately, have you?'

Something was not right. There was a hateful note in his tone that she'd never heard before. And yet he was relaxed, patient. He was like a cat, playing with his prey. He stepped closer and peered down into her face. 'What will you tell him now?'

'Who, Lord Marland?' she asked with studied nonchalance. 'I'll tell him your news, of course. What else?' She felt not a whit of guilt for lying to him. Cats, she knew, eventually tired of playing and moved in for the kill.

'What else, indeed? Perhaps I will tell him myself.'

He said the casual words with deliberate intent and intensity. Chloe's heart stopped. How? How could he know?

'I don't think it will matter either way—not for you,' he mused. 'He's not going to be happy with you.'

'Chloe!' Lady Ashton had come around a corner and was striding towards them, beckoning her.

'Oh, dear, it truly must be time for the dancing.' Grateful for the chance, Chloe took a step away.

Sir Thomas reached out and gripped her arm. 'I thought, since Braedon won't have you, you might be tired of acting as a glorified lady's maid.' Assessing, he looked her over. 'You have more grit than I would have accredited you with. I might be able to find you a situation.' He leered. 'I promise you—you would enjoy it.'

'It's nearly time for the introduction,' Lady Ashton called.

'Just remember,' he said.

Pulling free, Chloe hurried away.

Chapter Nineteen

Chloe's uncertainty was gone. She had to find Braedon.

Her mind raced as she moved through the congested house. Something was wrong. How could the entire antiquities community know already that the Spear had been handed off? Why was Sir Thomas acting so strangely? He'd been subtly hostile and almost aggressive. A dark sense of dread lay heavy in her stomach. Damn that Spear, and damn Sir Thomas, too. She feared telling Braedon that she had the weapon, but she knew his reaction would be far worse if he heard it from someone else. Suddenly her indecision felt nearly inconsequential next to her need to talk to him.

'Have you seen Lord Marland?' she asked his sister.

'No.' The countess's hands fluttered nervously. 'It's time for the performance.' She smiled to the left and right as she pulled Chloe along with her. 'We need to begin moving people into the ballroom.'

'I'll tell Dobbs,' Chloe volunteered. 'He can send the footman to begin gathering guests and you and I can inform them as we go.' And she could search for Braedon as she went, as well. She clasped Lady Ashton's hand for a moment. 'You'll be all right. I'll meet you in there.'

She went in one direction and the countess another, but Chloe didn't find Braedon until she had circled back around to usher a group of stragglers into the ballroom. He was there, though only his height allowed her to find him in the tightly packed room. She moved inside and stood on her toes to look. He stood at the end of the room, near the stage where the musicians had set up. Lord and Lady Ashton were with him—and just behind him stood Sir Thomas.

She started to push her way through the crowd just as Lady Ashton climbed to the stage.

Guests milled noisily about and the countess went unnoticed until the musicians blared out a single, brash note. Suddenly everyone turned to face them—making it twice as difficult for Chloe to weave her way through.

'Thank you all for coming to share this special evening,' the countess said from her vantage on the stage. 'As you know, this night is a celebration in honour of my husband.'

A smattering of applause broke out as Chloe ducked around a group of tittering ladies.

'Tonight we are all enjoying a taste of some of Lord Ashton's favourite things.'

A masculine cheer rolled through the crowd.

'I have cause to know that in his travels, he greatly enjoyed the Italian theatre. Though I suspect that he took the most pleasure in the gambling and the rampant flirtation, I do know that his favourite opera was Rossini's *La Sala di Seta*.' She smiled at the earl. 'Though I could not import a Venetian theatre troupe, tonight we are fortunate to have Angelica Orson with us. Miss Orson studied under Madame Catalani herself, and will perform for us a piece from the comic opera.'

The opera singer took her place. Lady Ashton stepped down from the stage and into her husband's embrace just as Chloe broke through the crowd.

Her gaze flew to Braedon. He looked magnificent in his formal wear, his shoulders twice as broad as any man's, his hair swept back and gleaming. He glimpsed her out of the corner of his eye and his first reaction must have come from pure instinct; his features softened and his hand half-raised as if to welcome her. Chloe breathed a sigh of relief.

But then she saw it—the moment his head caught up with his heart. His hand dropped. The light died from his eyes and his jaw set. Deliberately he adopted the remote expression she recalled so well from their days at Denning.

From beyond him, Sir Thomas looked on, mocking.

Her heart dropped as she joined their group. She almost wished that Sir Thomas had discovered that she was in possession of the Spear, that Braedon grew distant because his friend had filled his head with stories of her betrayal. Staring at his blank expression, she greatly feared that he had reached this state of withdrawal all on his own.

She heard nothing of the performance. Eventually the song trailed off, the noted singer gracefully bowed to enthusiastic applause. Lady Ashton stepped forwards again to signal the musicians to begin the first dance.

Just behind their little group, however, a disturbance started in the nearby crowd. Chloe heard exclamations of surprise and a few trills of laughter. Gentlemen moved and ladies swept their skirts aside to make a passage.

Rob's solemn, erect figure marched through the opening. A crack opened in Chloe's heart at the sight of him. In an obvious effort to dress appropriately, he had dug up a fancy morning coat from somewhere. It hung in wrinkles far past his waist, the tails dragging on the ground. He held Fitz tight in his arms and his expression was every bit as severe and remote as Braedon's.

With grave dignity, he marched up to the marquess. 'Dobbs says I'm to leave at first light. I knew you would not wish to say goodbye, so I've come to you.'

'There's no need for that,' Braedon answered harshly. He took an inexplicable step to the left. 'Back to the nursery with you, now. I'll come up in a bit.'

Chloe started at his callous tone. She stared in surprise, but Rob refused to be dismissed.

'You won't. I know you won't.' He swallowed and his chin lifted in defiance. 'I know what you think of me now.' His voice began to rise. 'And I don't care. You're not my da!'

'Braedon?' Hearing the commotion, Lady Ashton moved back from the stage. She stepped around her brother and caught sight of the defiant little boy. Her face abruptly drained of all colour. She staggered back a step.

'Mairi?' The earl reached out to his wife in concern.

'Back to the nursery, Rob,' Braedon ordered. 'Now!'

The lad jumped at the sudden increase in volume. The pup barked in alarm. 'No,' the boy answered quietly. 'I came to give you this.' He struggled to hold on to the spaniel with one hand while he fished in his pocket with the other.

Chloe saw the pain on Braedon's face when the hand emerged with a small, wooden figure of a dog.

Rob held it out to the marquess. 'I'm giving it back to you.'

Lady Ashton moaned out loud. 'Braedon,' she whispered. 'Who is that? Is he—?'

The marquess rubbed a hand over his face. 'I don't want it back. Just go now.'

The boy's face took on a dark, stubborn cast. 'I won't. I didn't hurt that girl, no matter what you think.'

A sob escaped the countess and she stepped closer to her husband.

Rob ignored her. 'I won't leave with this. I don't want it any more.' His gaze narrowed and cast about. Suddenly he turned smartly, hoisted the dog higher and strode past avid onlookers to a fireplace a few feet down the interior wall. A fire, lit earlier to chase the chill from the room, had been banked and was nearly dead. He didn't appear to care. He threw the little figure at the coals as hard as he could. 'There!' He turned to glare his anger at the marquess. 'I don't care!' he shouted. 'You can think what you like and it won't matter to me.'

'Oh, God—he is!' Lady Ashford groaned.

'Braedon! He's…he's Connor's? And you knew! How could you hide such a thing from me?' She stopped, her face contorted by a sudden torrent of tears. Harsh sobs ripped through her and she fell into her husband's arms.

Silence descended. The guests in the surrounding crowd watched avidly. Braedon looked bleakly between his sister and the boy, sorrow and anger etched deeply in his face. Her heart welling with sympathy and shock, Chloe reached for his hand.

He gripped it tightly for a moment, his head bowed as he absorbed the turmoil that had struck so quickly.

Sucking in a long breath, he let go of her hand. He lifted his head and her heart sank like a stone.

He had cast it all away. His gaze had cleared and his face was smooth, as calm as a still lake. 'Rob, you will return to the nursery. Now.' Even his tone sounded flat, expressionless. 'Ashton, take Mairi apart for a bit, let her recover in peace. Mairi, I believe I have the supper dance? I shall expect you back.' He gestured to the musicians on stage. 'The rest of us will begin the dancing.' He lifted his hands to the watching crowd. 'Everyone, please!'

The boy fled. The countess walked in the other direction, leaning heavily on her husband.

'Braedon,' Chloe whispered. The truth was

only beginning to dawn on her. His nephew. Rob was his nephew—his dead brother's child. An orphan, he'd told her, a tenant. But it had been a lie. Her heart clenched. The child had no one—and Braedon had been planning all along to send him away to live with strangers. No wonder the boy had been so anxious to prove himself. He'd been looking for Braedon's approval. Hoping for his care and concern. Tonight all he'd got was harsh words and dismissal. And tomorrow? By the boy's words—a hasty departure.

She stepped forwards. 'Braedon?'

'Hardwick. Perhaps you can help.' His tone was cold, impersonal, the everyday sound of a titled noble speaking to his servant.

She stared into his face. There was nothing for her there. No hint of tenderness or affection. No sign of the secrets and kisses and passionate sighs that they had shared. In just such a manner would he have regarded any passing acquaintance. Or stranger.

Just a few days. That's all she had asked for. It would appear that her time was up.

'Perhaps you could start the dancing?' he asked. He glanced over at his sparring partner. 'Thom will oblige us, I'm sure.'

Sir Thomas's mouth twisted and he held out a hand.

She shot him a look of disdain. Straightening

her shoulders, she turned her glare on the marquess. He might present the world with a blank mask devoid of any human feeling, but she was going to leave him with no doubt as to her hurt, betrayal and disapproval.

He frowned. 'If you don't wish to help…' he began evenly.

'Oh, I wish to *help*,' she snapped. 'But I think I shall focus my efforts on those willing to accept them.' She whirled away. Without looking back, she hurried after the boy.

Braedon wanted to go after her. He tensed every muscle, tightened every sinew in an effort to stay rooted in the ballroom, among his sister's guests.

This had to end. Anger lived in the pounding of his heart. Frustration flowed through his veins. Far more dangerous—need burned everywhere, lighting every part of him with the yearning to chase her down and erase the disdain he'd seen in her eyes. He felt as if he could not breathe without her smile, that he needed her approval just as he needed air. That he could not live without her love.

But he could. He would—because he would have to. He would don again the safety of his armour, reclaim the vast stretch of emptiness that protected him from such strife and discord as this. He looked around. Was this not proof enough of the sheer folly of lowering his defences? He had to rebuild, and he had to begin now.

Except that he could not quite abandon Chloe to her distress.

He took a step in the direction she had fled. Only to be stopped by a hand on his arm.

'You cannot leave as well,' Mrs Edmunds, Mairi's friend, gritted out through a determined smile. 'Think of your sister for a moment. This ball is extremely important to her. One of you has to stay and begin the dancing, act the host, or everything will disintegrate.'

Braedon frowned down at her.

'Don't look at me in that way. Mairi will be devastated if this falls into a disaster. So smile at me, damn you, offer me your hand and strike up the band. We'll lead the first set and your guests will follow.' She arched a sardonic brow at him. 'Otherwise, they will mill about a bit, call for their wraps and move on to the next social gathering, where they will gain a good bit of cachet by describing your family scandal and Mairi's failure in glorious detail.'

His gut seethed with frustration, but he offered her his arm. Before he led her to the dance floor, he looked after Chloe one last time. Inspiration seized him suddenly and he reached for Thom. 'Go to her, will you? Make sure she is all right?'

His friend was staring in the same direction, too—and his expression was not one of concern. He looked almost...predatory.

The strange look disappeared as Thom pivoted to meet Braedon's gaze. 'Yes. Don't worry. I'll go after her.'

'Tell her I'll come to her...later. As soon as I can.'

Thom clapped him on the shoulder and departed.

Braedon was distracted then, as Mrs Edmunds tugged him out to the centre of the floor. But he wasn't so preoccupied that he didn't notice Thom heading off in the wrong direction.

Chapter Twenty

Chloe climbed and climbed, leaving the noise and chaos of the party behind as she made her way to the top of the house. The upper floors were deserted, the servants' rooms empty of their occupants. Quiet, too, save for a lone thumping noise coming from the end of the corridor. She followed the sound, letting it lead her to a large suite of nursery rooms.

Rob was there, alternately trying to pry the lock off a fair-sized trunk and hitting it with a fire iron. She paused inside the doorway, as with a cry of triumph, he sprang it open.

His elation died away as he caught sight of her. 'Did *he* send you?' Rob demanded.

Good. The boy had latched hard on to his anger. It would mask the hurt and allow him to get through these first, difficult hours. An intelligent strategy. She rather thought she would adopt it herself.

'No.' She walked in and perched on a bed in the corner. 'I left, just like you.'

'Well, that's what I'm doing. I'm leaving— for good.' He had begun to rummage through the trunk, removing some items, leaving others. 'I'm not waiting for him, or going where he wishes me to. And I'm not taking nothing he gave me, either.'

'I understand.' She sighed. 'I think perhaps he doesn't intend to cause such hurt, but the end result is just the same.'

It struck her how painfully similar their situations were. She imagined Rob teetering on the same edge as she had as a girl, hoping someone would save her, realising with sinking despair that she had to find a way to protect herself. His last defiant statement illustrated the biggest difference between them, however. Braedon had given her nothing to discard.

Watching the boy, feeling the tug he exerted on her heartstrings, a far more difficult truth was driven home. Braedon wanted neither of them. He did not want, or could not accept, the emotional entanglement—the *intimacy*—that would come along with accepting either of them into his life.

'I'm leaving, too,' she announced suddenly.

'Why are you going?' he asked with suspicion. 'Does he think you hurt someone, too?'

Chloe shrugged. 'Not exactly, but close enough. I think he believes that I am going to hurt him.'

He grunted and continued his sorting. Chloe watched for a moment, thinking hard. The boy was wounded and justifiably wary. But surely, surely there was something she could do to help him. 'Where are you going when you leave?' she asked idly.

'I don't know. I'll find a place. On my own.'

She nodded understanding. 'As will I.' She stood suddenly and went to the window. 'I think I shall go to the seashore. I told Lord Marland, not so long ago, that I've always wanted to live there.' She fell silent again and waited.

'I saw it once,' he ventured after a moment. 'My ma took me.'

'Didn't you love it?' She shot a quick grin over her shoulder before facing the dark window again. 'I'm going to go down to the beach every single day. I'm going to walk for miles with the sun on my face and the wind in my hair. I'm going to throw rocks at the water and frolic in the waves and collect shells.' She was going to sit and feel the spray and allow the ocean to make her feel small—because at the same time, being part of the majesty convinced her that she was never truly alone.

She glanced over at the pup curled on the bed. The idea in her head was taking firm root in her heart. 'Too bad you can't come with me. Fitz would love to chase the waves and the seabirds. He'd have a high time.'

Rob blinked. 'Yes. Too bad.'

'Unless…' she glanced at him as if startled by the idea '…I suppose you could come along. I wouldn't mind the company and it seems a shame to deny Fitz the experience.'

He frowned as he sat down heavily next to the dog.

'Oh, I understand,' she assured him. 'Never mind. You have plans of your own.'

'Well, not really. That is, I don't have anything important to see to. I suppose we could go along with you—for Fitz's sake.' He ducked his head. 'If you don't mind, that is.'

'Mind? I'm finding it a brilliant idea.' She left the window and crouched before him. 'Why should we both set out alone? Lord Marland doesn't seem to need us. And I can tell just on our short acquaintance how fine a boy you are.' She smiled. 'Yes, you can come with me if you wish. I've plenty of money set aside and you and Fitz and I will have a grand time.'

Faint hope lit his gaze. 'We'll leave together, then? Tonight?' he asked, with a quick return of anxiety.

Chloe sucked in a breath. She didn't want to

leave tonight—because a part of her was still tempted to stay and fight, to convince Braedon that the love and laughter and richness of an open heart could outweigh the pain. But the vision of his empty eyes stopped her. It wasn't her that he'd been chasing so hard, but the Spear—and the seclusion that it symbolised.

'Tonight.' She sighed. 'Get your things together and we'll go along to my room. I'll write a note to the countess, pack and we'll go.'

'Not yet, you won't,' a masculine voice interrupted. 'I'm afraid I'll have to add one more item to that list before you leave.'

'Sir Thomas!' The unease he'd inspired in her earlier blossomed into fear that reached out with icy tendrils. She knew enough, however, not to show any sign of it. She pulled Rob to his feet and placed a hand on his shoulder. 'How kind of you to come and check on us. But you needn't have bothered, we were just on our way out.'

'Yes, so I heard.' He leaned against the doorjamb. 'You won't be going anywhere, however, before you turn over Skanda's Spear.'

She stared blankly.

The master swordsman took a threatening step into the room. 'Don't toy with me, Miss Hardwick. I was watching today—watching you and Conover. A very slick manoeuvre, I must admit. I nearly missed it. But I know you have the Spear.'

Reaching for her, he yanked her away from Rob. 'I've already been through your room. Either you've hidden it well, or you've turned it over already.' He reached behind his back, beneath his coat, and withdrew a flattened belt with a scabbard attached. He drew the blade, a short sword that glittered in the dim light. 'For both of your sakes, I hope it is the former.'

'Here, now!' Rob stepped forwards. 'You shouldn't be threatening a lady!'

Chloe gasped as Sir Thomas brandished the blade in the boy's direction. 'Keep back and keep out of this,' he ordered.

'Rob,' she said, fighting to keep her voice steady. 'Don't worry. It's in my room,' she said to Sir Thomas. 'Leave him here and I'll take you to it.'

'He comes.' He beckoned the boy with the blade.

'No! I'll give it to you without a fuss—but you leave him here.' She let him see her determination and the very real threat of the mayhem she would create if he did not bend on this.

Glaring at her, he nodded.

'Rob.' Bending over the boy, she caught his eye and widened her own. Significantly. 'You know the marquess hates for you to hide away, unseen.' She raised her brows and hoped he understood that she was trying to send him a message. 'Think of this like a game. You stay hidden here. He won't come looking for you—he's too busy with his guests. Then I'll be back in a moment and we'll be off.'

'To the seashore?'

'Right away.'

'Fine, then.' He sat on the bed and pulled the pup into his arms. 'But hurry.'

'I will.' She met the mad, mercenary gleam in Sir Thomas's eye and hoped she spoke the truth.

Chapter Twenty-One

Braedon could not shake his unease—or his urge to find Chloe and apologise for—something. Everything, perhaps.

He stayed, though, acting the host as the dancing began and answering questions with non-committal answers.

When Mairi returned, red-rimmed eyes the only sign of their difficulties, he welcomed her back by pulling her into his arms. 'I'm sorry,' he said. 'I should have told you. I didn't want you upset.'

'The upset was inevitable.' She gave him a tremulous smile. 'It was the timing that was atrocious. But I'm better now and Ashton has forgiven me.'

'You've done nothing for which you need forgiveness.' Braedon took her hand. 'And you don't need to worry further. The boy leaves in the morning for one of my estates.'

Her brow wrinkled. 'I'm sure I didn't mean—'

'Mairi.' He kissed her hand. 'Not now, please. I have to…' His voice trailed off. What was it that could be done, really?

His sister smiled. 'Go to her.' She squeezed his hand. 'They are gone now, Braedon. Connor and Father are dead. They can't hurt us any more, can they? We both need to remember that—and stop living in dread.'

He couldn't stop—couldn't change, at least. Mairi had a chance, but he knew that he was long past such a thing. Still, he couldn't let things with Chloe end without at least an explanation. A goodbye. He left the ballroom in a hurry, his heart starting to beat fast in anticipation.

His pulse doubled again, for an entirely different reason, when he encountered Rob racing down the stairs at top speed, terror in his eyes and a fire poker in his hand.

'Whoa there.' He caught the boy with both hands. 'What are you doing, Rob? Where are you going with that?'

Gesturing back up the stairs, the lad gasped for breath. 'He's got her. Your lady. I think she was telling me to get you. She needs help! Go!'

Braedon clutched his shoulder. 'Who has

her?' But he knew. That look. A denial lurked on his lips even as a chill swept over his soul.

'Your friend.' The boy still breathed heavily. 'The one you fight with.'

Something dark shifted inside him. Could it be happening again? Betrayal. By a friend of so many years. Someone he'd sweated, laughed and bled with.

He straightened. 'Where are they?'

'He was taking her to her room. To get something.' Rob shook his head. 'I don't think he means to let her go.'

'Stay here.' Braedon moved to climb the stairs, but Rob grabbed his coat. 'Here.' He offered up the poker. 'He's got a knife.' He shook his head. 'No, it's a sword, like you fight with, only shorter.'

Braedon grasped his hand for a moment. 'Keep it. Stay here— Wait, no. Lord Ashton, the earl. The man the party is for tonight—you know him?'

'Aye, I think so.'

'Find him, Rob.'

'But where?'

'Somewhere in the crowd. He should be with the brown-haired lady. Tell him what you've seen. Tell no one else! We don't want to start a riot and I don't want anyone else interfering. Tell Ashton to be careful.' He put his hand on the banister. 'And thank you, Rob.'

* * *

Rob watched the marquess move stealthily up the stairs. He climbed a few himself to peer upwards. His lordship stopped on the correct landing, but moved off to the right, instead of left to the lady's room. To get a blade of his own, likely.

Just below, a footman hurried past as Rob paused, indecisive. His head wavered back and forth between the emptiness above and the crowd at the back of the house. There were hundreds of people in the house and he figured the odds were high that Ashton wouldn't believe anything he said—if he could find him. He'd seen the look on the wife's face and knew from where it had come. It would take too much time. He could help on his own. Resolute, he squared his shoulders, gripped his fire iron and, pressing close to the railing, began to slink up the stairs.

'You are a wily one, aren't you?' Thom's voice was just audible. 'Twice I threw that bolster across the room and I never suspected... You split the seam and just tucked it in? Oh, my dear, I fear I have underestimated you in every way.'

Braedon eased up to Chloe's door and pressed against the wall. There was a hard edge to Thom's voice that he had never heard before. Suggestive and sarcastic both, the way he expressed his admiration caused Braedon to grip his blade even tighter.

'My God, but she's a beauty,' Thom breathed. 'Those jewels on the handgrip! Those alone could keep me debt-free for a decade. Ah, the gold point and the jewels there, too. It's hard to know whether it would be better broken up or intact.' He gave a nasty laugh. 'Laxton is a fool twice over if he thinks I'll be turning this over to him.' He huffed. 'For the trouble I've been through and the pittance he's paid me over the last months?'

Soundlessly, Braedon grasped the wall for support. The Spear! It had to be Skanda's Spear. God, had it been Thom who had frightened Chloe and stolen her notebook? Thom who had mimicked concern as he asked after Braedon's success in the hunt? He thought further back. Yes, Thom who had shown up unannounced at Denning, just after the first whispered rumours of the Spear.

And Chloe? Chloe had the weapon? How? For how long? He clenched his teeth against the pain in his chest. This anguish felt like too much to bear.

'What I want to know is—just how deeply did you have old Braedon fooled?' Thom demanded. 'Whom are you working for on the side?'

Braedon lifted his head. Yes. He wanted to know, too.

'I don't know what you are talking about.' Chloe sounded indignant—and a little frightened.

'Well, you didn't turn it over to him, did you? I confess, I had to brace myself to come tonight—I fully expected to find him crowing over his success.' There was a pause. 'I doubt you accomplished this alone. So who is it?'

'I have only Braedon's best interest at heart,' she said angrily. 'You are judging me by the short rod of your own behaviour.'

'So you were going to give it to him?'

Braedon held his breath.

Chloe held her silence.

Thom laughed. 'Yes—just as I thought. I'll wager you and Pisano were in cahoots.'

She didn't answer.

'Or perhaps you haven't even made up your mind. But it doesn't matter in any case, does it?' Thom sneered. 'The thing is mine now. Come on,' he said roughly. 'You are coming with me. The house is full and you will prove useful, in case Connor's little by-blow proves to be not as smart as I suspect he is.'

Braedon crouched into position, his blade at the ready.

'Wait,' Thom said. 'The bolster was a good idea.'

His ears straining to listen, Braedon's eyes focused on the blade before him. It wasn't his best, merely a practice sword. He started, realising it was the very one he'd been restoring the day both Mairi and Thom arrived at Denning. The day Hardwick had spoken of the sea. He wondered if that was the day she had first began to drift away from him.

'Let's go.'

Suddenly she was there before him, thrust first into the hall by his former friend. Braedon pressed a finger to his lips, but she could not suppress the start she gave at the sight of him so close. Her eyes widened and that was all the warning that Thom needed. He pushed her hard and she stumbled up against the opposite wall. Leading with his sword, he entered the corridor.

'That boy disappoints me,' Thom said with a shake of his head. 'Almost as much as your assistant, there.' He nodded toward Chloe, but Braedon was not naive enough to look. Sighing, Thom tossed a long, round bed pillow to the floor. It was split down the seam and amidst the stuffing he caught a glimpse of gold. 'None of the people around you is ruthless enough.'

'Except for you, it would seem.' Still crouching, Braedon took a step toward the centre of the corridor, blocking the passage.

'Not half as ruthless as the money lenders after my head, old man.'

He feinted, but Braedon didn't flinch.

'Oh? So that's the reason you've descended to terrorising women and children? Why you've betrayed one of your oldest friends?'

'Well, I am fond of my head. Attached to it, you know.' He gave a sharp, bitter laugh. 'And friends like you are expensive to keep.'

He slashed to the right, trying to shift Braedon out of position, but he'd trained with him for far too long to fall for such a manoeuvre.

'It's my fault, then?' Braedon laced his words with sarcasm. 'Convenient for you.'

'No, it's damned inconvenient, actually.' Thom straightened and let his blade fall a bit. 'You were a friend, but in the end, you were no different from the Royal Dukes or the rest of the blue bloods. Oh, you might invite a chap to stay for a week or two in your vast house, with servants and fine food and abundant drink, but you never consider what I'm going home to afterwards. You were one of the few who actually bothered to pay your shot for my services, but it was never enough to let more than tiny rooms in a dirty neighbourhood. Never enough to dress well or drink richly or play deep.'

His attack came fast and on his last syllable. Braedon was ready. Their blades crossed and the battle was on.

Eerie silence settled over the passageway.

There was no talk now, only harsh breathing and the sound of steel scraping steel as they clashed again and again. An odd echo drifted from below—the high clink of glass and silver sounding sharp over the swell of music and laughter. The servants, setting up the midnight buffet.

It reminded Braedon that he had more to focus on than just Thom. Chloe? Where was she now? He risked a glimpse past his opponent and found her crouching against the far wall of the passage. Deliberately he retreated, just a bit. He didn't want her hurt, but neither did he want Thom gaining access to the stairs and escape.

Thom took heart, though, from his apparent advantage. He spun, suddenly, and drew first blood, slashing a thin line in the narrow spot where Braedon's waistcoat rode high. *Damn.* Braedon let loose a hiss of pain and swiftly doubled his own attack.

The fight stretched on. They were too closely matched, too well versed with each other's strengths and weaknesses. Braedon knew that Thom was prone to resort to dirty tricks when he began to tire. He took it as a good sign when his former partner lashed out at him with a booted foot.

He avoided it easily. 'Growing tired, old man?' he taunted. He knew a few dirty tricks, too. The vast majority of Thom's experience came from private matches, from training and sparring with the gentlemen of the *ton*. Braedon had fought on battlefields, amongst the slick blood and fallen bodies of comrades and enemies alike. He'd brawled for his life with men armed with rage and fear and fervour as well as weapons of steel. He lunged now, lightning quick, striking hard and fast in a move designed to confuse Thom and leave him teetering off balance.

It worked. Thom hung suspended for a long moment, leaning back over one foot. Braedon relented, waiting.

It was a mistake. With an effort nearly beyond human ability, Thom somehow righted himself and surged forwards. Braedon was too slow to get his sword back up to defend. In a fiery blaze of pain, his left arm was laid open.

He stepped back. Too far. They'd reached the stair landing. He couldn't let Thom slip past. He had to end this quickly now. His coat grew damp from the rush of blood.

He swung, a vicious arc aimed for Thom's retreating arm, but the older man spun away and lashed out with his foot again, this time connecting with the wound at Braedon's waist.

He doubled over, nearly windless with the pain.

'You're not ruthless enough either,' Thom said through gritted teeth. 'It seems a damned shameful reason to die, but I know you. You'll come for me and that damned Spear and you won't stop. I have to have it, Braedon, or I'm as good as dead anyway.'

Braedon lifted his head. He saw the grim determination on his former friend's face. He saw him poised at the edge of the stairs, saw his arm lift high for a killing strike.

And then he saw a small form unfold from the railing several stairs down. Another, smaller arm raised high, poised to strike a blow with a fire iron.

Somehow Braedon launched to his feet, his sword arm held low. At the same moment that the fire iron hit Thom behind the knees, he thrust up, driving the point of his sword deep in the spot between shoulder and arm. He winced at the jolt and grind of steel meeting bone.

Eyes bulging in shock, Thom contorted impossibly. He hung, oddly twisted and suspended on his toes for a long moment, before he overbalanced and went tumbling down the stairs.

Braedon sank back to one knee. Clutching his arm, he stared at Rob. 'You scared the hell out of me,' he said.

Chloe approached. Her eyes fixed on the still form below, she reached out and pulled the boy close. Watching her, Braedon saw the moment she recoiled and glanced down to see Thom climbing slowly to his feet. He glared upwards with a snarl of pure hatred.

Braedon pushed the pair of them back, but the fight had gone out of Thom. Limping, his sword arm hanging useless, he started down the stairs.

'Follow after him, at a distance,' Braedon ordered. His head had begun to spin. He couldn't help it; he sank down to sit on the floor. 'He's lost and he knows it. He's hurt. Let him go, as long as he doesn't try to touch or talk to anyone.'

Chloe searched his face and then rose to do as he bid. Braedon waited until she had gone, and then he looked at Rob. 'Watch over her,' he said. And then he slid down and back into black oblivion.

Chapter Twenty-Two

Braedon roused once, when Chloe tightened a strip of cloth around his arm. He woke again, briefly, as many hands carried him from the corridor.

The next time, he came awake gasping, sitting up to find himself in his darkened rooms. Ashton sat alone at his bedside.

'Chloe?' he asked.

'She's still here,' the earl answered, handing him a porcelain cup. 'Drink that. I'm sure it's nasty, but the sawbones says you must take as much liquid as possible.' He sat back while Braedon drank. 'She says she's leaving in the morning. And she's taking the boy. She's in a high, fine temper, old boy. Won't even talk with Mairi.'

Braedon swung his legs over the bed. 'She'll talk to me.'

Understanding shone in his brother-in-law's eyes. 'Be careful, man. You've lost a lot of blood. And don't tell your sister that I let you go.'

Braedon didn't know why he was going, really. What was there to say? She'd had the Spear. Did it matter how long, or if she'd meant to give it to him at all? The answers felt unimportant, for the first time, because they didn't change the outcome of this night, couldn't save either of them from the end.

He found her folding her things into a portmanteau.

'You're leaving.'

She faced him, her eyes lighting with horror. 'What, pray, are you doing out of bed?'

'Just tell me. Just say it. You're leaving. Leaving *me*?'

Her gaze turned sad and inward. 'I'm afraid I have to.'

He sighed and leaned against the doorframe. 'Where did you get it?'

'Conover.' She turned back to her packing.

'Today? Yesterday, now, I suppose.'

She nodded.

'Are you going to him now? Is he hiring you? Or *courting* you?'

'How easily you believe the worst of me.' She sighed. 'But I suppose you do have cause.'

It wasn't an answer. He hesitated a beat. 'Are you taking it with you?'

Chloe breathed deeply and determined to take the risk. She had to try. She set down a roll of stockings and gave Braedon her biggest, most reassuring smile. 'I love you, Braedon.'

He flinched. Visibly.

She laughed. It was an ugly, bitter reflection of the hurt inside her. 'It's true. I know you don't wish to hear it, but it's the hideous truth behind…everything. It's the reason why I left Denning—yes, even then I was beginning to love you. It's the reason why I agreed to help you find the damned Spear. Why I made love with you.'

He breathed deeply and shook his head.

'I told you I was searching for myself. It's true. I told you I don't want to allow fear to rule my life—and I've finally discovered why. You taught me why. It's because fear blinds you to love. It blinded me at least, beginning back when I taught at that school. When I was your Hardwick—' She broke off, stifling a sob, but gathered herself after a moment. 'I let fear cut me off from any chance at letting love grow.'

She gave him a wan smile. 'Do you know, at first I fretted that I had wasted my time here in London with your sister? I worried that I had not found a new calling or secured a new direction for my life. But now I know that I did accomplish something big and grand and so important that it will affect all the days of my life.'

She read the question in his eyes, but he didn't speak, didn't ask. She told him anyway. 'I'm here, out in the open. I'm not hiding anymore, because I discovered that I want love, Braedon. Even more amazing, I discovered that I am full of it, ready to burst. It's like love is a great, gorgeous leafy vine inside of me—and it wants out. It wants to stretch and entwine with others to connect me to the world.' Her voice fell as she let her eyes roam over him. 'And the thickest, healthiest, most demanding shoot inside of me is reaching for you.'

He made an inarticulate sound.

'I know. It can't reach you at all. You draw your sharp swords and knives and you hack away at any attempt to make that connection.'

He looked angry now. No longer leaning on the door, he stood stiff and proud, his hands clenched at his sides. He opened his mouth as if he was going to object, but he sighed instead. His shoulders slumped and he moved to sit in the wing chair by the fire. 'You're right.'

She waited.

'But you are wrong, too. I don't waste my time fending off love, Chloe, because I don't believe in it.'

Her eyes filled. Lips trembling, she whispered, 'How can you say so?'

'Perhaps I should say that I don't believe love to be the panacea that most believe it to be. Or perhaps I should just say that love is just not for me.' He glared at her suddenly. 'It's a fantasy, Chloe,' he said harshly. 'And a *dangerous* one. How can I say so? I ask you the same! How can you and the rest of the world continue to perpetuate such a lie? Look around! Look at the misery around you. I refuse to believe in a fantasy that is not strong enough to keep the people who are supposed to love you from hurting you. Or turning away while it's done.'

He propped his uninjured arm on to his knee and dropped his head into his hand. 'Do you know why Rob is upset with me?'

She shook her head.

'I saw him bent over the form of a sobbing little girl. I thought he was hurting her.'

She understood. 'You thought he was like his father.'

'Yes,' he said harshly. 'Connor...' He swallowed. '*God,*' he swore suddenly. 'Not even Mairi knows how he died.' He lifted his head. 'But I'm going to tell you, because I want you to understand.'

She sank down on the bed, her heart pounding. Suddenly she was very much afraid of what she might hear.

'There was a girl in the village. You know the sort—not bright. Slow since birth, but pretty. And docile and sweet. Connor abducted her. He took that innocent girl to a gamekeeper's cottage in the woods and he used her horribly. It likely wasn't the first time he'd done such a thing. But he went too far. He killed her.'

Her hand went to her mouth, though she couldn't make a sound.

'My father found them,' he continued. 'And at last he had to face what he had done. What sort of monster he had allowed Connor to become. All those years, he'd ignored Connor's faults, because he *loved* him. But that night, for the first time he was ashamed of his eldest son. Sorry for what he'd wrought. And fearful for what might happen in the future, when he was gone and there was no one to check Connor.'

Braedon looked up at her with anguish in every line of his body. 'My father shot him—killed his son, the light of his life. He blamed both deaths on squatters. But he wrote the truth in a letter to me—and a few days later he had an "accident" while cleaning his gun.'

He started to shake. Chloe flew to him and knelt at his feet. On her knees, she clasped him tightly and, crooning, ran comforting hands over his back.

He didn't let her comfort him for long. Pulling away, he stood and moved back. 'Now you know, Chloe. Love doesn't save you. There's no magic in it.' He shook his head at the plea she could not hide. 'It was misguided love that created a monster like Connor. And twisted, thwarted love that killed my father.'

Her tears were flowing freely now. 'It's horrible,' she said. 'But let it go, Braedon. It's over.'

He snorted. 'It's never over. Look at what happened last night.'

'I'm so sorry for all that you have seen and suffered. But you are holding it close, deliberately choosing not to let it go. We all have pain. Everyone. But it is possible to move past it. It is *necessary*. I'm ready to help you. We all are.' She breathed deeply and narrowed her gaze. 'I'm asking you to try, Braedon. You have to start somewhere. Somewhere, some time, you have to trust someone.' Silently she asked him to begin now, with her.

'I know what you want,' he said. 'I can't give it to you. I can't make myself believe.'

Her heart was breaking. Climbing to her feet, she went to the dressing room and came back with Skanda's Spear. She stood tall in the middle of the room and planted it beside her.

'So many stories I've heard of the Marauding Marquess,' she whispered. 'About captured French pay wagons and battles won and treaties forged.' She choked out a small sob. 'A hundred more I've dreamed up in my head. But never, in all of those tales, did I ever hear you called a coward.'

He made a wordless sound of objection.

'You are making a choice,' she said. 'You are choosing fear and isolation—the things you never told me this Spear represented.' She picked it up and offered it to him. 'I didn't know if I was going to give this to you. But you've decided. So take it.' Unending tears spilled out of her. 'I hope you will be happy together.'

Chapter Twenty-Three

Just past a fortnight later, Braedon leaned back against the magnificent porcelain display that housed his Japanese pole arm. He was drunk, but that didn't keep him from pulling another long swig from the bottle in his hand.

Above him, the domed centre of his weapons wing arched. All was complete—the wing finished, his many beautiful weapons displayed to full advantage. He'd come in here every day for a week, ready to gloat, longing for the rush of victory, the warm flush of accomplishment, or even quiet pleasure in seeing his beloved artefacts showcased so well.

It wouldn't come. None of it. He felt only empty instead. He didn't understand—he'd thought when the project was finished, he would also feel complete. Here it was—a permanent, lasting mark on Denning, one that had nothing to do with either his father or his brother—one they would have despised, in fact. Their ghosts should have been defeated, permanently laid to rest. And yet Denning's halls still echoed with their disappointment and displeasure, just as it always had.

He drank again, but the bottle was empty. He stared at it, dangling in his hand, and wondered why the hell he didn't feel full?

He flung the thing away from him, scowling as it skittered across the marble floor. He knew why. He placed full blame on her—on Hardwick, who had helped him build this place, and on Chloe, who had left him unfit to enjoy it.

Oh, God. He reached for the Spear of Skanda. Never far away, it rested on the floor nearby. Pulling it on to his lap, he began to stroke along its burnished wood. All of those years, all of this effort to create the perfect retreat. All of the careful manoeuvring to maintain his emotional boundaries. Wasted. He was here, where he should be. Alone, as he should be, and still he did not feel safe, secure or fulfilled.

She had ruined him. She'd pressed her lithe body up against his armour and melted it with her warmth. She'd invaded his empty places, changed them with her presence, so that they no longer felt comfortable when she'd left them, but merely abandoned.

She was nothing but a thief. She'd robbed him of his contentment, of his future. Fury and frustration seethed inside him.

'Damn it all!' the scream tore out of him and bounced around the dome above. Fists pounding, he shouted again.

He thrust the Spear aside, got to his feet and began to move about the room. One by one he went to stand in front of his prized artefacts. Nothing. He was still hollow, still aching with emptiness. He went around to every one of his ancient treasures, but each failed him.

Broken, forlorn, he went back to the centre of the room. He lay down, spreadeagled on the cold marble, and tried to clear his mind. To cast back and find where it had all gone wrong.

He refused to let his mind dwell on his father or brother—he'd revisited that pain enough. Instead he thought of Thom, wondering what signs he'd missed, or if there had been something he might have noticed or done to change that disastrous outcome. He thought of Rob, and how in his rush to judgement, he'd inflicted the same sort of hurt on the boy that he'd resented himself.

And he thought of Chloe. How perplexed and distressed he'd been when she'd left this place. He remembered how he'd reacted to her in London with reluctant fascination and trepidation. How the hurt at her reluctance to give him the Spear had paled, because he'd already made the horrific decision to leave her behind.

And then, as the cold seeped into his bones and his gaze fixed on the precise pattern above, it struck him—the ultimately important question. Why? Why had he been so afraid of her? Why had he known, so firmly and deeply in his soul, that he had to set her away? To save himself pain? To avoid feeling the cavernous void inside of him? Well, he'd done neither.

In fact, he suddenly wondered if these weren't the same grievous emotions that he'd carried with him since he was a child. Perhaps Chloe hadn't changed them or added to them. She'd merely made him more aware of them, because she had fleetingly taken them away.

He sat up, struck by a sudden notion. His hands shaking, his heart pounding in sudden excitement, he climbed to his feet, flung open the display and carefully took out the pole arm. It felt awkward in his hand. He had no training with this sort of weapon, was not sure how to control it. He couldn't fight with it; he would be a danger to himself and to others. Understanding bloomed in his soul and gave birth to hope. Maybe love was the same. A thing of beauty, which could be twisted into a weapon in the wrong hands.

Perhaps, just as with a blade, all the importance, responsibility and power of love rested with the wielder. And that meant that the *real* question was not if he believed or trusted in love, but if he believed and trusted in Chloe.

He did.

My God, it was true. He trusted her. She held a number of substantial weapons in her personal arsenal, and from the beginning, she had wielded them *for* him. Her warmth, her generosity, even her commitment to finding the joy in her own life, had eased him. She'd agreed to help him on his quest, though she'd been under no obligation. She'd shared herself with him. She'd listened to his darkest secrets and given him back comfort and light. She'd taken away the hurt he carried and he hadn't even recognised its absence—he'd only feared its return.

Bemused, he dropped the pole arm and looked around with new eyes. At last he understood the question. Now what of the answer? His feet were moving into a run before he even finished the thought.

Chloe sat on the rock promontory and let the soft sea wind soothe her. The tide hurried by, on its way to rejoin the vast ocean stretching before her. Spray occasionally reached her, gentle at this time of day, touching her cheeks with bright drops of comfort. She looked over her shoulder, towards the empty shore, thinking that it was time for Rob to return.

For several weeks they had travelled the coast, exploring villages and beaches. They had tried out several cottages, but none felt like they were meant to stay. Until this one, perhaps. Situated alone outside the village of Deal, it had much to recommend it. An ideal location, tucked into a protective basin, a short, wide trail down to the beach, and this glorious curved arm of rocks, which allowed Chloe to climb right out to the turbulence that echoed in her soul, and at same time created a protected cove ideal for Rob to explore.

As their journey had begun, Rob had clung a bit, keeping to her side, watching her expression closely. But as the days had passed and they had grown used to each other, he had relaxed, and his confidence had grown. They had been in this place nearly a sennight now, and he'd taken to disappearing in the morning, exploring down the shore with Fitz at his side. Chloe suspected that he had found a friend, for he'd returned lighter-hearted these last few days, eager to share his treasures: pretty shells, coloured pebbles or fantastically smooth driftwood.

She looked again towards the shore and saw Braedon's figure striding along instead of the boy's. She closed her eyes against the vision and turned back to the sea. It wasn't the first time her imagination had forged a picture of what her heart wanted most.

It was the first time the image had shouted her name, however.

Looking again, she found him scrambling over the rocks towards her. He was here! Her heart stopped, then stumbled to a fast, hopeful pace.

He didn't speak as he drew nearer, just perched next to her and looked out across the blue expanse. They sat in silence. Chloe waited, her nervous fingers fidgeting endlessly with her skirts.

'No one has ever dared call me a coward before,' he said at last.

Disappointment swamped her. Now her fingers stilled. Had he come all this way just to quarrel? She straightened her shoulders. Very well, then. The time of her easing his way was long over. 'I'd say it was high time someone did, then.'

He laughed. 'I'm sure you are right.'

She stared at him in mock wonder. 'Well, that's a first, isn't it?'

He leaned back on his hands and smiled at her. Her breath caught. It was a true smile, open and unguarded.

'Ah, Chloe, I begin to think that there are far too many firsts between us to count.'

She couldn't stop looking at him. He looked

so...*there*. Completely present, somehow. As if he'd stopped keeping out a wary eye for something behind him, stopped blocking her from what lay ahead.

She bit her lip, afraid to trust it. 'I'm glad for it, then,' she said. 'But it's the lasts between us that worry me.'

He sat up and reached for her hand. 'They don't worry me.' His voice rumbled like the sea against the rocks, just as intense. 'I hope we have many of both.' He took her other hand. 'I hope you are the first and last woman I chase to the end of this island. I want to wake up every morning with your face the first thing I see, and the last before I go to sleep at night.' He moved closer and touched her cheek. 'I know that you will be the first and last woman I say this to: I need you, Chloe. I love you.'

She clutched him tight with one hand and covered her mouth with the other. 'I don't understand,' she whispered. 'What's happened?'

'I listened,' he said simply. 'I finally heard you. I opened my eyes and saw how generous you are and how blind I have been. I saw how I kept closing the door and you kept slipping through the cracks. I stopped and looked back and realised that with you, for the first time, I learned to accept tenderness and caring and concern and even to give it back a little, as well.'

He grabbed her hands again and she saw a bit

of desperation return to his eyes. 'I don't want to stop. You were right. It's the only way to move past the pain. I want to learn more, give and take more.' His fingers tightened on hers. 'Will you teach me?'

She bit her lip and searched his face. 'Yes,' she said on a whisper. 'Yes.'

He threw his head back and whooped with joy. She laughed along with him until, growing serious again, he assured her, 'I'm sure I'll be a horrible pupil. I've been hiding for so long. But I trust you to stay. You've seen what lurks inside of me and still you care. I trust you not to turn away when I slide back into darkness, but to lead me to the light.'

'You know I will,' she told him. 'But I'm so glad you took this first step—it had to be on your own.'

His eyes clouded. 'It wasn't easy—but you know that.'

'And I couldn't be happier.' She cradled her cheek into his large hand. 'But, Braedon, it's not only me you must worry about. There's Rob—'

She stopped as a sheepish grin stole over his face.

'I know.' He ducked his head. 'I hurt him first, if not deepest. I'm afraid I've been…not a coward, but cautious.'

'It's you—' she realised suddenly '—you he's been off with in the mornings?'

He nodded. 'I read your letters to Mairi. It's not her fault,' he said quickly. 'I had to find you. I'm afraid I made a pest of myself.' He grinned. 'I saw in them how close you and Rob had become. I felt like I needed his blessing.'

Her mouth twisted. 'And did he give it?'

'Look and see.' He motioned toward the shore.

Rob was there, at the edge of the rocks. Fitz frolicked at his feet as he jumped in the air and shouted something that the wind carried away.

'What is that he's holding?' she asked, shading her eyes and getting to her feet.

'It's Skanda's Spear.'

She knew her face fell as he continued.

'This morning I asked Rob what I should do with it.'

'And what was his answer?'

'Well, I was of the mind to throw the thing into the sea.'

She gasped and he shrugged. 'I meant to show you that I've finally and truly chosen you.'

She blinked back tears. 'Would you do that?'

'I'd do anything to show you how hard I'm holding on to the hope that you've given me.' He blinked hard and after a moment, he went on, 'Rob pointed out that the thing would only be likely to roll back in with the tide and make someone else miserable.'

Chloe laughed.

'I thought of a cave then, or a cache in the cliffs back home, but Rob had another suggestion.'

'What was that,' she asked, genuinely curious.

'He suggested that I give it to you. And further—that we make a baby girl and leave it to her—and to her daughter after that and on down the line, so that no man will ever be tormented by the thing again.' Nervous, he looked into her face. 'What do you think?'

Her eyes welled over. 'I think it is a brilliant idea.'

He smiled in relief. 'I promised him that if you agreed, I'd kiss you good and proper, so that he would know.'

Chloe laughed through her tears. 'Then let's not disappoint him.'

They didn't.

* * * * *

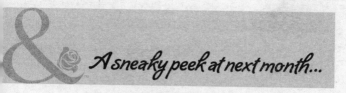

A sneaky peek at next month...

HISTORICAL

IGNITE YOUR IMAGINATION, STEP INTO THE PAST...

My wish list for next month's titles...

In stores from 6th July 2012:

☐ An Escapade and an Engagement — Annie Burrows

☐ The Laird's Forbidden Lady — Ann Lethbridge

☐ His Makeshift Wife — Anne Ashley

☐ The Captain and the Wallflower — Lyn Stone

☐ Tempted by the Highland Warrior — Michelle Willingham

☐ Renegade Most Wanted — Carol Arens

Available at WHSmith, Tesco, Asda, Eason, Amazon and Apple

Just can't wait?

Visit us Online

You can buy our books online a month before they hit the shops! **www.millsandboon.co.uk**

0612/04

Special Offers

Every month we put together collections and longer reads written by your favourite authors.

Here are some of next month's highlights— and don't miss our fabulous discount online!

On sale 15th June

On sale 15th June

On sale 6th July

Save 20%
on all Special Releases

Find out more at
www.millsandboon.co.uk/specialreleases

Visit us
Online

0712/ST/MB377

The World of Mills & Boon®

There's a Mills & Boon® series that's perfect for you. We publish ten series and with new titles every month, you never have to wait long for your favourite to come along.

Blaze®
Scorching hot, sexy reads

By Request
Relive the romance with the best of the best

Cherish™
Romance to melt the heart every time

Desire™
Passionate and dramatic love stories

Have Your Say

You've just finished your book. So what did you think?

We'd love to hear your thoughts on our 'Have your say' online panel
www.millsandboon.co.uk/haveyoursay

- 🌹 Easy to use
- 🌹 Short questionnaire
- 🌹 Chance to win Mills & Boon® goodies

Visit us Online

Tell us what you thought of this book now at
www.millsandboon.co.uk/haveyoursay

YOUR_SA